PRAISE FOR THE RIDER FILES

Masters File
Honorable Mention
2018 Readers' Favorite Awards

"Masters File: The Riders File Book 2 by CB Samet is a fast-paced tale of crime and unexpected humor. The plot development of CB Samet's novel is a combination of romance and suspense that lures the reader in, making it a one-sitting read."

— READERS' FAVORITE AWARD REVIEWER

(2018)

"Ooh! Insanely suspenseful and ... romantic .... Mix high-level medical skills, high-level retired Army Ranger skills, high-level tech/hacker skills, the Russian mafia, the Cuban mafia, a loser ex-husband with gambling debts and unlimited gall—the result is explosive!"

— BOOKBUB REVIEWER

MASTERS FILE

THE RIDER FILES BOOK 2

CB SAMET

AVANTSTAR
PUBLISHING

Cover Art: CirceCorp design - Carolina Fiandri

(circecorpdesign.com)

ISBN ebook: 978-1-54392-685-9

ISBN paperback: 978-1-7324525-5-8

To PMG Book Club and PMG Writers for their support and
encouragement

CHAPTER 1

$\mathcal{B}$eating helicopter rotors sounded seconds before Ryan looked up to see a half-dozen men rappelling through the open ceiling of the warehouse. Dark figures clad in black blocked out the sun and descended from the sky like fallen angels of death.

Ryan pulled his sidearm.

"Incoming!" Reece yelled.

Ryan glanced at his partner, dressed in a navy suit over Kevlar like himself, who had also drawn his weapon.

His gaze darted to the transport van where men loaded the equipment. The cargo could be the only reason for the sudden intruders. The automatic weapons strapped to the assailants who lowered themselves from the sky was testament to the fact that they weren't here to make a bid on the prototype.

Ryan fired, hoping to drop as many attackers as possible before they touched the ground and had a chance to take aim.

As Ryan's and Reece's bullets struck several of the rappellers, they opossumed upside down, held in place by their D-ring and harness.

"What the hell is going on?" Maxine Rider's gravelly voice sounded through Ryan's earpiece.

Reece spoke over the sound of his gunshots. "Well, boss, the prototype demonstration may be over, but the party's just begun."

Sharp Industries had hired Maxine Rider's Security and Investigation group as an extra layer of protection for the unveiling of their prototype weapon—a small drone capable of carrying a hundred bullet-size explosive devices capable of targeting individuals based on heat signatures or biosensors.

With the unveiling complete, prospective buyers had finished drooling and left. Only the prototype and a handful of security detail remained for the transport.

Three of the assailants touched down on the concrete warehouse floor and began laying down weapon fire for the next incoming wave. Very soon, Ryan, Reece, and Sharp Industries' security team would be outnumbered. So much for a deserted warehouse in North Atlanta being an ideal place for a semi-secret meeting.

Ryan and Reece took cover behind steel beams that stretched up to the rafters.

Ryan squeezed his trigger. As his bullet hit one of the black-clad men in the shoulder, he wondered at their credentials. Clearly ex-military, though not from an elite forces team.

He glanced at the van. The cargo was almost secured. Two of Sharp's security detail defensively shot at the intruders to protect two more who tightened the clasps around the crate. There wasn't much point in hastily escaping with a twenty-five-million-dollar piece of equipment if it was going to get jostled and broken in the back of a getaway van.

"Cargo's in jeopardy," Ryan said.

"Yep." Reece's mustache twitched.

"You wanna drive or shoot?" Ryan asked.

"Do you have to ask?"

Ryan grinned and loosened his tie.

Reece reloaded his Beretta before providing cover fire as he and Ryan dashed for the van. By the time they reached the vehicle, three of the four security guards had been shot.

"Just like Tokzar!" Reece hollered.

Shit, I hope not, Ryan thought.

He shoved into the driver's seat and cranked the engine. In the side mirror, he saw another six men touch down from the ropes connected to other choppers.

How many were they up against?

The automatic weapons' fire had ceased, and sharp shooters took aim. Apparently, they developed the good sense not to destroy the equipment they were attempting to steal.

When Ryan heard Reece slam the back doors shut, he hit the gas. "We've got the cargo, Max. Need a destination."

"Claire," Maxine snapped.

Claire's strained voice sounded through his earpiece. "Working on it. Head north on Highway 19."

"Copy."

"Injuries?" Maxine asked.

"Only one of Sharp's boys made it. He's in the back with Reece."

"Well, this is a Charlie Foxtrot," Maxine complained.

"Sharp has a storage facility near Lake Lanier. I'll talk you there," Claire said.

Reece said, "Max, what're you going to do to make sure we get there in one piece? Those Little Birds are going to be on our ass soon."

Ryan knew Reece was right. Having a destination was pointless if the enemy helicopters kept them from reaching it.

Twelve rappellers. Ryan did the mental calculation—from a capacity perspective, that meant four choppers at least.

"How many birds?" Maxine demanded.

"Four." Ryan and Reece simultaneously answered her.

Ryan added. "Black Killer Eggs with shooters."

Maxine swore before she went offline.

Ryan took a left on Old Roswell Road heading north.

Claire spoke. "She's calling Bob Sharp now. Keep straight onto Westside Parkway."

Ryan imagined the blue-haired girl frantically typing in front of three computer screens. She rarely had to extricate them from dangerous situations, and she wasn't military trained, so she would find the pressure challenging. However, he had faith and confidence in Maxine that she would find a way to get him and Reece out of this mess.

Hopefully.

He heard Reece fire shots.

"Come on, Reece. Save your ammo. You're not taking out a chopper with a nine millimeter."

"Not the bird. Just a shooter. Or two."

The blades thumped through the sky. Like Tokzar. Ryan, Reece, and four other rangers had scrambled like hell to get through the abandoned town outside of Tokzar, Afghanistan, and to the extraction point where a Black Hawk approached to take them to safety. Enemy fire racketed relentlessly. They ran, hoping not to get shot. Except, unfortunately, Reece had gotten shot that day.

Ryan swerved the van around a slower car.

At a cruising speed of 155 miles per hour, the helicopter would have no problem keeping pace with the van. A good pilot could maneuver close enough for a gunman to take out a tire. Fortunately, at the moment, the power lines streaming above forced the pilots to take caution. When Ryan reached Tanner MacDonald Parkway, the choppers would be less inhibited to get closer.

The clink of a bullet striking the metal of the van had Ryan gripping the wheel even tighter. Both he and Reece swore simultaneously.

"'Rangers lead the way,' man. Get us out of here." Reece's voice sounded strained, and Ryan guessed the bullet had landed too close for comfort.

"Working on it." Ryan maneuvered around vehicles with a white-knuckle grip. A certain familiar adrenaline rush coursed through him.

"Left on Haynes Bridge," Claire instructed.

"Hold on!" Ryan shouted to his passengers—Reece and Sharp's security man.

Ryan took the turn sharp without a blinker. The car he cut off slammed to a halt as the driver honked the horn furiously. Ryan straightened the screeching tires and accelerated.

"Parkway's coming up," Claire advised.

"Crap." Ryan needed to first cross the parkway and then hang a left to head north, but upcoming traffic would slow him down, making the van an easier target. He swung wide to the left and then cut a sharp right at the intersection.

Honking horns erupted as he zipped past cars.

"Uh, Walsh?" Reece poked his head up by the front seat.

"Yeah?" Ryan's eyes never left the road.

"You're getting on the off-ramp."

Ryan swerved, avoiding a head-on collision. "Yep."

Reece crawled into the passenger seat and buckled his seatbelt. "Okay. So long as you know. So long as you're not having desert flashbacks where you can drive wherever the hell the truck won't get stuck or mined."

Ryan sailed across oncoming traffic, over the median. He cut left before slamming on the brakes.

Reece jerked forward, his seatbelt holding him in place, as he released a grunt. "Kidding man. Only kidding."

The security guard in the back seat swore as he collided with the wall of the van.

Ryan looked through his window, craning his neck to see the choppers as they flew past.

Reece peered toward the sky, upper lip curled toward his mustache. "Under the overpass. Nicely done, Walsh. We've got roughly sixty seconds before they close in on us from either side and we're riddled with bullet holes."

Ryan put the van in park and reloaded his gun.

"Claire, watcha cooking for us, honey?" Reece asked.

Maxine's voice came back over the coms. "Sharp's got drones in the air. ETA three minutes."

"We'll be dead in two," Reece said with mocked cheer.

Ryan and Reece hopped out of the van.

Maxine ordered, "Defend the prototype, stay alive, and I'll send the two of you to the Caribbean when this is over."

Ryan supposed that was a better offer than he'd ever gotten from the Army Rangers for risking his life.

Black helicopters descended on both sides of the overpass. Armed men in black combat attire sat on either side of the choppers.

Ryan sighed and aimed his Beretta. "Yeah. Just like Tokzar, except choppers instead of all-terrain vehicles."

⁕

JENNA MASTERS SKILLFULLY inserted the long, slender needle between the vertebrae in the back of her heavily sedated patient.

She tried not to be distracted by the elaborate tattoos spanning his skin. Based on their macabre appearance—skulls, black roses, a viper, and ghostly figures—she judged he would be an interesting character once he recovered from his illness and was awake. She had to give him enough sedatives to disable an elephant to finally get him lax.

Her nose itched beneath her mask, but she couldn't break the sterile field to scratch it. As she pulled the stylet out of the needle, she wiggled her nose in lieu of being able to rub it.

Clear liquid dripped from the end of the needle.

Magic.

She would have to try that Bewitched trick more often.

Wonder if it would work on making my ex vanish?

After measuring the opening pressure with a digital manometer, she collected the cerebral spinal fluid as it trickled. She preferred to have completely obtunded patients when inserting long, sharp objects into their spine.

When she'd collected a sufficient amount of fluid, she removed the needle.

And for all that ... you get a Band-Aid.

As she secured the it over the tiny puncture site, she admired the large elaborate cross on his upper back. With three sharp points at the apex and arms and the swirls of decoration on the interior, it looked both holy and deadly.

She stepped away from the bed, finally able to rub her nose with the back of her gloved hand over her facemask while simultaneously arching to stretch her back. Rolling off her gloves, she flung them into the trashcan. As she peeled off her cap, gown, and mask, a nurse stuck her head in the door.

"Need anything, Dr. Masters?"

Jenna looked up at Kat and smiled. "All done. Check out that champagne tap."

Kat's eyes fell on the vials of cerebrospinal fluid on the nearby table. "Nice."

Jenna wriggled her eyebrows at her. "I've already placed the orders. Can you get that to the lab right away?"

"Sure thing."

Kat stepped into the room as Jenna stepped out of the room.

Jenna had paused her normal rounds to get the lumbar puncture done, and now she needed to get back on track.

SIX PATIENTS, one chest tube, and one cardiac arrest later, Jenna sat at the computer workstation typing notes and sipping a fruit smoothie. She typed rhythmically to the beat of 'Can't Buy Me Love' that she played in her imagination.

"What are you chipper about?" Mike, one of the nurses, asked.

"Antigua. Three days away."

"Ah. That time again?"

"Indeed."

"Oh, to live the charmed life of Dr. Masters." He gave her a toothy smile.

Jenna smiled back and nodded.

If you only knew the sacrifices it took to get this far.

"Dr. Masters, room six has family requesting an update," April, the charge nurse, informed her.

"Oh, right. Didn't the patient have an uncle or something coming all the way from Russia?"

"Ye-ah." April's voice was hesitant.

"What's wrong?" Jenna asked, blinking as she sipped her smoothie. The strawberry, mango burst danced on her tongue.

"Well, they look a little imposing."

"They?"

"Do you want me to call security?"

Jenna had heard that some family members had been gruff over the phone with the staff. However, having a first-time conversation flanked by security would shatter any opportunity to build rapport with the family.

"No thanks, April. Can you put them in the family conference room, see if they want any drinks and then tell them I'll be there in five minutes?"

"Will do." She shrugged and left.

Jenna thought about the patient in bed six. He'd been the one who received a lumbar puncture earlier in the day. The twenty-six-year-old had seen some hard living, judging by the scars and tattoos that covered the majority of his arms and torso.

His muscular body was extremely fit, though, which made restraining him challenging. They had to keep him from inadvertently harming himself or yanking out any of his lifelines—breathing tubes or intravenous access. His metabolism churned through sedatives like a piranha through flesh. Fortunately, he was young and recovery would be swift.

Five minutes later, Jenna straightened her scrub top and entered the family conference room. She stifled her surprise to see a broad-shouldered man in a suit with short, spiked, peppered hair and a tattoo crawling up his neck. Men, the size of linebackers, flanked him on either side.

"I'm Dr. Masters. I can give you an update on your nephew. Would you like to take a seat?"

"I am Vladimir Pronin. Thank you for your punctuality."

He sat stiffly, and his men remained standing.

If Jenna had ever formulated a mental image of what an older, modern Vlad the Impaler would look like, this man would have supplanted it. Adding to the persona was his English, heavy with a Russian accent. His tailored gray suit and sleek, expensive obsidian watch only magnified his aura of strength and power.

Jenna sat opposite him at the conference room table.

Before she could start with explaining her medical assessment and provide and update, Vladimir spoke. "Mikhail is good kid, Dr. Masters. He has college education, and he looks out for the family. And we look out for him. So I was livid to have this Dr. Pasha tell me my nephew is in critical condition from drug abuse."

His palms rested flat on the table, and his jaw ticked like a man working to control his temper.

Well, now she knew why Dr. Alik Pasha had asked her to take his patient. And it had nothing to do with his patient load being high.

Jenna recognized dangerous men when she saw them, but she also knew that simple, respectful conversation about their medical concerns could diffuse the situation. She waited quietly for him to finish.

"My nephew is not flunky or junky or whatever you Americans call it."

"I agree."

He started to open his mouth and then closed it. He regarded her through narrowed eyes. At last he said, "You do?"

"Yes. He has no track marks to suggest intravenous drug use. There are no finger stains to suggest use of a crack pipe. His drug screen had opiates and benzodiazepines, but he got those in the ambulance and emergency room to control his delirium."

Vladimir's anger and defensive posture deflated.

"So what's wrong?" He lifted his hands, palms upward.

Jenna tugged at her earring stud. "Has he been in the woods or wilderness recently, maybe hunting?"

Vladimir arched an eyebrow and looked from side to side at the men to his right and left as he seemed to consider whether or not to answer her question.

"*Da.*"

"Lyme disease."

"*Da*?" The uncle's eyes widened.

She resisted the urge to respond with *da*. "Yes. I'm told when he came in he was confused, agitated, and febrile. On my exam this morning, I noted a particular sort of rash. Then, I did a lumbar puncture. There is evidence of meningitis. I'm still waiting on the Lyme titer, but I've already started the appropriate antibiotics."

He took a long moment to consider her. His eyes held a glint of admiration.

Rapport achieved.

"Why did not the other physician find this? Why was I told it was drugs?"

Eh ... because he stereotyped your nephew.

Jenna tried to think of an answer that wouldn't incriminate Dr. Pasha, but the truth was he'd assessed the patient's age and tattoos and decided that drugs were the statistically probable culprit for his behavior rather than the less common meningitis. Jenna didn't believe drugs caused his current state because she had looked closely for track marks; the man's skin and overall hygiene were too immaculate.

She chose her words carefully. "Lyme disease can have a misleading presentation, especially in the young."

Vladimir had obviously been insulted by Dr. Pasha in a way that conveyed he wished him bodily harm. The Russian appeared to have two men at his side capable of making his wishes come true.

"But you were not deceived." His eyes flashed as though taking all of her in—physician, woman, and sleuth.

She shifted uneasily as he stared at her with a little too much interest, his smile turning wolfish as he leaned back. He seemed to be committing the details of her appearance to memory.

Rapport gone overboard.

"The rash gave it away," she mumbled. She began to sense some vague familiarity with the man. A growing unease crawled along her spine—this was someone notorious—someone she should neither cross nor with whom she should endear herself.

"And the recovery?" he asked.

"The breathing tube should be able to be removed in a day or two. After that, he'll be observed for a few more days."

Vladimir stood, and Jenna felt a wave of relief as their family discussion came to a close.

"Family can visit him now?"

"Yes, of course."

Coming around the table, he extended a hand which Jenna politely accepted.

The firm but coolness felt like gripping the handle of a pair of pliers. The handshake conveyed a similar precaution—*you don't want to be on the wrong end of it.*

"*Spasibo*, Dr. Masters."

With that, he abruptly planted a kiss on either cheek and then excused himself. Jenna didn't know whether to be glad or worried about his behavior.

CHAPTER 2

Maxine Rider drank her morning coffee and stared out of her window at the gray February sky in Atlanta. She had assigned Ryan and Reece to their next job and sent them to the Caribbean, as promised. Perhaps her statement—made while the men tried to escape with Sharp Industries' prototype and their lives—had implied a vacation to the beach rather than work, but that was their own fault if they misunderstood her or made assumptions.

In truth, saving the prototype was worth a vacation in Antigua rather than a spy mission, but Maxine had no intention of setting the expectation that rewards for a job well done would be so lofty.

Because Sharp's equipment reached its way unharmed—shaken not damaged—back to one of his warehouses, Bill Sharp had thanked Maxine, promised to speak highly of her team, promised to use her services again, and paid handsomely. His quick access to his company's drones helped ensure the safe return of his equipment and Maxine's team.

Unfortunately, the drones weren't idling armed and ready to fly so he had to sacrifice the drones themselves into the enemy helicopters. After they took out two of the Killer Eggs, the other two helicopters abandoned the siege on the van.

A lesser team than her two former Rangers might not have gotten to the van and escaped. A lesser team might have been killed or maimed. But her men, practically part of her family, remained unharmed. Of all of them, tender Claire was the most rattled, but she'd recovered and grown a little more spine in the process.

Sharp was genuinely appalled at the lives of his employees that had been lost in the attempted theft. He didn't know who had plotted such an elaborate heist of his cargo. He asked Maxine to use the investigation part of her company to unearth the perpetrators. Maxine set Claire to the task. Ryan had suggested it felt a bit like his former employer, before his Rider SI work.

Maxine recalled the first time she met Ryan and recruited him. He'd left Titan Enterprises disillusioned—transitioned from army strong to a hired mercenary who lacked the programming to be someone's minion. She found Ryan in a Las Vegas fight club, center ring. She suspected he took physical beatings in front of a beer-drinking crowd as a way to punish himself for what he'd allowed himself to do in the past.

Titan Enterprises focused on making money without a moral compass. The criminal activity of their clients and the injuries to the innocent were of minor consideration.

Maxine had stayed until the end of the fight and entered the locker room when he was alone. Ryan had showered and wore a pair of blue jeans as he towel-dried his dark hair.

"Kickboxing for money hardly seems like an adequate use of your talents," she said.

He regarded Max carefully, but didn't seem bothered by her intrusion into the male locker room.

He shrugged.

"You could've beaten him long before the third round," she said.

Ryan didn't seem the type to put on a show for the crowd, but he also wasn't the type to let himself lose, no matter the self-flagellation he sought. So he took a beating until he'd had enough, she suspected. Meanwhile, the crowd got their entertainment.

"Yeah," he agreed.

"Ever bet on yourself?"

"I don't gamble."

"Says the man who lives in Vegas."

"Can I help you with something?"

She liked that he remained cordial while assessing her. He hadn't dismissed her despite her intrusion and her appearance—stocky in cargo pants and a t-shirt.

"You tell me." She extended a hand to him. "Maxine Rider."

"Ryan Walsh." He eyed her warily as he shook it. Then he turned, grabbed his clean shirt, and pulled it over his head. "I can't help you."

Max felt a twinge of pride. Reluctance restrained him because he knew who she was despite her small company. Good man. A worthy hire knows the playing field—knows who's a contender.

"Why is that, Walsh?"

He packed a bag with his gym clothes and shoes. "Maxine Rider? Of Rider Security and Investigations?"

She nodded.

"I don't do that type of work anymore."

"You're right. You don't work for a manipulative bastard lining his pockets."

Ryan smirked, revealing a dimple on his cheek. One cheekbone swelled from a hit he had taken during the fight. "You know Lucius Titan?"

"I know all the major private security companies, both legitimate and feigning legitimacy."

Ryan leaned against the lockers. "By your tone, one might think you consider yourself legitimate."

Maxine stuffed her hands in her pockets. "We're good people helping good people. We're the reason you joined the military long ago. We represent a brighter future for those who leave the military because they want more ... want better."

"I don't regret the service to my country, but I'm not as naïve as I was the day I enlisted."

"Of course you're not. That's why I want to recruit you. I don't want boys handy with guns who blindly follow orders."

His eyes flared, revealing a hint of skepticism in his otherwise calm body language. "So says the former marine."

She smiled. "I want men and women who can think critically and help clients out of tough situations." She pulled a business card from her back pocket. "Research me. Call me when you're ready. If you don't like an assignment I offer, you're free to pick a different one."

Ryan took the card but didn't reply.

Walking away, she added, "And call your buddy, Reece. He needs to get out of the bottle. I'm willing to hire both of you."

⁂

JENNA SAT AT THE AIRPORT, waiting for her flight to Antigua and thinking of warm sand and lapping waves. She sipped her overpriced coffee as she watched the bustling pedestrians making their way through O'Hare. Outside, the sky was pale blue and snow from a dusting a few days ago covered grassy areas. She was happy the precipitation had passed and that today there were no flight delays.

Her phone rang.

"Hi, Brody."

"Jenna, you're off to Antigua?" her boss asked in his deep, rumbling voice.

"At the airport."

"You're good? Work's okay?"

"Yes." She drew out the word, wondering about his odd inquiry now, while she was on her way to vacation.

"You're coming back?"

"I always come back, Brody."

"I heard about one of your recent patients."

"Uh-huh."

"Sounded like the kind of shady celebrity none of us want the responsibility of caring for."

Jenna suspected Vladimir Pronin's visit would sustain hospital gossip for several weeks. "It's all good. The patient is fine. His uncle is fine."

Jenna had researched Vladimir on the Internet in the evening after his disconcerting stares and gushing appreciation. It was better she hadn't known at the time who he was or she may have taken the security guard with her.

Thou shalt not antagonize the leader of the Russian mob.

"And you're okay with everything?"

"We got along fine," she reassured him.

"Okay. And you're coming back?"

"I'll be back at work when I'm due back."

"Okay."

"Can I start my vacation now?"

"Okay." He hung up the phone.

She stared at her phone before putting it on airplane mode. Soon, she would forget about the young Russian and his Lyme meningitis. He'd made great strides in recovery on appropriate therapy and had been liberated from life support. A few more days in the hospital, and he would be stable for discharge home or wherever Pronin's next escapade propelled him.

Mikhail's girlfriend, who came to his bedside after Jenna met his uncle, was none other than Russian supermodel Natasha Bodrov. The gaunt yet angelic beauty with cascading auburn hair had towered over Jenna as she expressed her gratitude.

Jenna had updated Vladimir on the progress of his nephew on her last day at work. He had thanked her again with kisses again.

"No problem," she had replied with a forced smile.

What else did one say to the alleged leader of a major Russian crime syndicate?

"You saved Mikhail's life." He had said to her during their farewell.

Normal rapport re-established ... with the Russian mafia. Thanks for that. Dr. Pasha.

Vladimir kissed her cheeks yet again.

"If you ever need anything, Dr. Masters, you call Vladimir Pronin. *Da?*"

"Yes."

"*Anything.*" He leaned in and ensured unwavering, uncomfortable eye contact.

She'd never had a godfather, but felt like she had suddenly acquired one. A godfather one did not dare cross.

"Yes," she replied.

He patted her cheek and left.

But she'd already eliminated the trouble in her life, so she knew she wouldn't be calling in any favors to the Russian mafia.

CHAPTER 3

*J*enna fixed her eight hundredth drink of the night as Jimmy Buffet crooned leisurely through the speaker.

"Honey, can I take you back to the States with me?"

"No, Chuck," Jenna replied. "You need to take yourself back to your room and sober up." She placed a glass of water in front of him.

"You could make an honest man out of me," he insisted through glassy eyes and tobacco-stained teeth.

"No one can pull that feat off, I'm sure." Her tone remained light, but she hoped Chuck would call it a night and stop wasting away in Margaritaville.

She enjoyed vacationing in Antigua and the slow pace of the Caribbean compared to the ICU, but filling-in bartending at her parents' resort could tax her ability to remain congenial. She poured ginger beer over ice and did a slow pour of Gosling's rum. After slipping a lime on the edge, she slid it down the bar to another customer.

"The Dark and Stormy," she announced.

"Thanks," a female customer said.

Jenna restocked clean glasses at the bar as she looked beyond Chuck to watch a courtship gone awry. A cute brunette in her early twenties had been flirting with a half-dozen college football players. She seemed to enjoy making a sport of getting them excited about her and then walking away from them. Promising everything, delivering nothing.

It reminded her of someone she cared to forget.

"Stop it!" the woman cried, which seemed to be more of a cry for help than her usual playful tone of the night.

The football players were advancing down the field. Ogling eyes turned to groping hands, disinhibited by beer consumption.

Jenna started to miss her real job. Well, she'd be back there soon enough.

I am many things, but a bouncer isn't one of them.

Besides, this was an island resort. They weren't supposed to need a bouncer.

She moved to come out from behind the bar to intervene, when two men approached the football players. She recognized them as guests of the resort for about ten days—long enough for her to nickname them.

The slightly shorter one with the handlebar mustache was Wyatt Earp. His wingman was a silent, brooding David 'Bruce' Banner. He looked mild and calm, but she wondered if he would transform into the Hulk when provoked. Each night he remained at the bar long after Wyatt had taken his catch of the night for a moonlit stroll or whatever else two consenting adults might do at an island resort.

The two men conversed calmly with the football players who seemed to inflate their chests out further like blow-up dolls.

She hoped Banner was warning them not to make him angry.

"You wouldn't like me when I'm angry." Because that would make her nickname spot-on.

When the six football players pushed out their chairs and stood, Jenna's heart pick up pace. Wyatt and his friend were woefully outnumbered. Oddly, they didn't appear disconcerted.

Incorporating some higher brain function for the first time that evening, the brunette slunk away from the impending fight and over toward the bar.

Jenna pulled out her medic bag from under the bar, partly in anticipation of the impending fight and partly hoping to ward off any major medical injuries.

RYAN STOOD as tall as most of the football players—well, kids really. Kids who foolishly thought three-to-one odds were in their favor. He and Reece had asked politely for them to find more willing companionship than the girl who seemed to be toying with them. He wasn't intending to start a fight, but then this was a bar with a concentration of testosterone and alcohol.

Based on the boys' body language, they itched to fight—glassy eyes narrowed, cheeks turned crimson, and knuckles tightened.

Ryan's challenge would be to achieve surrender without causing any lasting injury. The boys needed to learn a little humility without suffering career-ending wounds.

The blond brute swung first, a slow and clumsy move that Reece easily dodged before kicking a leg out from under him.

A second thug swung with a beer bottle in hand. Ryan caught the bottle-wielder by the wrist, pivoted, and, bending his knees, flipped the man over his shoulder.

The largest of the football players picked up a nearby wooden chair. His face contorted in misplaced fury as he swung as hard as he could at Reece.

Ryan envisioned the chair's trajectory and wanted to yell out a warning, but he was preoccupied blocking another attacker.

Reece ducked the chair with ease, and as it continued its course around and struck another boy. One of the chair legs connected with the boy's neck and the football player crumpled to the ground, clutching at his throat.

Friendly fire.

The one who swung the chair stood in shocked disbelief at having clobbered his friend to the ground.

Ryan punched his attacker in the jaw. He had planned to avoid head and knee shots, but it was time to end this charade. The boy on the ground was seriously injured after that blow.

Reece casually fended off another attacker.

When Ryan got a clear look at the one on the floor, his mouth went dry. The college boy's lips turned blue as he struggled to breathe.

Collapsed larynx.

Ryan had seen it before—caused it before. It was certain death.

From around the counter, one of the female bartenders appeared at the boy's side, a bag in tow. With green eyes intently focused, she felt his neck even as he struggled. She grabbed an open bottle of vodka from the bar and knelt back on the floor.

"Hey, Banner," she snapped at him, "keep these assholes at a distance long enough to let me save this kid's life."

Banner?

Ryan nodded. He glanced around the room. So far, Reece had the remaining two football players that had rebounded under control. He saw the other bartender on the phone, hopefully dialing for an ambulance. He turned his attention back to the woman.

Jenna.

He knew because he'd heard the other bartender talking to

her one night. "Jenna, where's the Grand Marnier?" And Ryan remembered because he'd seen Jenna several times over the last few days, intentionally, from a distance.

She jabbed a syringe of something into the boy's thigh. Then she pulled off the vodka spigot and doused it with the liquor. Snapping on a pair of gloves, she rapidly wiped his neck with an alcohol pad. From her bag, she produced a scalpel.

"Whoa!" Ryan exclaimed.

Blazing green eyes glared up at him as she suspended the blade an inch from the suffocating boy's neck.

"If I don't do an emergent crich, he is going to die."

Her voice contained such absolute and unwavering certainty that he believed her. He believed that she fully intended to save his life and had the ability to do so.

"Okay," he conceded. "Can I help?"

She grinned at him. "You can make sure he doesn't clock me with a right hook."

Ryan moved to secure the kid's hands, which were wrapped around his lower neck in the universal sign for choking. There wasn't much fight left in him as the crushed larynx slowly swelled shut, but in his last few panicked breaths he could thrash violently enough to interfere with Jenna's work.

Which is what, exactly?

"Don't watch if you're squeamish."

Ryan watched with fascination as Jenna, with surgical precision, slit a hole in the young man's throat. She produced a wad of gauze, dabbed away a thick trail of crimson blood.

After a quick inspection of the spout from the vodka bottle, she inserted it into his neck. She put her lips to the spout and blew out a breath. As she breathed out in a slow, timed fashion through the spout, the college kid turned from ashen to rose-colored. He had slipped into unconsciousness, so Ryan released his grip.

Reece had the rest of the room under control. The boy's friends, who were licking their wounds, had gathered around the medical emergency. Aside from them, there were only two other bar patrons, one other bartender, and the girl who had been flirting with the football players. She sat in a corner looking sullen.

Between breaths, Jenna cleaned the wound and prepared strips of tape.

A pair of gloves landed in Ryan's lap as he knelt opposite Jenna beside her patient. Dutifully, he put them on and awaited instructions.

She gave another breath. "Since you are neither incapacitated by fear nor unconscious from the sight of blood, be a champ and hold that in place."

Ryan obeyed, grasping the spout that protruded from the boy's neck between his thumb and index finger. Jenna secured the pourer in place with wide medical tape over his neck. She seemed careful not to apply too much pressure.

Jenna spoke without looking up from her work. "Those were some wicked fight moves."

So says the woman wielding the scalpel.

"Former Ranger," he replied.

She gave him something of an appraising look, and he immediately approved of her eyes roaming his body.

She breathed again through the spout, and he marveled at her ability to remain calm given the situation.

"And you would be doctor—?"

"Masters."

"Dr. Masters ... who moonlights as a bartender?"

"Something like that."

She breathed again, strands of copper hair falling forward.

"Are you in witness protection or something?"

She started to chuckle before seeming to realize he'd asked a serious question. Her mouth thinned to a straight line and her eyelids lowered. "Yes. Witness protection. Now you've forced me to reveal myself. I'll have to change my identity and go on the run again." She cracked a wry smile, and her eyes sparkled at him. "That would make a great story, but no, I'm not in witness protection."

Ryan watched her, amused and intrigued. "Then why?"

She flashed him a sidelong glance. "My business, Banner." Her voice remained friendly.

"Banner?"

"Sorry." She shrugged. "Every time you come in here, you sulk in the corner while your friend, Wyatt, has a good time."

Ryan felt a rising excitement to think she'd been taking notice of him ... repeatedly. But then, didn't bartenders notice everyone in their bar? Except, she was also a physician. He would get the story behind that career divergence.

"I do not sulk," he said. "Also, I don't think you're supposed to mingle Westerns and comics."

She breathed again into the makeshift tracheostomy.

"Brooding then. And my imagination, my rules."

Ryan laughed.

"Ah, so he does lighten up. Trauma brings out the lighter side?"

He arched an eyebrow and refrained from pointing out that she was the reason he was laughing and smiling and not the unfortunate circumstances.

JENNA PASSED off care of the unconscious boy to the emergency medical technicians when they arrived. They rigged the adaptor onto the bag-valve mask so they could breathe for the patient.

After starting an intravenous line, they loaded up the stretcher and headed to the hospital.

Police arrived and initiated questioning, starting with the football players.

Jenna used the time to clean up the mess on the floor and then to clean behind the bar.

Banner took a seat at the bar.

"Bar's closed."

"Yes, I imagine so," the Ranger replied, a smile playing on a set of full lips.

"You gonna linger here and see what other trouble you can get into, Trouble-Maker?"

"I like Banner better."

She chuckled. As she dried a wine glass, she looked up at him. His brown eyes radiated warmth and an unspoken invitation, different from when he'd been brooding in the corner. She noticed faint traces of a few scars on his face, making him ruggedly handsome and obviously no stranger to fights. She caught herself before she lingered too long in anything that could be called a stare. Spinning around, she shelved the wine glass.

She turned back around to face him. "Okay, Banner, I don't cover the bar again for another five nights. Should I make sure I have the necessary equipment to place a chest tube in somebody on Friday?"

He gave her a wolfish smile.

He thinks I'm asking if he's going to be here next Friday. Not my intention. Was it?

"Somehow, I think a woman like you already has the necessary equipment."

Jenna felt herself blush. He was right. She had the hose, the bottles, and the scalpel, of course.

"Emergency Medicine?"

"Critical Care," she explained.

He nodded as he seemed to quietly reflect on her identity. "Dr. Jenna Masters, critical care physician."

She capped a jar of maraschino cherries.

"—and weekend bartender?"

Hmm. He's fishing.

She wasn't biting. Her past belonged to her. She came to Antigua because this was the one place she could go to forget the past. It always had been.

"And you? You're not local. So what? One long vacation you don't seem to be enjoying? Or maybe you're the one in witness protection. You were a professional kickboxer, and you witnessed racketeering. You're in hiding here until you testify."

He smiled. "Kickboxing?"

Jenna shrugged. "Okay. Former hitman who turned on the mafia."

Something dark flickered in his eyes but then just as quickly vanished.

"So I'm the Hulk or a kickboxer or a hitman?"

"I'm making this up as I go." She wiped down the countertop.

"That's a lot of speculation when you haven't even asked me my name."

Jenna froze. She swallowed hard. She liked bantering with the man and liked how he was easy on the eyes. But a name? No. She decidedly didn't want a name.

"What's in a name?" Handsome by any other name would look just as delectable.

No name. Nice and superficial.

CHAPTER 4

yan woke early the next morning and prepared his coffee. He stepped outside for his morning routine of sitting in the Adirondack, watching the sunrise and catching a glimpse of Jenna going for a morning beach run. Her long, shapely legs were a touch sun-kissed and her strawberry hair gleamed in its ponytail.

She remained oblivious to his watching her, as she had been the entire time he was here. He'd been working his way up to an encounter with her in between the information gathering he was sent to Antigua to do.

Last night was the first time a real conversation transpired between them rather than only drink orders. He was learning so much about her, but more was waiting to be discovered. She kept her distance, corralled her trust like a prized steed.

Hands off, Banner.

She genuinely seemed not to want to know his name. Before he could advance the conversation further, the police had come for statements. After than, she'd left before he could speak with her. Instead, he talked to her bartending counterpart, who explained that Jenna's parents owned the resort. Another fascinating fact.

Reece approached from the door of the adjacent bungalow, disrupting his calm morning. "Well, last night was a disaster."

Yes and no, thought Ryan.

Reece followed Ryan's gaze to the beach, then to the woman on the beach.

Reece shook his head. "I don't understand, Walsh. You tell me she's off limits, then you never make a move on her. Normal people don't stalk women. They ask them out."

Ryan sipped his coffee. Up until last night, he'd found her attractive, but he wasn't sure that he wanted something based solely on attraction, especially if she lived here and he was based in the US. He'd had enough superficial relationships. Now, knowing she had some confounding depth, he had every intention of 'making a move.'

"If I'd approached her the first time it had crossed my mind, she would've shut me down for good." He felt certain of that now more than when he'd first begun to take an interest in her. "She doesn't think she wants a relationship."

Reece adjusted his khaki shorts and sat next to him even though Ryan hadn't invited him to do so. "All I'm saying," Reece drawled, "is reconnaissance is for the assholes we spy on, not for women you want to have dinner with."

"Can't be too careful."

"Bullshit. You're not watching her because you think she has deadly secrets. You're watching her because you're too scared to ask her out."

Was that it?

It hadn't begun that way. Initially, he didn't want to know her. A man in his line of work didn't secure lasting relationships easily. A man with his past didn't deserve one.

After seeing her bartend one evening, he subsequently caught sight of her on the beach the next day. She lounged under an umbrella with a laptop open and sipping tonic water and lime. Long, shimmering copper hair spilled over her shoulders. A medical journal lay on the table. To his surprise, she unleashed a beautiful, heartfelt laugh.

What he wouldn't give to make a woman laugh like that. He realized she was having a video chat with someone—someone who made her look vibrant and made her laugh richly. Someone who wasn't here on a tropical beach sitting beside this gorgeous, tan woman in a bikini with her lean runner's legs, perfectly curved hips, and round breasts. Day after day, this someone never came to the island in the flesh.

At first, Ryan kept his distance because he thought there may be a special someone. Now, he realized, perhaps he didn't have a good explanation for his hesitation. Last night changed everything. Last night she kept cool under pressure. She saved a life as simply as if she had poured a Tom Collins. Then, she casually stood back at the bar, not expecting fanfare for her efforts.

Suddenly, she wasn't just a pretty bartender; she possessed more depth and character. Even more intriguing was that she didn't boast about her skills.

"It's complicated," Ryan finally admitted.

"*She's* complicated. I like simple," Reece said. "Who works at a bar when she can put in an emergent tracheostomy in under two minutes?"

"I think I like complicated," Ryan mused.

"You want me to have Claire run a background?"

"No," Ryan said hurriedly. Reece was right. Ryan's behavior had already bordered on stalking. "I want her to tell me about herself when she's ready."

Reece shrugged. "I take it we're still on for today?"

"Kayak at ten."

"Okay. Reece plays wingman. I'm on it." He stroked his mustache.

"One more thing. During the kayaking, I'm Banner and you're Wyatt."

"Beg pardon?"

"Dr. Masters didn't want to know my name last night. I'm not volunteering it. If she wants to know, she'll have to ask."

"You've got some deranged courting tactics. You know that, right?"

TOURISTS WALKED toward the kayak dock as Jenna prepared to take them on an enjoyable day around the islands. So many fascinating details awaited to be shared, not to mention the thrill of the boat as it noiselessly cut through the waves.

She startled to see Banner and Wyatt walking toward her, shirtless with black swim trunks. Their arrival shouldn't have been unexpected; after all, they were hotel guests. She searched Banner's expression for some hint of mischievousness or scheming. His face, partially hidden by his sunglasses, was an indiscernible mask.

Coincidence that he's here on the one day of the week that I'm the tour guide?

His expression remained neutral as he approached.

Don't flatter yourself, Jenna. You didn't even have the courtesy to ask his name.

When the number of registered tourists matched the count on her sheet, Jenna boomed, "Good morning, everyone! Gather around, and we'll go over a few details before we start the kayak tour."

She explained the sequence of the excursion—kayaking, island tour, refreshment break, then reef snorkeling. After reviewing the safety tips, including no sparkling jewelry that may attract barracuda during snorkeling, everyone donned a life jacket.

"Okay, pair up. Two to a kayak."

One by one, she helped them from the deck to the boats, mostly couples. The two men waited last and certainly didn't need her assistance. She held their oars as they boarded.

"Dr. Masters," Banner said with a grin.

Her heart sped up a few beats at the sight of his handsome dimples. "Dr. Banner."

He chuckled, a sound she was deeply starting to enjoy. She had the feeling he seldom partook of simple pleasures and suspected creating a light-hearted moment he enjoyed was an achievement with a man like him.

"And how are your parents—the owners of this fine establishment?"

She narrowed her eyes at him. Sometime between the bar fight and walking to the morning kayak tour, he had researched her. That information would have taken some digging, but not been impossible to unearth. She bit her lip.

What else had he uncovered about her?

She climbed into her single-passenger kayak all the while staring at his muscular arms and legs. When his mouth gave a wry curve at one corner, she knew she'd been caught.

Damn dark sunglasses.

She needed a pair of those. She hadn't been able to tell he was watching her ogle him. Her face flushed, and he probably saw that too. Taking a deep breath, she focused on the tour. Fortunately, she'd given this tour a hundred times so today's muscular attraction wouldn't cause misguided distraction.

"Okay, folks, let's review kayaking basics. If you're in the front, your job is paddling. If you're in the back, you are the rudder. Your job is steering and synchronous paddling. Please try not to smack your co-kayaker in the head even if he or she forgot to take out the trash before you left for vacation."

Her crowd graciously chuckled.

Joking aside, she didn't want any more emergencies.

"If you get tired, Phillip and Sal will be close at hand with the pontoon boat. They also supply the rum punch at the end of the tour, so you might treat them like your new best friends."

The tourists gave a few excited cheers at the mention of rum punch. The boats bumped carelessly together as they tried out their paddles.

"A few facts about Antigua. First, that is the correct pronunciation—An-tea-ga, not An-tea-gwa. We are one hundred eight square miles of arid land. Our population is roughly one hundred thousand, and we are entirely dependent on tourism for our economic survival. Our major sport is cricket, but football—that is, soccer—is also popular."

When they set out from the coast, she tasted the salty breeze and enjoyed the gentle rock of the kayak.

With the trail of tourists in yellow kayaks following her, she imagined she looked something like a mother duck with her ducklings in yellow kayaks dutifully in tow.

Hah!

Maybe this was what it felt like to have one's ducks in row.

She cut through the aqua ocean with the blade of her oar. Left, right, left.

Not too fast, can't leave the duckies—err—tourists behind.

She glanced back, seeing Banner and Wyatt bringing up the rear. With a little effort, they could have easily taken the lead behind her. Perhaps their nature forced them to take a protective flank the same way they stepped in to protect the woman in the bar.

Former Ranger.

Stopping at an alcove, Jenna waited as the boats gathered around her.

"I mentioned that Antigua is arid. That's because our highest elevation is only thirteen hundred feet, so we have no high mountains to capture precipitation." She went on to describe the plant life and wildlife, including the Antiguan racer, a harmless but endangered species of snake.

"One of our big events is Antigua sailing week—a series of boat races with some two hundred participants. It's absolutely magnificent to sit on the shore and watch hundreds of boats gliding through the water."

She led them to a shallow reef with a nearby island and sandy beach. She instructed them that they had one hour to walk the beach, sunbathe, or snorkel before they needed to be back at their boats. As the tourists climbed out of their kayaks, Phillip and Sal secured the boats to ensure they didn't drift away from the coast.

Jenna docked her kayak at Sal's boat. She hopped on deck, tugged off her lifejacket, and grabbed a bottle of water out of a cooler. She twisted the top off and turned, almost bumping into Banner's tall, broad body.

She stifled her surprise.

"Did you want a bottle of water?" she offered.

She swallowed, staring at his bare chest. She felt like she needed to pour the cold liquid over her head to cool off the sudden swell of teenage-like hormones.

He smiled at her ... that damned charming, I-know-what-you're- thinking smile.

Trouble with a capital T.

"Actually, I was wondering which of the activities you recommend—beach or snorkel or sight-see."

She blinked at him.

He was supposed to ask that question back in the group at the part where she gave instructions and then asked, "Does anybody have any questions?" Instead, he chose to ask her alone on the boat.

"You can try one this time and then come back on your next vacation and try a different activity," she offered politely.

"Are you asking me back?"

Her face heated, probably turning three shades of red. Her usual reply to the tourist group took on a whole new meaning when alone with an attractive man. Suddenly a friendly "Come back and visit Antigua!" transformed into a seductive "Come back and see me."

He lifted his dark glasses. "Call me old-fashioned, but I think we should have dinner before you ask me out on vacation."

"What? No, I ... that's not what I meant." She narrowed her eyes at him. He was twisting words in his favor.

His smile widened, and the corners of his eyes crinkling in enjoyment of her squirming discomfort.

She frowned, then stuck the water bottle in her mouth and drank. It seemed better that she keep silent lest he continue twisting her words or she keep stumbling over them.

"You don't want to have dinner?"

Yes, yes, yes ... and no.

She looked into his eyes. Maybe if he wasn't standing so close, her traitorous body would stop trying to gravitate toward him. She focused on remaining motionless.

"I can't." She finally got the words out of her mouth.

He frowned. "Because I'm a customer at the resort?"

She sighed. That line only worked when people didn't know

she was the daughter of the owners. "There's a storm coming, and after this tour, I have to get all these kayaks in the shed to prevent the high tide and waves from washing them away."

He nodded and stepped back from her. "I understand." Stepping off the edge of the boat, he plunged into the shimmering water.

Jenna stood under the baking sun surrounded by a dozen tourists and felt cold and alone.

RYAN WATCHED Jenna in the distance, rowing her kayak with ease and apparent enjoyment. Her smooth, light caramel skin glistened from sprays of ocean water that beaded on top of her. From behind his dark glasses, he had watched her apply sunscreen while she stood on the boat and he relaxed on shore.

She had missed some spots, but he thought it might be too much to offer to help her. She was already a bit nervous around him. Her behavior remained unwavering in an emergency, relaxed and cavalier as a bartender, fun and spunky as a tour guide, but skittish around him.

Curious.

Caution permeated her actions, as though she trusted neither herself nor him.

Good for her. Cautious was good.

He could work with cautious. Careless behavior and manipulative behavior were traits he couldn't stomach, and she didn't seem to have those.

"You ask her out?" Reece asked as he rowed in the front of the boat.

Ryan matched Reece's pace, rowing in unison.

"Yes. She said, 'no.'"

"Oh, sorry, Walsh."

"Worry not," Ryan replied. "Her brain said no, but her eyes said something else entirely."

"You and your nonverbal communication skills."

"It's an art," Ryan retorted. He knew Reece appreciated his skills when they worked on the job.

"Isn't that like cheating or playing dirty to use those skills in dating?"

"So asks the one who has been with three different women this trip."

Reece experienced a moment of uncharacteristic silence.

"Anyway," Ryan added, "it's working in her favor. If I hadn't noticed her body language, then I might've taken her at her word and accepted the rejection."

"Which she didn't mean?"

"Exactly."

In front of him, Reece shook his head.

When they reached the kayak dock, Ryan waited as all the other tourists, including Reece, made their way to the pavilion for the all-inclusive rum punch.

Sal and Jenna began to pull the kayaks out of the water. Ryan joined them to help.

"Banner, what are you doing?" Jenna asked.

"Helping."

"You're a *guest*," she reminded him in a harsh, scolding whisper.

"And you can't go on a dinner date because you have all of this work to do. So I'm helping."

And don't think I don't notice you staring at my biceps as I pull the kayak out of the water.

She turned, took a few steps, and bent down to pick up the opposite end of the kayak. Together, they carried it through the sand and hung it in the shed. With the three of them working, they moved the kayaks in no time.

Jenna stood motionless, looking out toward the horizon.

Ryan stood beside her quietly enjoying the sound of lapping waves and the smell of her coconut sunscreen.

She took a sidelong glance at him before resuming her gaze at the mesmerizing glisten of the water.

He kept quiet, waiting. He had holed up in the caves in Afghanistan for days at a time; he possessed an abundance of patience.

She wrung her hands together. "Yes. Okay. Dinner. But I'm exhausted, so is tomorrow night okay?"

Turning toward her, he scooped up a hand and kissed the back of it. "I'll pick you up at six tomorrow."

He released her hand and walked back to his room at the resort.

⁂

RYAN BUTTONED his blue cotton shirt.

Reece sat in the chair in his bungalow, pouting. "I can't believe you're going solo, ditching me for a date."

"You've seen women on this trip. I didn't harass you."

"You did actually, with those judgmental eyes of yours. Did you even ask this woman if she has a friend? We could have had a double date."

"That is not at all appealing."

He and Reece were brothers in arms and had battled through more tight spots than a hermit crab. They were inseparable on missions and liked each other in the relaxed company of a bar and a few beers. But they didn't—would never—double date.

"You asked me to play wingman for the kayaking, and what is my return on investment? A night alone."

Ryan tucked his shirt into his khaki pants. He turned to his friend. "You're acting like I'm leaving you behind on a mission."

"Aren't you?"

"Jenna Masters is not a mission. She is a beautiful woman with whom I have a date."

"You've treated her like a mission. Caution. Reconnaissance. Conquest."

Ryan gave him an expression of reproof. "Caution, yes. But there is no conquest. I'm hoping for an exploration of mutual attraction."

"Conquest."

Ryan sighed and abandoned the conversation.

"And I'm left behind," Reece added, smoothing fingers over his mustache.

"Take in a sunset. Relax on the beach."

"And don't wait up for you?" Reece teased.

Ryan considered his friend's playful question. Ryan could be charming and enticing, but anticipating sleeping together on the first date seemed a lofty goal to attain. "I have no idea where the night will take us."

⁂

"Jess, I need your help," Jenna said.

ICU monitors beeped in the background through Jessica Ong's phone. Jenna had caught her friend at work.

"What's wrong?" Jess said, alarm filling her voice.

"I have a date."

"Jeez, Jenna." Jess released a sigh. "I thought you were going to tell me you killed someone. You sound so worried."

Jenna stared at her wardrobe. "What? Why would you think I had killed someone?"

"I'm the cool friend someone would call if they needed to hide a body." Jess's tone sounded absurdly matter-of-fact. "But, now that I think about it, you calling me and panicking over a date sounds more like you."

Jenna frowned. She wasn't sure if Jess meant she would panic more over a date than a dead body. She let the silence settle, unsure of how to respond to her friend's insult.

"Okay, so date. What's the problem?" Jess asked.

"The last time I went on a date was ..." Jenna's voice trailed.

"Oh, right. That is a problem."

She could hear the sound of Jess tapping her fingernails on a desk.

"Did they even make contraceptives back then?"

"Hey!" Jenna paced her room. "I am not worried about sleeping with him."

"Good for you."

"No. I mean. I'm not sleeping with someone on the first date."

Jess's clicking fingers on the keyboard stopped, and she let out a grunt. "You have no sense of adventure."

Jenna ignored the comment. "I'm worried that it's been so long since I've been on a date that I don't know how to act normal."

"Right. Here are the rules: don't mention your ex; don't mention your son."

"You've eliminated three-quarters of my life from the conversation," Jenna said flatly.

"Talk about your childhood. Talk about work—but don't inundate him with the gory details. Talk about Antigua—all those cool facts you've shared with me."

"He got to hear all of those on the kayak tour."

"You're dating a tourist?"

"He's more than that. He's a former Ranger, and he clobbered a bunch of drunk guys in a bar as easily as if he were rearranging the furniture."

Smooth. Practiced. Flawless.

"Huh."

"Huh, what?"

"You sound a bit enamored. It's not a tone I've heard in your voice before."

Jenna flopped down on her bed and stared at the ceiling. "I'm nervous."

"You'll do fine." Jess added, "If all else fails, take your clothes off. You still remember how to do that, right?"

"Not helpful, Jess. Not helpful at all."

He was tall, dark, handsome ... and a level of danger she wasn't sure she was ready for.

CHAPTER 5

Ryan escorted Jenna to the dinner table.

"May I have your name?" Jenna asked.

Victory number one.

"Ryan Walsh."

"Nice to meet you, Ryan."

He admired her green cotton dress that showed off her legs and silver jewelry around her neck that made a V toward the gentle swell of cleavage. Her legs tapered down to silver-heeled sandals. Freshly coated pearl-colored toenails betrayed extra preparation for tonight's dinner date.

He led her to a table and pulled out the chair for her. He caught a waft of floral soap and a hint of coconut as she brushed past him. For an instant, he imagined burying his face in her neck and smelling the scent fully.

As he sat across from her at the small table, he admired the glow of her caramel skin by candlelight.

She picked up a menu, but he could see her eyeing him over the top.

"You're persistent, Ryan."

"I've been called worse."

She granted him a smile before looking back down at her menu.

He said, "I enjoyed the guided kayak tour."

She raised an eyebrow. "You and your friend had enough muscle power to tour twice as many islands in a day. You hardly needed a guide."

"Then we would've missed out on all of the amazing facts about Antigua." He made sure to pronounce the name correctly. "And I would have missed the opportunity to invite you to dinner."

The server introduced himself, poured water, and left a wine menu.

"Resourceful guy like you would have thought of something."

"And the critical care physician is giving guided tours because …"

She frowned, but it looked more like a pout. "You're not going to let that go, are you?"

"I watched you save a man's life and treat it like a day at the office. I can't let that go."

He thought of her leaning over, focused. A nick, then a trickle of blood. Next, in slid the makeshift artificial airway.

Jenna raised her eyebrows. "If it had been a day at the office, I'd be worried about completing my documentation and not getting sued."

She set down her menu and leaned on the table. "I work nine months of the year in critical care. The other three, I come here. Usually spread out over the winter months. My parents own the resort. I come here to work and help and escape from everything dismal and dreary in the world of medicine."

Was sharing that so hard, Jenna?

"Is that all you come here to escape?" Ryan knew he nudged her, but her self-preservation attitude toward something as benign as dinner with him didn't stem from her medical experiences. It could only come from a bad relationship. The question he sought answered was how bad was it? Irreconcilable differences or inconsolable damages?

Jenna bit her lip. "Wine sounds wonderful."

Maybe I need a different approach.

"Can't be all bad. I noticed somebody made you happy the other day. I saw you lounging on the beach. You seemed to be on a video chat with someone."

As though recalling or reliving the moment, her face illuminated, green eyes sparkling and almost filling with joy. It was a sight to behold. What if this woman's face had such a reaction thinking of him someday? Yet, surely he couldn't compete with whoever could bring her such instant delight.

He started to have doubts about dinner. What had he done? She clearly loved—

"That was my son, Cal."

—her son.

Her son?

"He's in a boarding school outside of Boston. It's a special school for competitive skiers. Hey," she snapped. "Don't make that face. He's the one who wanted to go. It's crushing me not to see him every day, but I'm trying to be supportive of his dreams. He's going to Austria to ski next week on a school trip."

Ryan considered the difference in weather. Currently, it was tropically pleasant in Antigua, chilly in Atlanta, and snowing in Austria.

The waiter arrived, and Ryan ordered a Meridian Vineyards Chardonnay.

"He used to come to Antigua with me every summer." Her voice trailed off as though rippling through a sea of a thousand memories.

He wanted to know them all, hear each of them as he watched her face radiate with the memories of her son.

"How old is he?"

"Fifteen." She took a sip of her water. "You can stop struggling to do the math. I was nineteen when I had him. I was a child, having a child, and married to an even bigger child. At least two of us grew up."

The server returned with the wine and poured two glasses.

"What happened?" Ryan felt as though he sat on the edge of his seat, desperately needing the mystery unraveled.

"Ugh. Okay, but this is degrading into a story about my son's father." She took a sip of the wine.

She hesitated as though waiting for Ryan to stave off the discussion, but he wasn't backing out now.

"We got pregnant, married too young, and stayed married too long. I thought that by staying married, I protected Cal from having a broken home. Turns out it was pretty broken anyway.

"Brad was charismatic, so much so that I hadn't noticed his gambling problem. Once I did, I carefully segregated our finances and hid any moonlighting funds I earned. Resident and fellowship hours are brutal. He never knew—or didn't care—which shifts were required and which were the few extras I worked. Because I didn't want Cal growing up without a father, I stuck it out—college, medical school, residency, fellowship. I basically kept Brad on a stipend, like a second mortgage. Of course, it meant we never had any savings—no nest egg."

She sipped the wine again, and then lowered it, staring into the glass. She seemed tortured and nervous retelling so much unpleasant past, but Ryan wanted her to know she could speak openly around him.

"I brought Cal out here every year ... our little getaway."

"But you left Brad," Ryan prompted.

Please, Jenna, tell me you left this jerk.

"His choice, and I was happy for it." She nodded, looking up into his eyes. "One day Cal turned to me and said, 'Mom, Dad is an ass to you. Why don't you leave him?' So I did. Officially divorced for over a year."

"Smart kid."

She chuckled. "So smart. He's such a gem. I look at him and wonder what I did to deserve someone like that in my life. It's amazing. I'd go through everything again to have the same outcome with Cal."

When the waiter reappeared, she ordered the Mahi Mahi and he ordered rock lobster.

Ryan sipped his wine. The buttery vanilla flavor coated his throat.

He asked, "Brad didn't ... he wasn't violent?"

"No. Brad was not violent. A lying, gambling cheater, yes. Abusive, no."

Ryan soured at that thought. He felt that those crimes against a woman were in fact abusive.

"When we married, he was charming. Then, he transformed. It was like watching Sméagol deteriorate into Gollum. Gambling was his *Precious*. By the time he started cheating—or by the time I noticed—I was so disgusted with him I didn't even care. I just didn't want Cal to know. He deserved a better role model.

"Of course, that all got shot to hell since Brad went to jail for drunk driving about six months ago."

Ryan sighed. "I gotta say, I'm hating this guy."

"I'm over it." The words came out bitterly.

She's nowhere near over it.

He felt utterly revolted. She sacrificed seeking her own happiness with someone else to keep the scum in his son's life only to have him screw it up anyway.

"So maybe we can move to a less depressing conversation. After all, what's a former Ranger doing in the tropics with a side-kick? Other than starting bar fights at my parents' resort?"

"Reconnaissance," he answered. Ryan had already decided prior to dinner that he would be upfront about his job.

She blinked at him.

"I work for a security and investigation company. We do the sort of background checks needed in the corporate world. Our other jobs involve protection."

Maxine Rider had started her company from scratch, and keeping it going meant sometimes getting paid to be barriers between people with money and those that wanted to hurt them.

"Background checks?"

"Yes. Who's engaging in corporate espionage. Who's embezzling funds."

"In Antigua?" she asked skeptically.

Ryan nodded. "A New York broker embezzled funds. We came down here and confirmed it."

The food arrived.

Jenna took a bite of fish and swallowed. "So you're like a high-tech, high-stakes private detective?"

"We detect privately ... perhaps covertly is a better term. Lots of leg work, stakeouts, online investigation." He dipped his lobster in butter and savored the taste.

"And Wyatt is part of the team?"

Ryan smiled. "Yes. Reece is one of my co-workers."

"And you got this particular skillset in the Rangers?"

"Not all of it." He took a deep breath. He wanted to earn her trust with the truth but not chase her away with it. She had also been extremely, painfully truthful with him. He owed her the same. "The Rangers got me the experience I needed to do private security with a large corporation."

. . .

Jenna sensed something sinister lurking in the memories of his work with the large corporation. The way he'd said the words 'private security' and the way his eyes darkened betrayed buried emotions.

"Like Blackwater," she ventured quietly.

"Like Blackwater." His voice sounded deep and full of sorrow.

She swallowed another bite of fish, barely registering the heavy salt and blackened seasoning.

She knew a little from media coverage of private security companies in the Middle East. They were said to have committed atrocities. Atrocities that, as a physician and as a mother, made her gut wrench. Reportedly, they succeeded in achieving goals beyond the standard US military scope.

Ryan continued, "I left, later than I should have—"

Not unlike my marriage, she thought.

"—but there are some things you don't forget—can't forget—can't forgive yourself for letting happen."

Jenna looked down to see that she was holding Ryan's hand. She stared into the darkness that had overtaken his expression until his eyes came back to her.

"I'm sorry," he said. "I think first dates are supposed to be more fun than this. I don't have enough experience with them."

Jenna shrugged. "This is only my second first date ever, so I've no set expectations."

He smiled at her, and the shadowy darkness of his past vanished from his eyes. The warmth from his hand spread into her arm and then through her body. She let go, afraid if she didn't, sparks would start flying.

"Tell me about Cal's skiing talents," he said.

As she talked, Ryan's listening skills amazed her. Was this what a normal relationship could be like—long conversations over dinner? She could picture many more nights like this with such an amiable man.

Which is ludicrous.

She barely knew him. Their lives existed eons apart, and not even the magic of the Caribbean would bridge that distance.

THEY FINISHED DINNER, but Ryan wasn't ready for the night to be over. Truthfully, he wasn't sure he ever wanted it to end. This amazing woman, physician, and mother mesmerized him. He asked a dozen questions about her son and her work, never tiring of hearing her talk enthusiastically about both.

She asked him about his work, but never directly about family so he had offered it up—no kids, never married. The few serious relationships he'd had didn't survive the nature of his work. Depending on his assignments, he could be gone for weeks or months at a time. It didn't help that during his prior private security job, he'd suffered a constant state of—*what had Jenna called it?* —brooding. That behavior wasn't conducive to relationship maintenance.

Ryan convinced Jenna to walk on the beach with him after dinner, and she didn't withdraw when he took her hand. She carried her sandals in her other hand and stared into the ocean as they continued their conversation.

"What's the most difficult assignment you've been on?"

"Kidnapping."

Her green eyes widened.

"We had a five-day travel through the Colombian jungle. I hate the jungle. Too humid, too many snakes, too many bugs."

Jenna squirmed adorably. "Snakes I can handle. But not the bugs."

"We were outnumbered and outgunned. All of our high-tech equipment failed from jungle moisture."

Jungle rot.

"Did you rescue the hostage?"

"Yes," he said gravely. "Judging by the torture, they had no intention of making the ransom trade they had demanded. The rescue saved his life."

"Bugs," Jenna said with disgust. "I once had a patient in my ICU with maggots boring through his gangrene flesh. To this day, anything that wiggles or crawls reminds me creepily of that leg."

Ryan and Jenna reached her bungalow.

She squeezed his hand tightly. "Do you like your job now?"

"Love it. Maxine, Reece, Barry, Dorian, Billy, and Mason. They're like family. I trust Maxine's judgment. We all do. She picks great assignments and makes us remember why we joined the military in the first place—to help people."

"A rewarding job. That's a keeper."

"Absolutely."

The moon cast long shadows from the Cretan date palm trees and beach umbrellas. Jenna's eyes were sad, which wasn't the look he hoped to see. Was she sad because the date ended or sad because she braced herself to distance herself from him?

He leaned in to kiss her, and she met him halfway. The taste and softness of her mouth sent tantalizing waves of excitement through him. He tasted and teased, his body heating.

What wonders awaited beyond that kiss? As he pulled away, he could tell by the look in her eyes that she, too, was carried away in the moment.

Then those beautiful green eyes came back into focus and saddened once again. She placed a hand on his chest as though to force herself to keep her distance. She intentionally squelched the fire.

"I like you, Ryan. I also like my freedom, my safety. I spent over a decade in a rotten relationship, and I'm finally free. I want to keep my freedom. I don't want to get mixed up in someone else's dangerous life."

Ryan's eyes roamed her face, the contour of her jaw, and the smoothness of her slightly parted lips. A row of delicate freckles crossed the bridge of her nose.

From his pocket, he produced a business card.

"Then I respect your wishes, Jenna, even though I'd like to convince you otherwise."

Leaning in one more time, he kissed her again, richly, savoring her. When she made the slightest motion to move her body a little closer to him, he used every ounce of willpower to pull away from her.

He tucked the card into her hand. "When you change your mind." Turning, he forced himself to follow her wishes and walk away from her.

CHAPTER 6

Ryan and Reece sat in the airport terminal waiting to board their plane back to the States. The terminal was filled with sullen faces, dozens of people not wanting their vacation to end.

"Nice of Max to send us to the Caribbean," Reece commented.

"Yeah."

"She was a bit misleading when she made the offer, though. She might have mentioned it was for a job and not entirely a vacation."

"It had its moments."

"So you kissed this woman, and that's all?" Reece's tone was incredulous.

"She said she didn't want a relationship."

"Did she say she didn't want a one-night stand?"

Ryan cast an irritable glance at Reece. "No. But I didn't want a one- night stand."

Reece snorted.

"She would have slept with me. Her body gave one message

and her brain another. She would have let me kiss my way into her bedroom."

And what amazing kisses they would have been.

Reece stared at him. "And that's bad because …?"

Ryan sighed. "If only half of her wants intimacy, then she's going to feel guilty and awkward and self-flagellating after a night together. Not a good way to start a relationship."

"But you didn't tell her you were flying out the next day?"

"No."

"Because?"

"Because relationships and love are about strategy. If I had told her I was leaving, then she may have either slept with me because she wouldn't have to face any regrets the next day or slept with me because she's thinking it's her last chance."

The announcement came over the loud speaker for first-class boarding.

"That sounds like a win-win, Walsh."

Standing, they picked up their carry-on bags.

"Short term, sure. But then we're back to the guilty, self-flagellating bit again. Love is chess, man. You have to think several moves in advance."

Reece smiled. "I thought love was a battlefield."

"Only if you're thinking only of yourself."

And only if you grew up in the eighties.

"Ouch. Thanks for that insinuation."

Since Reece had been through two divorces, logic dictated he would see love as a battlefield. The first he openly admitted was his fault; he wasn't home half the time and didn't make the effort the other half. In the second marriage, he had genuinely tried, even produced two beautiful girls—teenage nightmares now.

His second wife seemed unsuited for his line of work. Although he left the military to be home more, being closer to home didn't soothe her labile temperament. When the relationship failed, he followed Ryan into Maxine Rider's Rider Security and Investigation.

"Anyway, what makes you wise about relationships? You haven't had one in how long?"

The flight attendant scanned their boarding passes.

Ryan replied, "I've screwed up enough of them to know to make strategic moves and not go for immediate gratification."

They found their seats and stuffed their baggage overhead, pulling out their electronic tablets.

"Think she'll call?" Reece asked.

"I hope so, man. God, I hope so."

After they had finished their assignment in Antigua, Reece had been the one to suggest they stay for an extra few days. Of course, he'd seen Ryan eyeing Jenna, and Ryan knew this was Reece's attempt at matchmaking.

Ryan had agreed partly because he wanted to see if he could conjure a conversation with her and partly because, well, who wouldn't want to stay longer in a tropical paradise? The more he observed Jenna, the less he wanted something rushed or fleeting.

A woman of her strength and personality had real long-term potential. She must have felt the same way because she'd turned him down as though she were considering what they would be like in a long-term relationship.

She wanted her freedom. She didn't want danger.

He didn't bring danger, a point he could argue later with her. Truthfully, he brought boredom. He'd had women pining away, counting the days until he returned from assignment—military or otherwise. It wrecked emotional havoc on them. Someone like Jenna, engrossed in the fascinating aspects of her own life—medicine and Cal and the resort—wouldn't be troubled by interval absences.

JENNA ANXIOUSLY AWAITED the video chat connection as she sat in the lounge chair. Cal appeared. Rosy cheeks and dark, disheveled hair filled the screen.

"Hi, Mom."

"Cal, how's skiing?"

"We practiced aerials and Alpine skiing. Freestyle is my favorite—tricks, you know—zero spins, corkscrews. I wiped out yesterday doing a triple cork."

She let him ramble for a few minutes about practice, simultaneously missing him terribly and thrilled that he was truly having a great experience. She tried not to envision his many tricks and maneuvers, any one of which, if done incorrectly, might result in broken bones and torn ligaments.

"Mom, what's wrong?"

"What do you mean?" She shifted the tablet in her lap.

"You were all bubbly the other day. You seem down."

Bubbly? Am I ever bubbly?

"I had a date last night," she confessed.

"Cool. That's a good thing, right?"

"I blew it." She groaned, burying her face in her hands. She thought about how she'd turned Ryan down with such finality. And blamed his career for it instead of her own insecurities.

Couldn't she have simply told him that slow would be good? Noncommittal would be good? She didn't mean to convey that she wanted no relationship at all. But that had been the message she'd sent, so he'd left her standing, card in hand.

"So what?" Cal asked.

She let her hands fall away from her face as she looked back at the screen.

Cal shrugged. "So you blew the first date you've had in like a million years. Big deal."

She blinked.

"So you probably did the lame adult thing and told the dude you got out of a crappy relationship. Am I right?"

She pursed her lips.

"So the dude—what's his name?"

"Ryan."

"So Ryan will either like you and figure you're going to suck at dating after what you've been through, and he'll keep at it. Or he's not interested and jets, in which case he's not worth it anyway."

Jenna couldn't argue with Cal's logic. How had she gotten so lucky to have such an amazing son?

"You're right." She looked down at the business card that she flipped between her fingers. Gold embossed. Rider Security and Investigation. Ryan Walsh.

"So ... are you going to let him know that you're still interested?"

"He's gone." She went to find him in the morning. She wanted to reword what she had said last night, offer more dates. Pace themselves, if such a thing were possible on a tropical island.

Ryan Walsh.

Because she could access the guest list, she had learned that Mr. Walsh had checked out at six o'clock that morning. Had he known he was leaving and failed to mention it? Or did he take off because she had rejected him?

But he had given her his card, which implied he knew his departure was imminent and wanted her to reach out to him anyway—at her pace. He allowed her to set the pace. Did he understand her desires even despite her botched attempts to convey them?

"Oh. He left. Then, you have your answer. He's a loser."

She laughed. She disagreed with him but didn't say so. She also hadn't mentioned the business card, which wasn't visible to Cal.

"When are you back in Windy City?" Cal asked, chewing on a stick of something that looked like beef jerky.

"One week."

"ICU?"

"Yep."

"There are a couple other kids here whose moms are bigwigs —radiologist, CEO of something, and a senator."

She smiled. The notion that he thought she was a "bigwig" was cute.

"I was looking for jobs on the northeast coast."

An advantage of ICU shift work was the ability to pick up and move with ease, provided the opportunity was right.

Cal rolled his eyes. "Mom, you don't have to be here."

"Well, not *right* there, but I thought I could find something within a few hours driving distance in case you wanted a place to hang out on the weekend."

"Okay, but we do a lot of skiing on the weekends." His tone suggested she wouldn't see him much regardless of where she moved.

Then he leaned close to the screen. Too close. She could see some dark hairs on his chin that needed to be shaved.

His voice dropped to a whisper. "Mom, there is this girl that I like. I see her skiing sometimes. What should I buy her, you know, to tell her I like her?"

Jenna frowned. "I'm pretty sure the best way to let a woman know you like her is to spend time with her, take an interest in her interests and listen ... really listen to her."

And after all that, give her a kiss and your business card.

Cal rolled his eyes.

Jenna sighed. "Well, if she likes skiing, what about a new hat or goggles?"

Cal grinned, and his eyes became unfocused as though thinking over gift options.

"No sex though," she added. They had already had the birds-and-the-bees talk, probably in excess given she had been pregnant at nineteen.

Not hypocritical; speaking from experience.

"O-M-G, Mom!"

He leaned forward to turn off the computer.

"Love you!" she called before the video call disconnected.

Sitting on the beach of a tropical paradise, she stared out over the ocean and still felt the linger of Ryan's lips on hers.

⁂

JENNA WASHED dishes from lunch in the sink.

Elizabeth Tanner came up behind Jenna and rubbed her hands along her shoulders.

"Thanks for lunch, Mom."

"Are you okay? You seemed distracted at lunch."

"Yeah, Mom."

Her mom stepped beside her and dried the dishes Jenna handed to her.

"Cal?"

"I do miss him. This is his dream, though."

"We are so proud of you, Jenna."

Jenna looked at her mother. Her long gray hair was pulled back in a soft bun. Her parents had had her later in life. They were nearing seventy now. Despite being spry and active for their age, they couldn't have more than another few years in them to keep up the resort.

"Thanks, Mom."

Jenna had no desire to run a resort on a tropical island. Her passion was medicine. Yet, thinking of a stranger owning the estate saddened her. Investors would want to rip down the bungalows and put up hotel towers. Such changes would destroy the appeal of staying in quaint bungalows and sitting on the porch watching the waves.

"Did you and Cal go to that superhero movie before he left for school?"

Jenna smiled. "Yes, we did. Big screen. 3-D." She saw all of the superhero movies in theaters with Cal. One day Cal would find movies with his mom 'uncool,' but until that day, she would readily arrange movie outings. Popcorn was mandatory. Extra butter.

Her mother crinkled her nose. "I don't understand why all those PG movies have foul language."

Jenna blinked. "That's why they're rated PG, Mom."

"Well, you can't watch a movie without swearing unless it's a cartoon."

"They're called animations now."

Her mother gave her a sour look. "You know what I mean."

"PG movies have violence, too. Swearing and violence kind of go together." She knew from experience that when she stubbed her toe, there would be cursing involved.

"But the violence is fake," her mother replied.

Jenna's mouth quirked. "Well, since actors are swearing, guess that's fake, too."

"Oh, Jenna." Her mother shook her head at her.

Jenna chuckled as her mind drifted to the bar fight. Had there been swearing? Yes. The football players had been on the floor, writhing in pain and cursing. She hadn't given it much thought as she raced to help the one that couldn't breathe.

The bar adventure had led to the kayak adventure which had led to the date. The date she had immensely enjoyed—right up to the point she botched it.

Her mind drifted to imagining Ryan walking from his bungalow and lounging on a hammock by the ocean. He wore only his swim trunks as he had on the kayak tour. He stretched out on the hammock and then winked at her.

Her knees went weak. One of the soapy plates in her hand crashed into the sink.

"Oh! Sorry." She fished it out of the water and inspected it for cracks. Intact.

Her mother gave her a pitying smile. "Is this about Cal or a different man?"

"No man, Mom. Maybe when Brad is a distant memory."

"It's been over a year."

"*Distant* memory."

"Okay, dear. You've been so self-sufficient and alone for so long. It doesn't have to be that way."

"I don't know any other way, Mom."

"I know."

⁑

Jenna wiped down the bar countertop.

"Earth to Jenna. Come in, Jenna."

She looked at the rotund resort manager with his friendly hazel eyes and rosy cheeks.

"You've been distant tonight," Scott said. "Not your usual peppy self."

She refilled his diet soda. "Slow night."

He frowned. "I think it's that fight from the other day. It was too much like your day job."

She grunted but didn't speak. She would let him think that was the reason. Scott was a nice guy, but she wasn't going to discuss her romantic life—or lack of one—with him.

"He's okay, you know. Your mom went to the hospital to inquire about the football player. They said you saved his life."

Jenna nodded. It had felt good to save a life, but the event had been an unfortunate blunder by one of the boy's friends. Drunk kids.

Had she had the 'responsible drinking' talk with Cal? He was fifteen, but kids were resourceful to their own detriment. She would need to talk to Cal.

"You went away again," Scott said.

Jenna started shelving clean glasses. "Sorry." She hadn't meant to be rude to Scott.

Since kissing Ryan, her mind drifted, unfocused.

"So you won't be back until after the summer?" He drank his soda.

"Nope, too hot. I only come during the cooler months."

Scott already knew that, but he seemed to be struggling to make casual conversation. Why? He had asked her to dinner six months ago, and she had declined. Since then, he didn't interact with her much. Now, he sat at her bar.

"You had a date with a guest?"

Bingo. Someone must have told him. Small island. Small resort. Big gossip chain.

She resisted the urge to sigh as he sulked in his diet Cherry Coke Zero no ice.

"Yes. Great guy. Former Army Ranger."

Scott's shoulders sagged slightly. Surely he hadn't been pining away for her, waiting until she felt ready for a relationship. She'd told him she didn't want any dates during her time in Antigua and certainly not with someone who worked for her parents. She wondered if Scott thought she'd broken her own rules by dating a guest.

"Are you going to see him again?" he asked.

"I certainly hope so."

A woman in a floral dress ordered a mojito.

Jenna proceeded to crush the mint and add sugar.

"How is Cal?"

"He's good. He's been pestering me about driving lessons. Apparently several kids in his class have learner permits, and I am woefully neglecting my parental duty to educate him if I don't sign him up for driving lessons."

Scott gave a blank stare as one who neither has children nor took a true in interest in them. Ryan had taken an interest.

She poured the rum and walked the drink down to the patron at the other end of the bar. She lingered and struck up conversation with the woman who had ordered the drink.

The woman talked about her plans to tour the island. Jenna listened politely, but couldn't help glancing in the far dark corner of the bar, wishing Ryan sat back there, waiting for her.

CHAPTER 7

axine Rider sat at the conference room table as she presented Ryan and Reece's next assignment.

Reece's brow furrowed in disappointment. "You don't have another case on a tropical island?"

Maxine looked flatly up at Reece for wasting her time with useless questions. Claire annoyingly clicked away on her laptop. No doubt she was simultaneously hacking NSA, planting a computer virus, shopping for shoes, and playing solitaire.

When Maxine adjusted her chair, her belly bumped the table, causing her coffee to crest the rim of her cup and spill. She cursed.

Ryan stared out the window.

"Eugene Thomas," she continued with her briefing, "is suspected of fraudulent billing, embezzling and child pornography."

"Suspected by whom?" Reece asked.

"His wife. She wants him arrested, gone, and no longer a threat to her and their children. And she wants none of it traced back to her."

"So snatch and grab," Reece summarized.

"Data snatch and grab," Maxine confirmed.

She sipped her coffee, glaring over her mug at Ryan, who had yet to join the conversation. "Are we boring you, Walsh, with talk of gainful employment?"

Without taking his eyes off the window or altering the pensive expression on his face, he replied, "Expose embezzling scumbag. Got it, Max."

She turned her annoyed glare to Reece. Ryan's behavior troubled her, and perhaps Reece knew the inciting factor. Ryan was one of her best investigators, the most rational and meticulous of them all. Ryan Walsh did not daydream out windows during a briefing.

His last assignment had been on a tropical island. She would have expected the experience to clear his mind not jumble it. Furthermore, Claire had let slip Reece and Ryan remained in Antigua several days after the mission was completed; therefore, they'd even had an actual vacation.

Reece did poorly tried to suppress a grin. "Walsh is in love."

Maxine stared in stunned silence before a rush of emotions assaulted her. Her perturbance that Ryan's feelings distracted him mingled with a twinge of joy that such a formidable man might have found a match. Rational Ryan would not fall for anyone less than his intellectual equal. Would he? Anger and fear rushed to the surface of her feelings. Would a relationship threaten his desire to work at Rider SI?

She cleared her throat, and kept her voice detached from her rolling emotions. "Really?"

"Don't worry. She turned him down," Reece said.

"Temporarily," Ryan interjected politely, still not turning to fully engage in the conversation.

"In Antigua?" Maxine asked doubtfully.

The island was the only place Ryan had been since Maxine last saw him. Surely, he hadn't fallen for some tropical floozy.

Reece leaned back in his chair. "She was working on her parents' tourist estate. She lives in Chicago, working as an ICU doc."

Maxine swallowed hard. The brief description fit the profile of a woman who would be suited to Ryan—not only a physician but one who had the calm detachment to work with critical patients.

"Walsh?"

Ryan finally turned and looked at Maxine. He seemed to study her expression. His brow furrowed before his expression softened. "No worries, Max. I'm not going anywhere."

His simple, heartfelt statement assuaged her angst. It was as though he lifted the teapot of boiling water off the stove before it erupted into a screeching howl in her chest. Despite feeling the pressure of worry relieved, Maxine pursed her lips in a sour expression. She refused to give him the satisfaction of knowing he'd correctly deduced her concerns and diverted them.

"Good," she said simply.

Ryan winked at Maxine, another annoying yet reassuring gesture.

⁂

JENNA AWOKE from a deep slumber and found her way to the shower in her small Chicago apartment.

After cleaning and dressing for work, she fixed a cup of coffee and curled up on her couch. She held the cup in one hand and a copy of the April issue of *Critical Care Medicine* in the other.

Antigua had been a welcome reprieve from work and 'real-life,' as Cal called it. As always, it recharged her batteries. Those getaways were one of the reasons she could enjoy her work as a physician despite the demands and the stress while her colleagues suffered burnout and midlife career changes. Few, to be sure, had the luxury of taking an extended trip to a tropical island several times a year and only having to foot the bill for the flight.

Besides the relaxing ambience, Jenna could relish in the memory of everything her and Cal had done together in Antigua— his first steps in the sand; the first time he let the sand sift through his fingers; the first time a little wave knocked him over, giggles filling the air; the first time she took him snorkeling and kayaking.

Funny after all that he would choose to pursue skiing.

Follow your dreams, my little Cal.

Just don't knock-up any girls in the process.

Maybe Brad would have made better life choices if he hadn't been a kid with the onslaught of adult responsibilities.

But she had turned out okay, right?

She had a good job with great colleagues. Her boss, the ICU Director, was a bald-headed Mr. Clean—if Mr. Clean traded his scouring pads for donuts. He looked broad and tough with his polished head and wide girth, but he was a puppy dog, sweet and fluffy, as long as his workers showed up and did their job.

The nurses and respiratory therapists consisted of a conscientious and lively group dedicated to patient care. The efficient charge nurse always wore a scowl, except when she escaped to smoke a cigarette. The half-deaf nurse, a few years past retirement, made Jenna thankful for electronic medical orders so nothing was lost in communication. A younger, eager nurse had bushy red hair framing a perpetually flushed face behind thick-lensed glasses.

Then she had Kat, a nurse about her age. They had bonded over a long discussion when they discovered they shared a common terrifying experience of being robbed when they were both in their twenties. Kat's had been at gunpoint in Chicago and

Jenna's by knife in Miami, but the experience had left them both shaken for weeks.

Following that experience, Jenna took self-defense classes. She hadn't been harmed since she had fully cooperated with the robber and surrendered her purse. Nevertheless, she couldn't help wondering if the outcome would have been worse if the couple strolling through the park hadn't approached, causing the thief to bolt.

To this day, she still shuddered to think of the man's cold, dead stare. He looked at her like she was prey, like she wasn't the same species as him. Perhaps that's how a person came to view their victims to make the crime easier on themselves.

Jenna picked up the Rider SI business card from her kitchen counter and stared at it. Ryan Walsh.

She wasn't in the habit of self-deprecation. She spent many nights alone over the years when she longed to be held and comforted. The first reason she hadn't followed Brad's footsteps in adultery was because it wasn't an acceptable message to send Cal. His parents' marriage floated along dysfunctionally, but at least he would know what it meant to be faithful. The second reason was time limitations. When she wasn't clocking eighty hours per week, she wanted to spend time with Cal, not sneak around in a relationship.

By the time she rejoiced in being single again, she'd wanted to enjoy the space and freedom. She felt like a wheezing asthmatic taking a breathing treatment—the air rushed in with a deep sigh of relief extending down to the diaphragm. She reveled in the calm, soothing sensation that life was turning out better than expected.

Now that she could breathe freely, why would she expose herself to another irritant?

Ryan wouldn't be an irritant. He would be like breathing liquid oxygen. Smooth. Sensual. Electrifying.

How did she start something with a man who didn't live in the same state?

After draining her coffee, she brushed her teeth. She donned her winter coat, and she ventured into the crisp April air and gusty wind to catch the Chicago L to ride to work.

JENNA WAS HALFWAY through her patient rounds on her first day back at work. The adjustment always seemed more taxing coming back after vacation.

She spent the first hour of the morning discontinuing or changing orders on patients. Dr. Pasha had been working last night, and she disagreed with his management of most of the patients admitted overnight.

At her fourth patient, she flicked her pen at the computer she had been wheeling around during rounds.

"Are you kidding me?" she asked no one in particular. She stood beyond earshot of the patient, but the nurses could still hear her.

"What's wrong?" Kat asked.

"Bed four is on noninvasive ventilation."

Kat looked from the patient back to Jenna. "Yeah."

Jenna stared at the mask on the patient's face as it delivered pressurized air. The patient lay slanted in bed, breathing thirty-eight times a minute, according to the monitor above her head. Her heart ticked away at a hundred twenty beats per minute.

"She has pneumonia. She is not hypercarbic. She is not volume overloaded. She has no indication for positive pressure ventilation. And she looks obtunded."

Kat scrunched up her nose. "She is a bit somnolent."

"Can you page RT please?" Jenna asked as she snagged a pair of gloves.

Kat walked toward the phone to summon the respiratory therapists. "The usual cocktail?" she asked before picking up the phone.

"Yep."

Jenna introduced herself to the patient who made no response.

She examined the patient, including her neck and jaw. With her short neck and obese body, she had the potential to be a difficult intubation. She had a lobar pneumonia and floundered in respiratory failure because of it. She needed a breathing tube before she exhausted to the point of stopping breathing entirely.

Within a few minutes, the respiratory therapist had wheeled a ventilator to the bedside. Kat assembled medications and was filling and labeling syringes.

Jenna stood at the head of the bed wearing a mask and eye protection as she set up the equipment she needed for the procedure.

"Time out?" she asked the group.

Kat nodded.

Jenna recited the patient's name and medical record number. "We are performing urgent intubation for respiratory failure. Our blood pressure is set to cycle every two minutes. We have the necessary equipment for intubation and a bougie for good measure. We have drugs—midazolam to find a happy place, propofol for the deep slumber, fentanyl because propofol burns like a Floridian bonfire at Christmas, neosynephrine for the extra blood pressure oomph, and roc to ward off evil."

She liked rocuronium or succinylcholine at the bedside for intubations but never liked having to paralyze people. If an intubation turned critically difficult, there wasn't time to wait for someone to pull the medication from the electronic, password-protected dispenser.

She popped the tip of the suction catheter against her gloved hand, testing the strength. Adjusting the mask on her face, she tried to pull the eye shield component away from her face to keep it from fogging. A bag of IV fluid dripped into the patient's vein.

"I need a 'go' 'no go' for induction." She pointed the plastic suction catheter at Kat. "Nursing."

"Go."

"RT."

"Go."

"Nate." She pointed over to the ICU secretary. "Nate?"

He looked up from his iPad. She suspected he was playing Fruit Ninja judging by his rapid finger movements across the screen. He nodded and then looked back at his screen.

He made her want to grab his scruffy beard and shake him about to make him care about his job. However, she felt determined to get through to him in other ways.

"Nate, you're leaving me hanging here."

He was as enthusiastic about his job as a bedside urinal was about its job. Jenna tried to make a point of having him enjoy one moment of his job each day. She'd done a lot of odd jobs over the years, especially at the resort and including scrubbing toilets. Opportunity always existed to create fun in the workplace—like turning an intubation into a pre-launch sequence.

"Yeah," Nate replied, not looking up at her and the team.

"You know, as a little girl, I wanted to be an astronaut. This is the closest I'm going to get. You wouldn't deny a little girl's dream?"

Nate smirked. "Go."

Victory!

"Copy that. We are go for induction."

CHAPTER 8

Ryan arrived at his temporary apartment in DC and took off his suit coat. His and Reece's cover as two reputable businessmen was taking time to construct. In another week or so, their cover would be strong enough to infiltrate their target's office.

As he loosened his tie and slipped off his shoes, his phone rang.

"Hey, Sonny!"

"That was a rather cheery greeting," Ryan's brother replied. Technically, Sonny was his half-brother, but after growing up together, neither of them considered each other less than whole.

"It's nice to hear a friendly voice after a day under cover."

"Who are you this time?"

"Faceless businessman." He didn't tell him he portrayed an investment broker like Sonny.

"Sounds boring. Tell me about Antigua. I mean the parts you can."

Sonny knew Ryan didn't discuss clients or job details.

Ryan pulled out a head of lettuce, a green pepper, a tomato, a cucumber, and a packet of smoked salmon from his refrigerator. "Antigua is phenomenally beautiful."

"Oh? Do I hear a repeat trip in your voice?"

Ryan rinsed the ingredients for his salad. "If it works out."

"Good. You can bring me next time."

Ryan chuckled.

"You could always use the Red Funds. Buy a little bungalow on the beach."

Ryan's voice hardened. "Those are off limits."

"Yeah. Yeah."

Ryan's Red Funds were money earned during his previous employment. He'd been so sickened by the work he'd taken part in, he didn't spend a dime of his paycheck. Finishing his two-year contract and keeping his mouth shut was his only way out of the organization.

If he broke his contract or squealed on the things he'd seen, he would have been black listed from working in security or law enforcement ever again—that is, if they let him live. That unspoken threat extended to his family. Ryan understood the full wrath of the company, if betrayed, would affect more than only himself.

"You should at least know how much it's earned. It's growing like a football player on steroids."

The Red Funds had been so named for the blood on Ryan's hands. He hadn't stood up to the contracted bullies. People died because of it. Maxine and Rider SI were different. He hoped he could atone for his silent cowardice.

Ryan put all of his ingredients in a bowl and poured rémoulade dressing on top. "I don't want to know. Keep doing what you're doing."

Ryan trusted his baby brother to move and invest the funds as he saw fit. Ryan hadn't decided how he would use the money. For now it was back-up to his back-up money.

"I could invest it in property in Antigua."

"No." Ryan ate his salad.

He needed to steer this conversation away from blood money. "I met someone on the island there who'd be worth seeing again."

"Oh?"

"She's a physician."

Sonny's voice turned dull. "You met someone on a tropical island. You're supposed to be describing her appearance, not her vocation."

"Five, five. Tan skin, copper hair, green eyes like Caribbean waters. Fit with the right amount of curves."

"That's more like it. I just pulled into the driveway. I need to help Emily with the kids. But I want to hear more about this woman. Bye, for now."

Ryan turned off the phone and resumed eating his salad in the quiet of his apartment.

Jenna Masters.

He would finish this job, and if she hadn't called him by that time, he would call her.

After Ryan finished his dinner, he stripped and headed for the shower.

The two years he'd spent employed at Titan Enterprises and earning what would become the Red Funds marked a low point in his life. Six months into the job, he'd fully grasped the dubious nature of the company. With nearly a hundred employees, Lucius Titan didn't know each personally other than the few that closely guarded him. Ryan had only met the man once—slick hair and a polished appearance did nothing to mask his soulless black eyes. He wasn't from a military background. Rumors abound that he had wanted to be a military pilot but didn't qualify based on his poor eyesight. Regardless, he had amassed his own small army. The attrition rate was high, but the contract stated that what was seen or heard on the job, stayed with the job.

Most decent men kept their mouth shuts, heads down, and got out as soon as they could, which was what Ryan had done.

He'd known one man who had made the mistake of trying to take down Titan Enterprises. Jeremiah had worked on a few jobs with Ryan. When Ryan left, he urged the former Marine to come with him.

"I can't walk away from what's going on here," Jeremiah had explained. "I have some ideas about how to take Lucius down."

Ryan shook his head. "You're one man against the Kraken with no head of Medusa. Don't do this. Think about your family."

Jeremiah's expression darkened. "I am thinking about my family, Walsh. You think I can look my two little girls in the eye knowing I turned my back on hundreds of others sold into slavery?"

Jeremiah's gaze made Ryan feel like a coward. He loathed the underworld sex trafficking. He wasn't taking a stand, but also knew the impossible odds.

Ryan never heard if Jeremiah had assembled any incriminating evidence, but four months after Ryan left Titan Enterprises, Jeremiah's sister called to tell Ryan that Jeremiah and his family had died in a terrible car accident.

Cold with despair, Ryan knew it'd been no accident. He was certain of it. Undoubtedly, Lucius had him murdered, and to ensure no one else bred ideas of infiltration, he made an example of the man's family.

As time passed, no one targeted Ryan, and he suspected Titan Enterprises hadn't discovered that Ryan knew Jeremiah's plans to incriminate Lucius' organization.

Ryan let the hot water from the shower pour over him.

He'd dealt with all of the emotions and pain and anger and infuriating sense of impotence. Now, hollow guilt remained ... and a small savings he kept for emergencies only.

AFTER HER SEVEN-DAY stretch on the ICU, Jenna met up with her friend, Jessica Ong, to unwind.

"How's being back?" Jess asked.

They ate at a wing restaurant a few blocks off Michigan Avenue. The atmosphere was casual. Muted televisions hung on every wall, displaying various football games. The women sat at a two-seater high-top table.

"Good. It was such a nice break."

"Bartending and guided tours?" Jess asked skeptically.

"And running on the beach and swimming in the ocean. Oh, and then there was an emergent crich."

Jess dropped her chicken wing. "You're shitting me."

At a hundred pounds—soaking wet and carrying a bowling ball—no one would know the cute button-nosed Asian swore like a sailor. One of their critical care fellowship friends had affectionately dubbed her the 'Ragin' Asian,' which Jess quite liked.

"Bar fight," Jenna explained. "Guy took a chair leg to the throat and shattered his larynx. Probably his hyoid, too. Anyway, I did a cutdown crich."

"With what?"

"I keep a scalpel in my medic bag, but the actual trach was one of those liquor pour spouts."

"Holy crap. Okay. That wins out over my emergent pericardiocentesis. Took off three hundred milliliters of pus."

"Thanks for that image during dinner." Jenna took a swig of

her beer. She added, "That wasn't the best part though." She wriggled her eyebrows.

"What's the best part?" Jess asked through a mouthful of chicken.

"Tall, dark, and ruggedly handsome."

"No shit?"

"Nope."

"This was the date you called me about?"

"Yep."

"Did you get laid?"

Jenna frowned. "I just met the guy."

Jess stared at her with a bored expression.

"We had a nice date."

"What's he do?" After saturating a carrot in ranch dressing, she crunched down on it.

"Some type of private investigative work. Like when a company board wants a CEO investigated or vice versa."

"Sounds very James Bondish."

"No bondage. But yes, sounds dangerous."

"I said Bondish, not bondage."

Jenna shrugged. Jess had said it with a mouth full of food, and with Jess, anything was possible.

Jess guzzled her water. She couldn't drink alcohol thanks to Asian genetics. Alcohol metabolized to acetaldehyde causing flushing and nausea. Even a few sips were toxic to her.

Jess set down her water glass with a thud. "Holy crap, Jenna. You turned him down."

Jenna's cheeks burned.

"You had a hot date on a tropical island, and you shut the door on it."

Jenna poked a carrot in her ranch dressing but didn't take a bite.

"How much longer are you going to continue to deprive yourself?" Jess demanded.

"I didn't mean to run him off. It came out wrong. I don't want another Brad."

Jess rolled her eyes. "You were nineteen when you married. I guarantee there will *not* be another Brad. You cannot possibly make that mistake again."

"Not him specifically, but rushing into a relationship." Jenna abandoned the carrot on her plate and ran a finger along the condensation on her glass of beer.

"Still thinking of moving?" Jess changed the subject.

"It would be nice to be closer to Cal. I miss him."

"Can I have your job?" Jess worked as a critical care physician also but maintained two different part-time jobs at different hospitals in town, one of which was the same as Jenna. She'd explained to Jenna on multiple other occasions that she preferred Jenna's ICU. "My other boss is a chauvinistic jackass, and I get stuck with more night shifts than anybody else. I feel like I'm slowly turning into a drooling zombie."

"If I leave, you can have it." She didn't have any control over who they hired, but she could remind administration what a great intensivist Jess was.

Jenna enjoyed her colleagues in Chicago and loved running down Michigan Avenue and through Lincoln Park. She wondered if she should sit tight for three years; after all, she could uproot to Boston only to have Cal choose college in Denver.

The other option was to travel to him on her weeks off, but since she spent her paycheck on his exorbitant boarding for ski school, extra travel would break the bank. The nice thing about working for her parents in Antigua—in addition to being at a tropical paradise—was free room and board.

Jenna added, "It might be tough though since Boston is saturated with physicians ,and so far I haven't seen an offer without night shifts."

She empathized with Jess. Night shifts were tolerable in their twenties during training. Now, if she worked a series of nights, she spent the next four days acclimating and getting little of her chores and errands done. She wouldn't enjoy her time with Cal if she were—as Jess put it— feeling like a zombie during her days off work.

"Brody is way cooler than my other boss."

Jenna sipped her beer. "Yeah. He's a nice guy. He's been a little strange lately, checking up on me and asking if I'm doing okay, if I'm happy on the job."

Jess shrugged. "He's an ICU Director which means he has one of the highest physician burnout rates in the medical profession. I'm sure he checks in on all his employees." She considered her statement. "Well, not Dr. Pasha. He might do better to find a post-burnout nonclinical career."

Jenna raised her beer in a toast to Jessica's words. Jess clinked her glass of water against Jenna's bottle.

⁂

MAXINE STARED AT HER PHONE, then moved her bishop to take her opponent's rook. The Russian she competed against possessed a plethora of tricky moves. They had been playing Internet chess against each other for almost a year now. He held the lead currently by three games, but she felt confident she would win this one.

She slipped the phone into her pocket, grabbed her gloves off the kitchen counter, and plucked her jacket off the hanging rack. After slipping her layers on, she stepped outside and into her garden and began the cathartic work of pulling weeds and tilling the soil. In another few weeks, she would drop seeds. She enjoyed watching the miracle of Mother Nature. A little nurture and seeds yielded something wholesome. She felt the same way about her employees. They were good seeds in need of a little nurturing.

The March sun shone through the wood planks of one wall, illuminating her honeysuckle vine. She looked forward to May and June when the flowers would bloom and her garden would fill with the sweet aromas. For now, the light rain and earthy fragrance of the few blooming delphiniums along the edge of her fence suffused the air.

For one blissful moment, life seemed as it should. Business was good, and she needed new hires. The security detail on the tennis circuit was lucrative, though not intellectually stimulating. Ryan and Reece had proven to be a dynamic and effective team, from saving the Sharp Industries' prototype to successfully and covertly gathering information in Antigua—despite the delay in returning to Atlanta. Claire continued to be a hidden gem with her computer skills.

Best of all was the lack of drama. All of her employees seemed to have their personal lives under control.

Well, all except her.

She washed the dirt off her hands at the outside hose as thoughts about her son, David, poured through her mind. He was probably elbow-deep in blood and guts from a trauma case. He worked too much.

Can't imagine where he got his work ethic.

Sure as hell wasn't from his lying father.

She thought about calling David. She often thought about it. But what could she say? "I'm sorry I missed some of your childhood. I'm sorry your father took you away from me."

By the time she returned from her latest military tour of duty, David had already been poisoned against her. She failed to restore their relationship when she only had weekends and holidays to spend with him. She had offered to fight for custody, but David had told her not to bother. He wanted to stay with his father. After all, his father hadn't been the one to leave him and go into combat.

When she had apologized, David rejected it. Later, he didn't invite her to his high school graduation. College, too, passed without invitation followed by his medical school white coat ceremony then graduation.

A lack of invitation didn't keep her from going, but she kept her distance since distance seemed to be what David wanted. She hadn't sent cards either. What was a piece of paper with someone else's sentiments spewing from it going to achieve when a face-to-face genuine apology had been rejected?

She loved her military career. Loved the thrill of battle, the sense that she helped make the world a better place with a skillset only a few possessed. To claim she would trade that part of her life to win David back would be a lie. Yet, she could have done better to nurture their relationship when she had been home. She could have done more so he would have been impervious to his father's negativity of her. Perhaps if she'd known the lies he wove in her absence, she would have known to work to counteract them.

Naïve Maxine. Always thinking you'd come home to a hero's welcome and instead you were met with emptiness. An empty, broken home.

She sniffed and spat on the ground.

Maybe she should have sent the damn graduation cards.

CHAPTER 9

Ryan straightened his suit before entering Sharp's office.

He extended a hand. "Thank you for agreeing to meet with me."

Bill Sharp accepted the handshake with a smile. "No problem. I wouldn't turn down the team that saved me millions of dollars. Not just for the prototype, but all the R and D that went with it. Rider SI saved my hide that day."

"Maxine is working on identifying the perpetrators. Any thoughts on your end?" Ryan's gaze roamed the large office, from the plush carpet to the family photos on his mahogany desk. A photo of him, with his dark hair and gray above the ears, had him standing with an attractive blond wife and two teenage children.

Bill pursed his lips. "Speculation. Not too many organizations have both the intel and the forces to pull that stunt against me in broad daylight. Perhaps Titan Enterprises."

Ryan kept his face neutral. He and Maxine had discussed the same possibility.

Bill stuck his hands in his suit pant pockets. "Yeah, Max gave me the same silent expression."

"You understand that pointing a finger at a rival company without proof could reflect poorly on us."

Bill nodded. He walked around and sat at his desk. He motioned to the chair opposite him. "Please, have a seat."

Ryan unbuttoned his coat and sat.

"You didn't come to talk about the attempted heist. What can I do for you, Mr. Walsh?"

"Maxine has us on a different job entirely. We are trying to infiltrate a dirty lawyer. We have to finish building our cover as investment brokers."

Bill knit his brow. "You need my company to be a reference. This lawyer's company calls to verify you, and I confirm we've done good business?"

"Yes."

"You know for sure he's dirty?"

"Embezzling, fraudulent billing, adultery."

At that last dirty deed, Bill's face soured ever so slightly. Interesting, Ryan thought. He wondered if the weapons designer and CEO held the same loathing for cheating scumbags as Ryan did.

"Nothing strong enough for the legal system—yet," Ryan added. "Once we can get close enough, we can get the information we need."

"Seems a small favor considering what your company did for me."

"Maxine's company. I'm only the hired help."

Bill nodded. "Army, right? Delta Force?"

"Ranger."

"Okay, Ranger Ryan. Get me a one-page summary of your ghost company so I can be prepared to authenticate it."

"Thank you, Mr. Sharp." Ryan hesitated. "If Lucius Titan does, in fact, have your prototype or your company in his sights, you'll want to be exceedingly cautious."

"You sound as though you're speaking from experience."

"I might be."

A moment of silence settled between them, as though Bill was giving Ryan the opportunity to elaborate. Ryan wasn't interested in divulging his past.

Bill gave a slow nod. "Since the incident, I've doubled security. No one is touching my prototype or any of my other weapons."

⁂

Jenna tried calling Cal, but didn't get an answer. She would have to catch him another time.

She pulled herself into a ball on the couch and pulled her laptop to her. She felt sad and lonely and needed a moment of memories.

This empty-nest crap is for the birds.

She chose a video from the 'family video' folder. Cal had been eight, and they had driven to Austin, Texas. Jenna had a week off after medical school, and Cal said he wanted to see the Alamo.

It was the last trip Brad took with them. He usually didn't mind being the one to take pictures or videos, especially if it meant sightseeing would progress at a less leisurely pace. From Jenna's perspective, it meant she had a collection of videos post-divorce that didn't have her ex-husband in them. She wondered if that was fortuitous or if she had subconsciously arranged it that way.

The Alamo had been surprisingly touristy. She had half expected it to look like the rundown fort from old western movies. Logic dictated that the over two-hundred-fifty-year-old fortress would have been restored and transformed into a museum.

The video began after they had already toured the Alamo and took a hiking trail outside San Antonio. Cal was thin with knobby knees and thick, tousled brown hair.

As they walked along the trail, Cal held her hand, because this trip had happened before he discovered how 'uncool' it was to hold his mom's hand. The image made Jenna's hand tingle with a sense of longing.

Cal let go of her hand and stopped to pick up a stick. He continued walking, poking the ground with it and turning over small rocks.

"Cal, come on, you're slowing us down." Brad's voice sounded close to the microphone.

"Whoa, Mom! Look at that!" Cal scrambled backward.

Jenna came into view and looked where Cal had been. The camera approached and then zoomed in before shaking.

"Get back!" Brad snapped.

Jenna kept still, inspecting the black and yellow speckled snake. "It's okay, Cal. It's a kingsnake. Not poisonous."

Cal came back into view, peering cautiously at the snake.

"Don't get close," Brad warned, the fear in his voice permeating through the video.

Jenna shot him an annoyed look as she stepped closer. She had worked an entire summer during medical school at a herpetological research center. Brad knew this about her, so he should credit her with some knowledge about snakes.

She spoke to Cal. "See the way the head and body are seamlessly together?"

Cal stared with an adorable expression of amazement.

"Nonpoisonous snakes look like that. Poisonous snakes have venom glands that make their heads triangular shaped. Except for coral snakes. Their heads are not obviously triangular, but they're distinguishable by their red, yellow, and black stripes. Don't poke him with your stick, sweetie. Kingsnakes eat rattlesnakes, so we want to be nice to them."

"Can we pet it?" Cal asked.

"No," Brad snapped. The camera moved farther away from Jenna and Cal.

In a gentle voice, Jenna explained, "Wild snakes might get scared and feel threatened if we try to pick them up. Even though it isn't poisonous, it can still bite. Snakes accustomed to being handled can be petted, but you still want to be careful. You need to pick them up by the body—not the tail or the head, and you want to stroke the body in case it's head-shy."

"Can we get a pet snake, Mom?"

Jenna glanced back at the camera with an amused grin. "I think, for the sake of your father's mental health, we'd better forgo pet snakes. But I will take you to the pet center and see if they'll let me show you a few snakes."

Cal slipped his hand back into hers, and they resumed walking on the trail.

Jenna watched a few more videos before she couldn't ignore her growling stomach. The Indian restaurant a block away beckoned.

BRAD MASTERS SCREAMED glorious victory along with the crowd. *Virginia Darling*, a magnificent thoroughbred sixteen hands high, had won the race. He could already imagine the weight of the wad of cash in his pocket.

Life finally brought the payday he deserved. Clouds had silver linings after all. He had thought Jenna divorcing him would be financial ruin for him, but so far she hadn't asked for a penny of the child support written in the papers. And she shouldn't. He'd paid for childcare while she idled through college and then medical school. Stingy bitch. As a physician, now she made more than enough to support herself and Cal.

The other serendipitous silver lining had been his jail time. Although the DUI had ended his career at the company he'd been with for two years, it had opened new possibilities—new relationships.

His new business colleagues had their own code, and they weren't squeamish about pastimes like gambling or minor incidents like DUIs. And they respected him.

Today, however, wasn't gambling. Today was outright winning. A few grand in winnings wouldn't put him near even by any stretch of the imagination, but it was a sign. Betting and succeeding on Virginia Darling would be the first in a long, luxurious winning streak. He could feel it the way one feels warm, moist air marking the arrival of spring. Leaves sprouted around him. And the leaves were the color of money. Luscious pale green.

This was the mare's third win in twelve months, an impressive feat in a male-dominated sport. Maybe she could be the next *Zenyatta*—the first mare to win the Breeder's Cup who retired after a monumental 19-1 record. It was only April and racing season wasn't fully underway, but it was off to the right start. A ripe, green start.

Brad knew he was due for a lucky streak. He smacked his lips, feeling the rush of excitement as he held his winning ticket.

⁂

JENNA SAT at the physician workstation beside Carmen Owen who started the nightshift. Every bone in Jenna's body felt tired. Another seven-day stretch in the ICU had taken its toll. She felt ready for a day off when she had no other responsibilities save eating, sleeping, and bathing. Well, bills needed paying and laundry needed washing, but she could procrastinate one more day on those items.

She could take one day to do nothing more than exist. On her day of recovery, she could lie in bed, staring at her pale blue apartment walls while playing the sound of the ocean and imagining she relaxed back in Antigua.

She peered at the patient list in front of her as she gave report to Dr. Owen.

"Bed one is in atrial fibrillation. The stress of his pneumonia is the likely culprit, so he's getting 'vitamin A.' He's also out of shock and needs to be net negative by the morning."

Carmen jotted down notes. "Amiodarone. Diuresis. Got it."

"Bed two is a lower GI bleed. They are still cleaning up the last bowel movement, so beware."

Carmen wrinkled her nose. "I thought I smelled it when I came in tonight."

Jenna nodded grimly. She dreaded the smell of bleeding intestines mixed with stool. It won second place in foul smells of the medical world. Gangrene was first.

"He's supposed to be going down to IR tonight."

"Embolization." Carmen wrote the word as she spoke it.

"I'm not sure how much more he'll bleed before they can coil the artery. I've already put two units on hold. Last hemoglobin was seven."

"Transfusion. Check."

"Bed three is brain dead post arrest from home. Once her metabolic acidosis is resolved, she can get the protocol." Jenna referred to the protocol to definitively declare suspected brain death by proving the absence of brain function through a series of tests.

"What? No brain transplant?" Carmen teased.

Jenna blinked at her colleague, unamused. She'd told Carmen a family member had once asked about a brain transplant for his loved one. Perhaps that worked for Frankenstein, but it had no role or feasibility in modern medicine. Jenna had spent an exhausting forty minutes explaining why brain transplants were not part of standard medical care. No, there were no other medical facilities to which the patient could be transferred to perform a brain transplant. At least, not in the United States. Who knew what other places were doing. Likely not brain transplants.

"Bed four," Jenna continued, "is a sweet old man with pulmonary fibrosis. I can't move him out of the ICU because he needs too much oxygen. The family and case management workers are trying to see if they can get him home or if he has to go to inpatient hospice. He'd burn through an oxygen tank every hour, so my suspicion is inpatient hospice. Keep him negative because he's got no room for fluid on his lungs."

Carmen nodded as she wrote diuresis on her patient list.

Jenna rubbed her temples. "Bed five had an iatrogenic pneumothorax after respiratory failure and intubation."

"Oh?"

"He has terrible emphysema so I don't think it took much over-inflation to blow a hole in his lung," she explained.

"Ah."

"Anyway. Seven days later, he still has an air leak."

"Bronchopleural fistula?"

"Yep." Jenna guessed one of the weakened areas of lung from emphysema ruptured and, given the state of his lungs after fifty years of smoking, healing quickly was beyond its capability. She had asked a surgeon about removing the lobe of the lung that still leaked, but the surgeon didn't feel the patient would tolerate surgery given his poor lung quality. Instead, the surgeon had suggested Jenna talk to the interventional pulmonologist about placing valves in the patient's airways to block the leak.

"Tomorrow, he gets endobronchial valves."

"That's a thing?"

"That is a thing."

"Cool."

Brody approached the two women, fluorescent light gleaming off his bald head. His white coat was worn with missing buttons and tears in the elbows. A rim of brown discolored the collar.

His smile spanned as broad as his shoulders and gleamed as bright as his head. "Hey. My favorite dynamic duo."

Jenna looked at Carmen who gave her an equally blank look.

He stood over them and clasped his meaty hands together. "How are you?"

Jenna replied, "I'm well, Brody. How are you?"

"Good, good. Any energy depletion? Feeling emotional exhaustion?"

They stared at him.

He chewed his lip. "How about feeling angry or cynical?" He looks back and forth between the women. "Worried about under-performance?"

Jenna's mouth quirked. "Brody, you don't have to survey us. If you want to assess if we're burned out, just ask."

"Okay. Are either of you suffering from physician burnout?"

"I'm not burned out." Jenna turned to Carmen. "Carmen, are you burned out?"

Carmen scrunched her face in deep contemplation before looking up at Brody. "I don't know. Is there a pay raise involved if I am?"

"No, but the hospital is offering free counseling."

Carmen's eyelids lowered as she crossed her arms. "No. I'm not suffering physician burnout."

"Great. Okay. Thanks very much."

He walked away with a spring in his step.

Jenna sighed. She wasn't burned out, but she did want to be horizontal in bed soon.

She made her way through the rest of her list of patients as she sipped her kiwi-kale smoothie.

Carmen chuckled at the last patient. "Dr. Johnson is still here."

"Yeah. As soon as I can wean him off his norepinephrine, I'll ship him out of the ICU."

Dr. Johnson was a crotchety old retired surgeon who didn't think women should be physicians. This posed a predicament for him since he was currently a patient and half of the physicians on the ICU staff were women. Due to his pedantic, pontificating personality and aura of self-importance, no one dared challenge his verbal abuse of the staff.

Except Jenna.

After learning about his preference, Jenna made sure he was always under the care of a female physician and male nurses. It would have been simple to trade a patient with Dr. Pasha, giving Dr. Johnson a male physician. Jenna preferred challenging the man's perceptions, not avoiding them.

She pushed herself back from the table, stood, and stretched.

"When is the next trip to tropical paradise?" Carmen asked.

"Not soon enough." Jenna sighed. "It will be too hot for the next few months. Cal will be on summer break soon, though. I thought we could take a road trip tour of the Northeast. Hike in upstate New York."

"Fun."

"What about you? Summer plans?"

"Florida beach with Dan's family. Every summer."

Jenna grinned. "You're brimming with enthusiasm."

Carmen grimaced. "The kids have a good time, but I know

what a week with my mother-in-law will be like. 'Carmen, how is the weight loss coming,' she'll say, looking me over with disapproving eyes. 'Carmen, you let your girls eat that terrible processed food.' 'Dan, don't worry about the dishes, Carmen can do them.'"

"Unpleasant."

"To say the least."

Jenna had been fortunate that Brad's parents were pleasant. They were sweet and blissfully ignorant to his faults, but always pleasant. Jenna and Brad's divorce had been a shock to them, only slightly less alarming for them than Brad asking to move back in with them.

She would never turn Cal away and would always welcome him back if he lost his way after college. Still, if he returned separated and broke fifteen years after leaving the nest, she would wonder if she had failed him as a mother somehow. As much as she ached to see him every day, he wasn't dependent on her so perhaps that was a sign of adequate parenting.

"Get some rest, Jenna."

Jenna nodded and bid Carmen farewell. "I'll see you in the morning."

Home.

Sleep.

She put her mind and body on autopilot and caught the L to the station near her apartment.

Dream of Antigua.

—and a tall, dark and handsome man standing outside my bungalow kissing away my loneliness.

CHAPTER 10

*R*yan finished another meeting, building his cover toward an office visit with Eugene Thomas. He pulled his phone from his pocket, took it off silent, and checked for calls. A missed call from an unknown number showed itself. No voicemail.

He dialed Claire.

"Accounts payable. Can you hold?"

"Funny, Claire."

"What can I do for you, Ryan?"

"I'm texting you a number. Can you run it for me?"

He heard her fingers working their magic over her keyboard.

"Sure. How's the sting coming? Seems awfully slow on your end. I mean, my program has been ready on my end for weeks."

"Oh, yeah. If you could break his company's firewall, we'd all be having chili dogs at the Varsity instead of trying to get into his office."

"My title is Genius, not Miracle Worker."

Ryan chuckled.

"Okay. The number is registered to the mobile phone of one Jenna Masters," Claire said.

Jenna. Ryan straightened. Jenna from Antigua.

A flicker of excitement quivered through him.

It wasn't a misdial since his phone number wasn't programmed into her phone. She didn't leave a voice message, which suggested hesitation on her part—that and the many weeks that had passed since Antigua until she called.

"Claire, can you run a trace on that phone and route it to my laptop?" he asked.

"You got it. Ryan?"

"Yeah."

"Are you coming to Dorian's bowling party?"

"I've got the job in DC. I'll miss it."

"Okay. It's just that Aurora's friend, Lizzy, is coming, and we thought you two should meet."

Ryan kept silent as he walked the block toward his apartment.

Claire continued typing.

He didn't want friends setting him up with women, but wasn't sure how to continually, politely remind them.

"Who's Jenna Masters? I did a search. Looks like she's a physician in Chicago. Ooh, pretty, too. Is she a client?"

Since Claire investigated and scrutinized each client, she already knew the answer to her question.

"She's a person of interest," Ryan replied.

"Huh. Work or pleasure?"

"Goodbye, Claire. Thanks for your help."

He disconnected the call as he reached his apartment complex. After pressing the code to let himself inside, he took the stairs two at a time to the third floor, and let himself inside the room. He opened his laptop at the kitchen counter and logged into the tracking program. Jenna was home, well at a minuscule apartment that was at least not in a bad part of town.

He wanted to call her, to hear her voice, but he wanted to talk with her at a time when he could definitively set a next date. With the job in DC, he couldn't be sure exactly when that would be.

———

MAXINE QUIETLY OGLED the handcrafted leather gun cases. Wall-to-wall tables of weapons and paraphernalia filled the large convention center. Prospective buyers meandered through the aisles, wide-eyed and mouths watering the way children wander through a toy store.

Guns and romance novels are the staples of life.

Neither of them would ever disappointment.

What you see on the outside is what you get.

Claire pranced up to Maxine, blue hair bouncing. "Maxine, you have to see these drones. We have to get one. Well, five actually."

Maxine scanned the various booths at the weapons convention. A potpourri of weapons dealers mingled with high-tech surveillance and reconnaissance gear. A few other tables hosted either security companies looking to hire men and women or applicant services for companies to find hires.

Maxine narrowed her eyes at Claire. "What part of 'man the booth, Claire' was confusing?"

"Man."

Maxine felt her left eye twitch. "Okay. Can you please maintain a Rider SI presence at the booth?"

"If someone is interested, they can take a business card. Besides, large burly men wearing camo pants are intimidating."

Maxine picked up a Luger off an antique booth display and

inspected it as she suppressed her annoyance at Claire's insubordination. "Many of my men are burly and used to wear camouflage. Myself included."

Claire flipped a blue strand of hair out of her face. "The ones here all have sticks up their butts. None of them are going to ask a blue-haired, twenty-eight-year-old about a job opening in security. You're better off if I'm not staffing the booth."

Maxine frowned. Claire had a point.

Dorian Chaplin appeared beside Claire and spoke in his flowing British accent. "I would approach your booth, Claire. I would want to know how you get such a radiant sheen in your hair." He flashed a dashing smile at her and Maxine.

The gray suit he wore made him look like he was hiring for one of the more affluent security companies. His style portrayed impeccable taste accentuated by his tidy peppered hair and smooth, dark caramel skin. Dorian was Maxine's oldest, and by far the most eloquent, employee. He was also her most stable with a wife and daughter soon to start college.

Dorian would be an attractive face to recruit for Rider SI, but he and Maxine coveted his past. Maxine wouldn't have his employment at Rider SI become public knowledge and have his past drudged into the present.

Claire's cheeks turned pink. "I'm sure you met a few blue-haired *devochki* when you worked for the FSB."

He gave her an amused grin.

Claire didn't know Dorian's secret past and had been instructed not to dig into it. Maxine's team made a game of trying to guess his origins, goading him to divulge some clue.

He betrayed nothing. Maxine betrayed nothing.

Claire turned toward Maxine. "Can I at least show you the drones?"

Maxine allowed Claire to drag her over to the showcase.

As Maxine followed Claire, they walked past booths with guns, knives, and tactical gear, including belts, vests, eyewear, slings, flashlights, boots, breaching tools, and laser lights. One leather-only shop boasted rows of bags and holsters. At another booth, a sales representative took a man's measurements for a custom concealed suit. A collector's table displayed antiques. Her eyes briefly fell on a WWII Mauser Luger as they walked past the rows of weapons.

Claire led her to a booth with video displaying 'smart dust' in action.

Maxine frowned and turned an irritated eyebrow up at Claire. "This is still experimental."

The tiny microelectromechanical systems were used for weather mapping as they monitored humidity and barometric pressure. Alternatively, companies installed cameras on the particles for spying purposes, but that would only work on large groups —say monitoring a crowd of protestors. For the type of discrete surveillance Rider SI did, there was no controlling the little pieces. A gust of wind and the company would be out ten grand. Attaching the sensors to something weightier, which could also be used to guide them, would defeat the purpose of making the smart dust barely visible to the human eye.

Maxine continued, "This is population surveillance technology, Claire. Not individuals."

"I know," Claire replied. She hooked her thumbs into her jeans pockets. "I want the insect-size delivery drone. Heat signatures, infrared, and biometrics. Combine that with remote fingerprint recognition software, and we're tracking and watching without having to attach a traveling device."

Maxine pondered the utility of such a contraption. "Perhaps—"

"Maxine Rider," a male voice purred.

She turned to see the dark onyx eyes and thin lips of Lucius Wallenius Titan. His indigo suit shimmered the color of blue kyanite, and although it accentuated his eyes, it did nothing to fix the flat deadness within them.

Claire visibly stiffened.

Maxine, in contrast, relaxed her posture. A rival with the power of Lucius would be more likely discouraged from confrontation if he perceived no fear from Maxine.

"Your band of merry men are creating quite the reputation for your company."

Maxine smiled at the snake—the sleazy competition with a multi-million dollar company and a hundred mercenaries at his disposal.

His eyes roamed up and down her as though puzzled at how such a seemingly insignificant woman ran her own security team. That or perhaps he was trying to find her green tights.

Jackass.

"Thank you, Lucy. We're a small group but effective."

His lips curled. "Effective," he turned his appraising eyes to Claire, "and eclectic."

Maxine felt a flare of protective instinct. "Helps to have a pretty face to attract new recruits." Maxine hoped Claire would have the good sense to keep her mouth shut.

Claire's cheeks flushed, but her lips remained pressed together.

Lucius was a scumbag, but he was a smart, conniving scumbag. He needed to believe Claire was someone unimportant and insignificant, no one worth knowing or investigating.

His mouth quirked.

Maxine's stomach clenched. Shit. He already suspected Claire was someone worth investigating. What else did he know about her team? Her eyes flickered briefly around them. Dorian had vanished, blending in somewhere. He was another asset Titan Enterprises needn't know existed.

"Well, I'll let you return to your browsing." Lucius turned and left.

Maxine watched him walk casually away from them before a furious Claire spun and glared at her.

"Pretty face?!"

Maxine grabbed Claire by the elbow and hauled her back toward their booth. "Judging by the way you froze, I assume you know that man was Lucius Titan, owner and CEO of Titan Enterprises. You probably also know that he's a ruthless, manipulative hyena who doesn't care whose lives he destroys on his quest for fortune. A man like that will go out of his way to eliminate threats—even perceived future threats. He needs to sense that you're not a threat, even though you and I know differently. To me, you are invaluable and irreplaceable. To the rest of the world, you are just a pretty face."

Claire's anger seemed to have dissipated, and she gave Maxine a wry smile.

Maxine frowned. Her words were intended to deliver a warning of clear and present danger. The only thing Claire apparently heard was "you're valuable and irreplaceable," and the compliment went directly to her head. Claire would be insufferable for the next month.

⚬

JENNA RETURNED HOME to her apartment off the Magnificent Mile. She had finished another seven-day stretch in the ICU. Having been back from Antigua and living in Chicago for two months, the long days of kayaking and running on the beach faded to a less vivid recollection.

This week had been filled with intubating patients, placing central lines, and inserting chest tubes. For every patient, there was at least one concerned family member needing status updates. By the time she had finished rounding on patients, writing orders, performing procedures, updating family, and completing documentation, her twelve-hour shift came to a close. Some days she was lucky if she had time to grab lunch.

She kicked off her clogs.

Nevertheless, she liked her job. She could treat the sickest of the sick and impact outcomes for both patients and families. After working a grueling seven days, she was off for seven days. Completely off. Not an ounce of medical work. When she finished chores, she spent the time cleaning, doing laundry, paying bills, exercising, and video chatting with Cal.

All of this activity was why she hadn't called Ryan. There weren't enough hours in the day. Sometimes, she would sit, twirling his business card in her fingers thinking of calling. But it was too late or it was too early, he might be sleeping, might be eating.

What if he was working in a different time zone? She didn't want to be a bother. What if he worked on a job—a stakeout or something—and his phone rang and all of the sudden she'd blown his cover? She could ruin his job with a phone call.

When she had finally called, she let it ring twice before she hung up; all the worries about causing trouble raced through her mind.

The other possibility was that he could be on a date. It had been weeks since their night in Antigua, but he could have started dating someone. She had, after all, erroneously said she didn't want a relationship ... and claimed his career was the reason.

Staring at the business card in her hand, she walked to the

refrigerator and absent-mindedly pulled out salad ingredients to make dinner.

Her phone buzzed. She snatched it off the counter. "Hey, Jess."

"I need a carb load. Deep dish?"

Jenna looked at the wilting lettuce on her counter. "Sounds good."

They agreed on a location. Jenna stuck Ryan's business card back in a drawer for safekeeping. She quickly changed from scrubs into blue jeans and a blue cotton shirt.

As she stepped out of her apartment, she was greeted by a large belly.

"Oh, Brandon, you startled me."

"Sorry," her neighbor said meekly. He scratched at his beard. "I came by to see if you wanted to grab some Chinese take-out. Looks like you're headed out."

"Yeah." She shoved her keys in her purse. "Girls' dinner night. Thanks though." She tried not to stare at the bits of food in his beard.

Brandon possessed a good nature, and he was a thoughtful neighbor who took good care of her fish when she went out of town. But he was lonely—lonely for female companionship and seemed to be fighting to work up the courage to ask her out on a date. She tried to avoid giving him the opportunity without hurting his feelings.

She thought of her own struggle to call Ryan. If she knew he'd found someone else, it would save her the internal strife of trying to call him.

"I met someone." She brushed a loose strand of hair from her face. "In Antigua. His name is Ryan."

"Oh."

She grimaced at the way his face deflated. Although she told the truth, her words insinuated more to her and Ryan's relationship existed than truthfully did. She didn't want to hurt Brandon, but wanted to help him move on and look for other opportunities. Hopefully with someone he had something in common other than proximal living accommodations.

"What's he do?"

"Consulting work. I'm off to dinner. Bye, Brandon."

He nodded glumly. "Bye, Jenna."

⁂

RYAN NURSED HIS BEER, watching the target slide his hand up a thin blonde woman's leg as she giggled.

"Tense much, Walsh?" Reece asked.

Ryan's eyes didn't leave the man's moves. "Jackass doesn't even care that his wife is home with the kids while he's out partying."

Reece gulped his beer. "Assholes are a dime a dozen, man. Why does this one bother you so much?"

He looked at Reece and blinked, forcing the scowl on his face to relax.

Damn.

He had been brooding, like Jenna had accused him of doing in Antigua. "He makes me think about how Jenna's ex-husband treated her."

"It's all good now, right?"

"Yeah. She's done with him. She still deserved better than that."

Reece leaned forward. "So show her better."

"I intend to, but she has to let me in first."

Reece leaned back in the chair. "Are you doubting your persuasive abilities?"

Ryan gave a slight grin.

Would he be able to convince her to let down her guard? Could he dissolve the barriers she'd erected to protect herself?

He looked back over at the smug lawyer—Eugene Thomas—in his tailored designer suit—probably some expensive blend of goat and rabbit hair. He was picking up a woman half his age at the other end of the bar.

Building his and Reece's reputations and establishing legitimacy had taken several weeks even with Bill Sharp's help. Now that they were part of a recognized investment firm, they had gained a lunch appointment followed by an office meeting with Eugene next week.

The gray-haired, blue-eyed lawyer raised his glass to Ryan and Reece as the blond curled her body closer like a purring cat. From his suit to his watch to his shoes, Eugene oozed money. He smiled at his new business acquaintances who were hiring his law firm's services.

Ryan flashed a white smile and raised his drink in return. "Enjoy your last weeks before your wife gets her share and your company sends you to prison." He sat too far from the target and the pub music played too loud for anyone but Reece to hear him.

"So much for keeping your job impersonal," Reece grumbled, raising his glass in mock celebration as well.

CHAPTER 11

*J*enna's feet hit the pavement at a steady pace. A smooth, cool breeze stung her cheeks and ears, but her core was warm from the jog. She brought her hands a bit further inside her sleeves to keep her fingers warm.

Running was cathartic. On her Miami runs, she used to imagine that sweating during her runs detoxified her from the negativity in her life. Chicago was so windy she hardly broke a sweat. She imagined instead the breeze carrying away all ill humors.

Today, she jogged the Lakefront Trail under a pale blue sky. To her left, cars clogged North Lake Shore Drive. To her right, the west side of Lake Michigan rippled and sparkled as it lapped along North Avenue Beach. In the distance, sailboats dotted the horizon.

She had started running during college after Cal was born. As a baby and toddler, he had delighted riding in the stroller as she jogged. When he got older, he would bike alongside her as she ran, usually goading her to go faster. After that, he was old enough to stay home while she ran. She tried to coax him out, encouraging him to cross-train by running, but he lacked interest.

Now he was gone.

Fifteen years of pouring her heart and soul into something that was always destined to fly away from her. It felt sad. Right, but sad.

How did the quote go?

If you love someone, set him free?

At the next beach, she turned around and headed back south.

Cal would come back to her. She was already planning summer fun. She would take him to all the great sites in Chicago —Navy Pier, Willis Tower, Millennium Park, Shedd Aquarium, and more. Somewhere in their weeks together, she would have to make time for driving lessons.

⁂

MAXINE TURNED OFF HER COMPUTER. Claire kept the latest spyware, firewalls, and antivirus software on all the office computers, but she still insisted they be turned completely off at the end of the day. Maxine wasn't going to second-guess the tech-savvy genius.

Maxine stretched, trying to ease a familiar ache in her left knee. The residual scarring after a torn meniscus from her active military days often gave her fits at the end of a long day. Her doctor had also told her she had osteoarthritis in the joint. She managed the nagging pain with anti-inflammatories, but these currently resided in her medicine cabinet at home. Stretching would have to suffice until she got home.

When she reached Claire's office, she knocked and gently pushed the cracked door open. The overhead fluorescent light was turned off. In the darkness, the LED lights strewn about the ceiling borders of her office twinkled golden. Claire wasn't in her office.

Maxine turned, walked past the empty conference room and stopped at the door to the company's exercise room. At the request of her employees, Maxine had converted a conference room into a space they could use for sparring or weight lifting. A large navy mat spread out on the floor.

Claire, dressed in yoga pants and a sports bra, moved around the mat kicking and punching at the air. She wore her 3D virtual-reality headset. An absurdly base-heavy, high-energy tune filled the room.

Maxine decided to have a little fun. She crept around the mat to position herself in front of Claire. Due to the volume of Claire's music, Maxine didn't have to be particularly stealthy.

When Claire took her next swing, Maxine caught Claire's fist in her hand.

Claire shrieked and recoiled. She stumbled back as she tore off her headset.

Maxine walked to the stereo and turned down the volume.

"Not cool, Max." Claire stared at Maxine, her expression of shock transforming into irritation. Her cheeks were flushed, and her short blue hair clung to the sweat on her neck.

Maxine grinned. "I know a good martial arts instructor if you want real lessons instead of virtual fighting."

Claire grunted as she walked to the weight bench and snatched her towel. She wiped her forehead and neck. "That involves me interacting with a stranger."

"Not a stranger. A friend of mine. He's good people."

Claire snorted. "I don't do people."

Maxine crossed her arms. A talented and cute woman like Claire—although with weirdly blue hair—provided a disservice to herself and others by remaining staunchly antisocial. "What about Drake somebody? Didn't you have a date last week?"

Claire scowled. "That was three weeks ago. Bear didn't like him."

Maxine smiled. "He's a good judge of character."

Claire's one-hundred-twenty-pound bullmastiff was the woman's family and protector. Any date had to first meet Bear. If the dog didn't like him, the date ended before it began.

Even Maxine had been subjected to his nasal interrogation one day when she had dropped by Claire's house to bring her chicken soup.

Maxine's expression sobered. "How's Dorian making out?"

Claire flopped down on the mat and bent over to stretch. "He landed at Ezeiza at fourteen thirty-seven. Now, he's off the grid."

Maxine nodded.

"You think you'll get the hire?" Claire asked.

"I don't know. Dorian thinks so."

Mort Hutchinson was former CIA and would be an immense asset to her team if she could hire him. However, there were reasons he isolated himself in South America.

When Maxine first met him five years ago, he gave her an honest appraisal that her company was too small and underdeveloped for his services. Since then, Maxine had grown her business. She hoped Dorian could convince Mort to at least work on an as-needed basis.

"What about the attack on the prototype?" Maxine asked. "Any clues as to who initiated it?" Maxine had come close to losing Ryan and Reece during the attempted heist. She wanted to know who they had been up against and fulfill the job Sharp had hired her to do.

Claire crouched into a face-down stretch and mumbled something.

"What?"

Claire raised her head. "I said no, but Ryan still thinks it reeks of Titan Enterprises."

Maxine didn't want to clash with Lucius' team, but she wasn't going to back away from helping clients because it meant butting heads with the security giant.

⁂

Brad Masters limped back to his apartment, let himself inside, and closed the door. Collapsing on the floor, his last ounce of adrenaline seeped out of him like primordial soup from a primitive ocean. As he sank deeper into the floor, the pain from the beating he'd taken pulsed throughout his body. Everything hurt. He felt as though he'd been cycled on heavy duty in a washing machine filled with billiard balls. He was covered in blood and sweat.

What have I done?

He felt genuine remorse, something he often felt. For some strange reason, feeling bad about something he'd done seemed to do little to change the course of another mistake.

When he'd been caught driving under the influence, he had felt terrible. It was one more reminder that Jenna was right to have left him. One more mistake to throw on the pile. He had thought he might be able to burn that pile during his jail time. Sure, he couldn't atone for all of his mistakes, but he could relinquish the hold gambling had on him the way one sends a sky lantern into the night for a lost love one.

Goodbye. You'll be missed. But there's no coming back.

As it turned out, he'd been able to continue to gamble in jail. What's more, he met people with access to more money ... because he always needed a little more to make the next score.

This time he'd win. He'd make it big. He could pay back Jenna the money he'd lost in the past—starter fees, he'd call them. He could win Cal's trust back and have money to fly out to one of his ski competitions.

"That's my dad," Cal would say proudly. "He flew all the way to Austria to see me ski."

But Brad hadn't made the big score. He won nothing since *Virginia Darling*. He wallowed in more debt than he'd ever been. It was Jenna's fault. She had fed the beast for all those years. Enabled him. Then she left and took her money and their son.

Maybe the Cubans will give her what she deserves.

No, that wasn't true. He had created his own mess, made his own bed, invested poorly in his own future. "We all pickle our own peppers," his mother often said.

The Cubans would go after Jenna because of him. If they couldn't get money out of her ,then they would take it in the form of drops of blood.

Twelve million drops of blood.

His accountant brain rummaged through the numbers. Assuming about twenty drops in a milliliter, that would be way too many. The human body had—what?—maybe a few liters? Jenna would know. Anyway, it was decidedly not a survivable blood-letting.

As far as he knew, Jenna had neither the money nor an allowable volume of blood to appease the Cubans when they came calling.

Her parents? Not likely. They had sunk their life savings into a tropical resort that has suffered a number of setbacks: hurricane, drought, and recession.

He had put Jenna in a terrible predicament. He definitely was a—what did she call him?—a troll. Crinkling up her nose and sucking in her frustration after a bad gambling loss, she'd say,

"You foolish troll." Although laced with venom, it was hardly an insult. Of course, he realized later that had been her way of avoiding foul language around Cal. Had she been unencumbered, more derogatory names would likely have been cast at him.

He licked a long, lazy tongue along the dried blood on his swollen, tender lip.

Despite being a troll, he needed to call Jenna and warn her. She could get somewhere safe and lay low. Antigua perhaps. She could be there now for all he knew. They didn't talk anymore. Hell, he didn't even have her phone number anymore. She had told him Cal possessed enough maturity to decide on visitation, so he needed to call his son directly.

He could call Cal, but it wouldn't be a heartwarming conversation. *"Son, I owe money to the Cuban mafia, and now they're going to accost your mother to get it back. My bad."*

Not an option.

He could call Jenna's parents. Call the resort. Then they could warn her. Yes. He liked that plan.

He sighed. He needed a few hours of rest with all of this pain. Then, he would get up and call. For now, he needed to lie on the carpeted floor of his apartment and let the hurt subside.

Soon Brad fell asleep, face down, drooling on his carpet.

CHAPTER 12

"Is it that bad?" Jenna asked.

Jenna and Jess sat next to each other at the workstation lined with computers and telephones. Jess had worked overnight.

Jess's jet-black hair contorted in a disheveled heap, and her eyes drooped. "Screw you," her friend replied.

Jenna smiled.

Jess slid a piece of paper to Jenna with the patients' names with corresponding room numbers and top diagnoses listed. "We need to work out a better rotation where I'm not cleaning up Dr. Pasha's messes."

Jenna arched an eyebrow. "What'd he do now?"

"He paralyzed a patient with no sedation. Yeah, that's the same astonished face I made. He's such a—you know what? Never mind. I want to go home, take a hot bath, and forget my career choice for a while."

After rubbing her temples, she launched into her checkout on the patients. "Bed one is hypoxic respiratory failure—ARDS. And now he is appropriately on sedation along with his paralytics. He's on 80 percent oxygen and fourteen of PEEP. Bed two is a twenty-two year old with hypernatremia. Chick's sodium was 162. How the hell did she survive that? She's a lizard or from another planet. Or both."

Jenna let her weary friend ramble through the list. She feared if she interrupted, Jess would launch into an even longer tirade and keep herself longer at work.

"Anyway, her sodium is down to 156. Next lab draw will be at oh-nine-hundred. Bed three is tumor lysis."

"Lymphoma?" Jenna read off the list.

"Yep. Hydrate. Repeat labs also at nine. Bed four is in alcohol withdrawal. One more day and we're all done babysitting him for DTs. Bed five is a gram-negative rod sepsis. Getting IV fluid and weaning pressers."

"Bladder infection?"

"Yep. Bed six has mixed pulmonary fibrosis and emphysema with pneumonia. She's on high-flow oxygen. She's normally on six to eight liters at home."

"Yikes." Jenna knew patients with severe lung disease did not tolerate pneumonia well.

"I know, right? When she has one of her coughing fits, she drops her sats to 68 percent. The woman is an anaerobe. But she's rational. She knows if she ever gets a breathing tube, it's never coming out again. So she doesn't want life support."

"DNR-DNI?"

"Yep. And that's a wrap."

Jenna frowned. Such a small patient list meant the day would be filled with getting new admissions. "Get some rest."

"Peace out."

As she watched Jess leave, she drained the last of her coffee and readied her mind for the day.

. . .

LATER THAT DAY, Jenna cut through the chest wall and into the thoracic cavity of her patient. She parted the tissue between his ribs with sterile forceps. When she popped into the pleural space, dark red blood gushed out of the hole.

Hello hemothorax.

She slid in the hollow silicone chest tube.

This is a risk when we stick sharp objects into patients taking anticoagulation.

The patient had been on an antiplatelet drug for his heart. The hospitalist taking care of him decided to withdraw fluid off from around the patient's lung. Under normal circumstances and with someone skilled, the procedure—a thoracentesis—was fairly low risk. Inadvertently nicking an artery or vein running along a rib was a danger; therefore, blood thinners were usually held for several days before such procedures were performed. This unfortunate gentleman had the procedure performed emergently on anticoagulation, and he commenced to bleed three units of blood into the space between his chest wall and his lungs.

Now, the blood gushed onto Jenna's sterile drape, towel, and gown. The familiar copper scent diffused through the air.

After she connected the chest tube she had inserted to a drainage system, the blood flowed through the clear tubing and into a collection device.

And a red river ran through it.

"Mr. Jackson, we're almost done. I need to suture this in."

As she started the sutures, her hands began working independently with practiced motions. Her mind wandered to Antigua. She thought about her bar-side medical services, which led to thoughts of Ryan. Three months had passed, and the bungalow kiss had started to fade like a dream. If she didn't still have Ryan's Rider SI business card, she might have thought she'd imagined the whole thing.

My next break. On my next stretch of days off, I will call Ryan Walsh.

She would take one day of recovery and then call him the next day. No excuses.

———

ERNESTO BUSTA PULLED a handkerchief out of his suit pocket and wiped moist drops of blood from his face. Swearing softly, he looked at the red stains on his white handkerchief. If blood had gotten on his face, then it would also be on his suit. Tiny little flecks which may or may not be able to be removed.

He looked down in disgust and annoyance at Carlos lying prone on the floor. Dead. Next to his dead wife. Next to his dead children.

Sinfully, Ernesto's suit had been tainted because Carlos had gotten greedy.

Imbecil.

No one steals from Ernesto. He thought this was common knowledge. Apparently, he had to reinforce the point. And since Carlos had killed the first three men Ernesto had sent, Ernesto had to personally complete the job.

Incompetente.

His upper lip curled as he picked at the blood drying under his fingertips. He examined his hands, relieved to see no evidence of cuts or scratches on his skin.

Blood carried disease, and he wouldn't have someone he'd killed laughing at him from the grave while he slowly died from a contracted illness. Like hepatitis. His father had gotten viral hepatitis in jail. The disease combined with his affinity for alcohol had culminated in cirrhosis and a slow, miserable death. Ernesto was not, nor would he ever be, like his father.

"Señor."

Ernesto looked up at Juan. The short, stocky man had helped Ernesto manage the infestation problem Carlos had created. Together they had dealt with many obstacles over the years—from the first time they defended Juan's little brother on the streets of Miami to taking over the Miami base of the Cuban mafia to Carlos. *"Que bola?"*

"The Chicago team is assembled."

Ernesto blinked at Juan.

"Brad Masters' wife," Juan explained.

"Ah. *Si. Si.* Let's go back to the office, and I'll change first." To his chagrin, his empire never functioned without turmoil. He put out one fire only to have another arise. Carlos had been dealt with, and dealing with Brad's idiocy awaited.

Ernesto stepped carefully, avoiding stepping on splattered and congealed blood. He would not have blood soaking into his custom leather shoes.

He glanced at the bodies and turned back. "Juan—"

"The cleaners. *Si, señor.* It will be taken care of."

"Bueno."

———

RYAN PLUGGED the USB into the side of the desktop computer. Reece stared out the glass window.

"Seriously, Reece. You're supposed to be watching the door."

"How come we don't have offices like this?"

"Door."

Ryan glanced around the large executive office. It was fairly posh. Who needed a couch in his office? Somebody who spent too many hours in an office.

Or somebody who claims such.

"Clock's ticking, boys. You do know where the USB port is, right, Walsh? On the computer?" Claire said on the coms.

Ryan typed in the password.

Reece shrugged. "Don't worry. I put enough tetrahydrolozine in Eugene's iced tea at lunch to keep him in the bathroom for an hour. Poor restaurant. He'll probably report them to the health department, thinking its food poisoning. Course he's a lawyer, so he'll sue. Then again, if his wife is right about billing fraud, he'll be a little too busy to sue over the runs."

"Gross," Claire said. "Walsh? USB? Any day now."

Ryan growled. Claire loved to pester him the way a younger sister pesters her brother.

"Done," he said.

Claire couldn't pass the company firewall, so they had to physically get the information from the lawyer's email. They would all have preferred to have Claire do this remotely.

"Great, give me a sec to download," she said.

Two minutes ticked by.

"Okay. Got it. I'm done."

Ryan ejected the USB drive, stuffing it in his pocket. He put the desktop back in save mode. Pulling off his black gloves, he returned them to his briefcase and then straightened his suit. No trace.

Ryan and Reece left the office together, locking the door.

Claire spoke, "Are you guys out? Did you grab the jump drive?"

Ryan sucked in a breath through his teeth. "Damn. Reece did you get the drive?"

Reece grinned. "No, man, I thought you got it."

"Seriously?!" demanded Claire, her voice rising in high-pitched panic.

Reece snickered.

"It's not our first rodeo, Claire," Ryan said playfully.

"Not funny."

After exiting through the waiting area, where Ryan and Reece were supposed to be waiting, they took the elevator to the lobby. At the security desk, the lawyer's secretary argued with a bike courier about a delivery.

Ryan gave a wink to the bike courier who had done a remarkable job of keeping her distracted. Money well spent.

Ryan angled around and made eye contact with the secretary. "We can't wait any longer. Please tell him thank you for lunch. We'll reschedule when he's feeling better."

"Oh, I'm so sorry."

Before she had a chance to provide any further comments, the courier resumed the heated argument, flustering the poor assistant until she turned red.

Ryan and Reece exited the building and walked down the sidewalk. Reece took out the small communication device in his ear. Ryan withdrew his mobile phone and took it off silent.

"Did she call again?" Reece asked.

"No."

But Jenna had called.

"You gonna call her?"

Their rental car was parked a few blocks away from the lawyer's office building.

"Yes. We wrap up this case file, and I'm calling her." He adjusted the briefcase in his hand and took out his earpiece.

"Still stalking her?" Reece asked.

"I'm not stalking her," Ryan replied, his tone casual and not defensive. "When she called, I wanted to make sure she was safe. And she was."

"Yeah," Reece scoffed, "and you keep making sure she's safe."

Ryan didn't answer. He checked her location every once in a

while. He liked seeing where she was and imagining what she was doing.

She's at the hospital ... maybe leaning over a patient with her stethoscope pressed to someone's grandmother's heart or running an emergency, maybe another cricothyrotomy, preferably with numbing medication and the appropriate sterile equipment.

She's at home ... maybe curled up on the couch eating a chicken salad sandwich or laughing deliciously as she video-conferenced with Cal. He imagined her tossing her head back as she laughed, shimmering tawny hair spilling around her.

She's at the Indian restaurant ... probably getting takeout. He didn't like thinking of her walking in the dark from her apartment to the restaurant alone.

She's running along the lake shore again ... with her earbuds in, maybe playing ocean sounds so she'd feel like she was running along the beach in Antigua. He remembered those slender yet muscular legs and copper-haired ponytail swaying.

With the DC job finished, he would call her. If she pushed him back again, then he would leave her be and delete her phone from his tracking program on his laptop. But she wouldn't turn him away, not based on her body language in Antigua, not based on the fact that she had called him.

JENNA LEFT the gym after a midday workout routine. A cheerful May sun lit the sky. The brisk wind felt good on her hot cheeks. She slung her purse over her shoulder, across her chest, and chucked her towel over the other shoulder. Squinting down at her phone, she checked to see if she had any text messages from Cal. Nothing. Perhaps he was in class.

After taking a long gulp from her water bottle, she started

walking the few short blocks back to her apartment. She felt a zing of excitement. She would call Ryan today. No excuses.

A faded baby blue van caught her attention as it came to a screeching halt at the curb near where she was walking. She looked up startled as the door slid open.

Large masculine arms wrapped around her torso from behind her. She dropped her phone and water bottle in surprise. She screamed as the man lifted her and moved her closer to the open door and a masked man waited for her inside the van.

"Time to pay your husband's debts," her captor growled. His hot breath on her neck smelled like stale corn chips crushed in an ashtray full of week-old cigarette butts.

Fear coursed through her like an icy wave. If she remembered one thing from her college self-defense class, it was never get into the car. Once in the car, they could take their victim anywhere and do anything.

Never let yourself be forced into the car.

Struggling against the man's vice-like grip felt futile, but she did it anyway. Her eyes darted around, not seeing anyone nearby on the street who could help her.

As the man in the van reached for her, she gave a high kick and struck his chin. It was only a glancing blow, but it slowed his approach and made him more cautious.

The man holding her in his grip leaned back to lift her up into the van. Jenna arched back with him then positioned both legs on the edge of the van door frame and pushed with every ounce of quadriceps strength she could muster.

He stumbled backward, tripped on the curb, and fell back onto the hard concrete. As he released a grunt, his hold on Jenna slackened.

She rolled off of him and kept rolling right under the van, snagging her phone off the ground as she whirled. She tumbled into the street with a silent hope that she wouldn't get run over by a passing car in the process.

Clear of the van, she jumped to her feet and took off at a sprint.

Behind her, the van door squeaked open and the driver shouted, but she didn't look back at him. She didn't want to know if he was pointing a gun at her.

Brad's debts? What kind of shitstorm had he started?

Still racing, she held her purse with one hand to keep it from flailing and looked at her phone in the other hand. The screen had cracked, but it still worked.

RYAN AND REECE reached their rental car. As they got inside the vehicle, Ryan's phone rang.

Jenna. His heart skipped a beat.

"Hello?" he answered.

"Ryan!" Panic filled her voice, and she was panting.

"Jenna, are you okay?"

"I think ... I need ... consultation. How much ... do you charge ... per hour?" She talked between gasps for air.

She's running.

Ryan snapped his fingers at Reece and jerked a finger at his briefcase in the backseat. Reece obediently retrieved his laptop.

"What's going on, Jenna?"

"Think ex ... had some ... bad debt. Loan shark ... tried to grab me. Chasing me now."

Ryan logged in to his laptop and pulled up her location.

She was running down West 18th Street.

"Okay. Jenna. I want you to go to Roosevelt station, and you're going to take the L to O'Hare. You've got a mile dash ahead of you. I know you can do it."

By his calculation, she ran five miles every other day in Antigua. A mile under duress at full speed wouldn't be a walk in the park, but she was fit enough to make it.

He put her on speakerphone so Reece could listen.

"Airport?" she gasped. "But my … apartment?"

"Take your next left. No, you can't go to your apartment. An apartment door will not stop armed men. I want you layers deep in airport security."

A lump settled in his stomach envisioning her being chased by gunmen. "Jenna, are they armed?"

"Didn't stop … to ask. Kicked one … face … took off."

Reece pointed at the computer screen.

"Take a right in one-hundred feet. Next intersection."

"Sorry … circumstances," she huffed.

She's running for her life and apologizing for calling me?

He shook his head at his partner.

Pushing the mute button, he turned to Reece. "Get Claire on the phone. I need a full background on Brad Masters—her ex. Who does he owe money to and how bad?"

Reece pushed a speed dial button on his phone.

Ryan took Jenna off mute. "Jenna, you're doing great. You have I.D. on you?"

"Yes. Cramping … legs … already ran today." Heavy gasps of air came through the phone between her pained voice.

The sound of her exhalations over the phone stopped, and the sound of cars driving and honking emitted faintly in the background. Then Ryan heard the metro—the unmistakable rumbling and muted screeching of an above ground train.

She made it.

Ryan strained to listen to every sound. She had paused, perhaps to catch her breath or relieve a cramp.

A terrible scream ripped from Jenna's lips.

Ryan felt the blood drain from his face. "Jenna!"

He heard a few thuds and the sound of a door sliding shut, like a side door of a van. Muffled Hispanic voices talked frantically, and then the call disconnected.

"Jenna!"

Ryan felt suddenly sick and claustrophobic. He got out of the car, panting and fighting down the urge to vomit. Kidnapping!

He'd been on the retrieval end of kidnappings. He hated kidnappings, mostly because few victims survived. The next twenty-four hours would be crucial.

He felt Reece's firm hand on his shoulder. "Phone's not disabled. We're still tracking her. If her ex owes money then she's worth more alive than dead."

Until they figure out she doesn't have any money.

She'd explained to Ryan how Brad had burned through most of her monthly earnings like thermite, leaving nothing but molten iron and smoke.

Ryan sucked in a deep breath. "I need a plane to Chicago," he growled.

"Already on it. Claire is clearing a flight plan."

Ryan nodded. Good. Taking the private jet meant he could pick-up a gun in DC and keep it on him in Chicago.

"I need a gun."

"*We* need some guns," Reece corrected him.

CHAPTER 13

*R*yan felt restless on the plane. Nothing seemed to be moving fast enough despite his loyal colleagues all doing double-time.

Claire had arranged all the plane flights. He and Reece were leaving on a private charter out of a small hangar outside of DC. Maxine and Barry were flying out of Atlanta. They'd gotten an earlier flight so they would both arrive in Chicago at about the same time.

He received a text message from Claire with Brad's phone number.

Ryan called Brad from the plane—three times. He didn't care that it was now the middle of the night. Unless he was dead or dying, Brad would explain himself.

Prick.

On the third call, he finally answered, "Hello?" Brad's voice sounded cracked and groggy.

"Brad Masters?"

"Yeah." The shuffling of clothes or sheets and a deep inhalation of a bear post-slumber sounded through the phone.

"You want to tell me why you kidnapped your ex-wife?"

"What?"

That woke up his sorry ass.

Of course, Ryan knew Brad hadn't taken her, but the easiest way to get him to regurgitate his dirty deeds would be amidst proclaiming his innocence.

"Kidnapped?"

"What did you do with her, Brad?"

Reece gave Ryan the thumbs up as he listened to the recorded conversation.

"No. It wasn't me," Brad said, his speech pressured and panicked. "I didn't take her. It ... it must have been the Cubans."

"Cubans?"

"*Los Jaguares,*" he replied, butchering the Spanish pronunciation.

"Why would Cubans take Dr. Masters?" Ryan asked as though the idea was absurd, which it should have been in any rational universe.

"I owed them some money," he admitted meekly.

Yes, you do. You stayed in Florida after your divorce, got arrested, and hooked up with the Cuban mafia in jail.

"Jenna is suffering, maybe dying somewhere, because of your debt?"

"I—" Brad fell silent. "Wait. Who is this?"

The man who's going to get her back.

The man who's going to bury you alive if she's hurt.

"Someone who is going to send you back to jail," Ryan replied instead, since he and Reece were recording the call.

Ryan hung up the phone.

Although he hadn't gleaned any new information from Brad, his main purpose of hitting Brad with the consequences of his actions had been achieved. Brad needed to own the consequences.

He needed to sweat until he heard she was safe. A bottom feeder like that may not be worried about Jenna's safety, but he would certainly be worried about his own.

He felt a firm hand on his shoulder. "We'll get her back, Walsh."

Ryan looked up into his partner's firm expression.

"Thanks," Ryan replied. He tried to ease his grim expression back into neutral.

"It won't be like Kunduz."

Damn. That seemed like a lifetime ago. US military forces had been a day too late to save a small village north of Kunduz in Kunduz Province, Afghanistan. Insurgents had already devastated the area, taken food and supplies, and left the bodies.

One of the reporters he'd seen a few times—even had drinks with a few times—a fiery redheaded Canadian woman, had been among the victims. Ryan had taken the devastation hard. If the rangers had arrived sooner; if the woman had listened to his plea for caution; if the cursed war would ever end—

They wouldn't—couldn't—be too late for Jenna, not like Kunduz, his last tour of duty.

THIRTY MINUTES after Ryan landed and quit the plane, he felt relieved to see familiar faces. Reece had accompanied him of course, but Barry and Maxine now joined them at the hangar. Maxine Rider wore her usual bulldog face frown when she felt like her employees were spending too much money, which was the majority of the time.

Fortunately for Ryan, Maxine's secretly tender heart was a sucker for a romance story. Since Ryan had exactly zero of those since working for her, she would know this was a genuine cry for help. Thus, she consented to breaking the bank for the private flight.

He felt grateful Maxine had made the trip. She was an asset to have, owing to her experience as a former Marine. Although time and hard living hadn't been kind to her plump, aged body; her azure eyes never wavered from a fight.

Barry was always handy in a scuffle. From the waist down, he moved like a drunken sloth in a three-legged race, but he was the fastest draw and most accurate shot in any gunfight.

Reece, his Ranger brother, was a skilled sharpshooter.

Four-man team. Well, four-person team.

Some of the other members—Mason, Dorian, and Billy—were on assignments elsewhere. Mason and Billy had finished last year protecting a high-profile women's tennis professional so success-fully they'd been hired by another one. Dorian was assigned at some undisclosed location only Maxine knew.

Claire—affectionately referred to as the clairvoyant for the amazing facts she dredged up from her computer system—would be present for the extracting via coms. She was never on site, never worked outside of the home or office. As she was one of their most valuable team members, they felt comforted knowing their gifted gerbil would remain safely in her cage spinning on her wheel.

On a table in the hangar, Maxine connected a laptop to a portable projector. The image shone large and a bit unfocused on the wall.

She moved the cursor across the map. "This is the last location of Dr. Masters' phone from the coordinates you gave Claire. Rural Illinois."

She clicked from the scene to another image. Fields and trees peppered the landscape from a bird's-eye view. As she zoomed in, Ryan saw a few buildings.

"This is an abandoned farmhouse. There's a home, a storage unit, and a barn."

"Heat signatures?" Reece asked.

Maxine shot him a look of daggers as Barry chuckled. They operated on a tight budget and high-tech as heat signatures were not in their purview. Reece knew that but enjoyed being antagonistic anyway. Even the satellite imaging was still life and probably six to twelve months old.

"Actually," she said with a smug grin, "I called in a favor."

She clicked through to the next image. "Infrared drone over the property at 5 a.m. this morning."

Barry whistled.

A van and a car were parked outside the home. The black-and-white image revealed the house and barn in dark gray with tiny bright white bodies. Two in the barn, four in the house. Male from female and aggressor from captor were indiscernible in the gray-scale image.

Five thugs, Ryan thought. It seemed like quite a display of force for one woman. He wondered how much money was at stake.

Barry salivated as he watched the image. "How did you afford to rent an infrared drone?"

"Irrelevant," Maxine explained with a smug, satisfied smile. "What is relevant is that Ryan owes me. Ryan's gonna be my bitch for some time after we pull this off. Aren't you, Walsh?"

He smiled. "Yes, ma'am, I am."

"When do we go?" Reece asked.

"Now," Ryan replied sternly.

"Darkness would be better," Barry suggested in a nonconfrontational tone.

Ryan started to protest, but Maxine held up a hand. "While I concur that darkness would be better, I also agree that we are on a clock since we don't know what sort of injuries Dr. Masters has or if they plan to move her. So we go now, but we do full perimeter recon before we strike."

Everyone moved toward the vehicle, but Maxine stepped in front of Ryan. He halted and looked down at her scowling face.

She said, "I need to know that you're going to follow commands out their soldier, no matter what we find."

Ryan stared at Maxine and then through her. He tightened his jaw, knowing she suggested Jenna could be in bad shape ... or worse.

"We're a team, Max. I wouldn't do anything to jeopardize the team."

"Including not jeopardizing yourself?"

Ryan didn't answer.

Maxine sighed. As she turned and walked to the car, she mumbled something about being surrounded by a bunch of soft men who were falling over women, except her actual words were more crude.

⁂

JENNA WOKE to the sensation of pain.

Where does it hurt? she asked herself, as though asking one of her patients.

Everywhere, came the response.

Everywhere, burning, aching pain. As her mind and body reconnected to a state of consciousness, she isolated the areas by the sensations she felt. Skinned knees, right rib pain—not broken —, left shoulder pain.

At least she could improve the shoulder pain. Using her legs, she rolled herself off of her left shoulder. Her hands felt bound with something sticky but malleable.

Finally, she dared to open her eyes. She looked at her wrists. Black electrical tape wound around them.

She blinked as her eyes adjusted to the large windowless room surrounding her. Sunlight streamed in through the wood slats of the walls. The cold, damp floor chilled her as the mildew smell of wet hay filled her nostrils. A barn. Surely there were worse places to find oneself.

She stared at the tape on her wrists. Sweat and movement had loosened the restraints. To be so carelessly hindered suggested her captors hovered near her. She did a personal inventory check. She still wore her gym clothes. Her watch was gone. Her earrings had been taken as well.

Suckers. Good luck pawning cubic zirconium.

She would miss her watch, though. It was fashionable and waterproof.

Her eyes focused on a nearby wooden crate where an open bottle of water and half-eaten sandwich lay. After rising to her knees, she shuffled closer to them. Gingerly picking up the bottle of water with her wrists bound, she gulped it down steadily.

From one corner of her view, a Latino man emerged, zipping his pants.

"Hey! Punta! That's my lunch!" he cried angrily.

In the few seconds it took him to cross the room, she downed the rest of the bottle. With a growl, he slapped her hard across the face. Agony flared through her cheek and deep into her jaw as she was knocked back to the floor. She curled in a protective fetal position in case he struck again.

Her parched mouth felt revitalized, even though she could feel her cheek swelling.

Worth it, she decided.

When she looked up, he had sat back down, finishing his sandwich.

Gross.

He hadn't even washed his hands after peeing.

Laying on the cool floor, her cheek throbbed from the blow. She pressed it against the packed dirt, hoping the chill would ease the pain and swelling. As she closed her eyes, she imagined the coolness of the ground like snow on a mountainside.

She envisioned Cal skiing down packed snow, his body a lean string of tightly coiled muscle—so graceful. Pride swelled in her heart thinking of the skiing awards he might win. He wanted to work toward Olympic tryouts in a few years. He certainly possessed the work ethic to get there.

She needed to survive this. She needed to be there for Cal.

Curling tighter into a ball on the floor, she thought about what her captors might do to her—both now and when they weren't satisfied with whatever money they took from her. The natural course of the path she had been dragged onto included torture and misery. She shook uncontrollably, which was counterproductive to calculating an escape.

Then she thought about Ryan and the way he had called to her. His voice had been filled with so much concern, fear, and panic of his own. He conveyed so much emotion as he had screamed her name.

She hadn't made it to the L as planned. If she hadn't slowed down, perhaps she could have made the train. With lungs burning and calves aching, she thought she'd time for a twenty-second breath catch. She'd been wrong.

Ryan had been directing her where to go. Somehow, he must have been tracking her, probably by phone. He seemed like the type of man who could be so quick and efficient. Maybe he had those resources at his disposal in his line of work.

Was he still tracking her now? She had neither her phone nor her purse. Her captors could have tossed the phone out of the van at any time. Regardless, she sensed Ryan would try to find her and had the means to do so. If the worry and angst in his voice was any indication, he would pour every ounce of effort into finding her.

How long will that take? How long has it already been?

The abduction occurred midafternoon. Currently, she saw sunlight through a barn, which could only be outside city limits. She also felt cold, as if she'd been lying on the barn floor for hours, probably overnight.

Overnight.

That would correspond to her level of dehydration, too.

She liked to think the time lapse raised her chances of being found alive, but she also couldn't wait on a rescue and risk Ryan being too late. Just because she could slip out of her wrist restraints with minimal effort, didn't mean she could escape when someone's back was turned. Sure, she could physically exit the barn, but that was not a sufficient escape.

Given her dehydration, pain, and fatigue, she wouldn't get far. The next time she tried to flee, she needed to succeed or they might leave her with more debilitating injuries.

CHAPTER 14

Ryan, Reece, Barry, and Maxine had taken up different quadrants around the abandoned house and barn. Careful monitoring enabled them to see who moved about the premises.

Ryan grit his teeth at the slow pace of reconnaissance. Hurry up and wait. He'd been on a dozen infiltrative operations, but nothing like this. The usual spine-tingling thrill of the fight was supplanted by anxious dread.

What if she'd been injured? What if she'd been killed?

Claire had discovered that Brad owed money to *Los Jaguares*, a Miami-based Cuban gang. She hadn't pinned the dollar amount but surmised it was sizable—worth finding Brad's ex-wife, Jenna, to collect it, even if it meant traveling to Chicago, stealing a van, and kidnapping a woman.

"Activity." Ryan heard Reece's voice in his earbud.

He watched as three Latino men left the house and walked to the barn. They had a house but chose to keep her in the barn?

Animals.

Then again, maybe she was isolated overnight from five foul men for her own safety.

One man carried a laptop folded under his arm. They would need a computer to do a wire transfer, Ryan surmised. Once she gave them what they wanted, or as much as they could squeeze, she was a dead woman. That sickening thought mummified his intestines.

Maxine's voice came through his earbud, "That leaves one in the house and the rest in the barn. Barry, you take the house."

"Copy, Max."

Rustling sounded through the com device as Barry followed the command and moved to his position.

"Barry?"

"Ma'am."

"Shoot to maim, please. I don't want to have to explain to local PD why we killed people on their turf."

"Yes, ma'am."

"Ok. Everyone else will advance on the barn. Ryan and Reece go through the front. I'll take the side. No friendly fire."

They took their orders and moved cautiously from the woods to the field to the barn.

Ryan scanned the perimeter again. No movement on his side of the property.

ALTHOUGH OUTSIDE WAS A RELATIVELY warm day for Illinois in May, Jenna's bones felt cold in her moist exercise clothes on the dank barn floor. Fortunately, no breeze penetrated the wood walls or she would have felt colder. If her captors kept her out here for another night, she would die of either hypothermia or dehydration.

Escape sooner rather than later.

She forced herself to sit up slowly and stretch her major muscle groups.

Three Latino men entered the barn.

Four guys for one debt collection. Must be bad.

The kind of bad that maxing out her credit cards wasn't going to cover. The kind of bad that makes a group of men travel from Miami to Chicago. They had to be from Miami since that was where Brad lived in and out of incarceration these days. She'd hoped Brad wouldn't learn she'd moved to Chicago. She relocated when they separated, and she didn't have family in the state, only Jess. However, a little internet investigative search would have turned her up because she'd to get an Illinois medical license.

Alaska. Why didn't I move to Alaska?

One man's eyes were fixed in a scowl. Another man's dark circles surrounded his dilated pupils. A third averted his gaze, as though unable to look his victim in the eye. Perhaps he had some remaining humanity to at least feel remorseful for what they were about to inflict upon her. Whatever it was, it was bad enough to make a criminal bashful. His expression was the most terrifying. Lastly stood the man with droopy eyes, weary from being her overnight guard.

Four men. Grumpy. Dopey. Bashful. Sleepy.

Dopey and Bashful hauled her up by her elbows until she was on her feet. Her legs wobbled, but their firm grips kept her upright. Grumpy snapped open the laptop, causing Jenna to recoil. The men on either side of her kept her from retreating.

Grumpy ran his fingers over the keyboard. She recognized him as the one she had kicked in the face.

"*Listo*," he said.

He turned the screen to face Jenna.

Video chat with a loan shark. Splendid.

Wait. How do they have service out here? Hot spot?

The man on the screen wore a blue button-down dress shirt with an expensive-looking sheen. He was clean-shaven and well-rested. Both hands had tattoos, though she couldn't read the words.

"Do you know who I am, Dr. Masters?" His rich voice with Hispanic accent oozed a deadly calm.

My executioner?

Jenna swallowed. "No."

"My name is Ernesto Busta. I am the leader of *Los Jaguares*. Your husband owes me a great deal of money."

"Ex-husband," she croaked through a dry mouth.

She held her breath, waiting to see if Grumpy intended to get violent over her correction. Her mind raced. *Los Jaguares*? So Brad had landed trouble with a gang, not a loan shark? Or were they a gang that also loaned money? She pleaded ignorant about how the underworld operated.

Ernesto smiled, dark and sinister. "*Lo siento.* Your ex-husband owes me money."

He gave a long pause.

Jenna took slow breaths as she rode out the silence. If she admitted to having money, then they could demand access to her accounts now to prove it. Once they saw she didn't have enough (because surely she did not), they would kill her. If she openly admitted to having none, then she proved of no use to them and also as good as dead.

"He tells me you can get your hands on three hundred thousand dollars."

Jenna felt her jaw drop.

Three hundred thousand pennies, maybe.

Why would Brad tell them that? From what imaginary hat had he pulled that number?

Yet the number seemed familiar somehow.

Yes, life insurance. Brad's life insurance policy was for that amount. Had he kept paying it for a year after their divorce? Maybe he had for Cal's sake. Perhaps a gambling CPA had the wherewithal to make some appropriate financial decisions.

But the only way it would come to her would be if Brad were—

"Is Brad alive?"

The thought of Cal losing his father—well, what remained of the scum-sucking troll who signed her death warrant—sent a lump of ice hardening in her stomach. Her head began throbbing.

"For now," Ernesto said with a shrug.

A voice boomed through the barn like the celestial voice of a condemning archangel. "Rider Security. Nobody move!"

Ryan!

Hope jolted her heart into double-time.

He was dressed in brown camouflage. His gun was drawn and aimed at the men surrounding her.

She watched in horror as *Los Jaguares* did exactly the opposite of what they'd been instructed to do.

Sleepy, being unencumbered by either holding the victim or the laptop, drew his weapon first.

Ryan, seemingly unconcerned, kept his gun trained on the men holding Jenna.

A shot rang out from somewhere to Ryan's back left.

Jenna flinched.

Wyatt!—Er, Reece.

Ryan's mustached gunslinger was to the right of Ryan and two paces behind him.

Sleepy crumpled to the floor.

One captor released her as he reached for his gun. The other stammered back, standing behind Jenna but still holding her. Clumsily, he reached for his gun.

She had to free herself, or he was going to use her as a human shield as soon as he gripped his weapon in his hand.

Ryan yelled, "Jenna, get down!"

She was already wriggling out of her loose hand restraints. With one arm free, she spun her elbow into the man's face. He jerked his head to the side. Her glancing blow did little damage but forced him to release her. She felt vaguely aware of pain in her elbow where his teeth had come into contact with her skin.

She dropped to her knees and rolled backward, bracing her ears for Ryan to shoot. Adrenaline overrode the aches and pains she'd felt earlier as she sprang to her feet and bolted for the back door of the barn. Not bothering with the locked latch, she drew her leg back toward her. As she kicked the door with one solid strike, the weak and rusty lock crumpled and the surrounding wood splintered.

Gunfire erupted behind her, but she didn't stop to look.

A cold breeze swept across the farmland. It struck mercilessly at her bare legs and arms. She ran, legs pumping ferociously over the uneven ground. The area must have once been a crop field because the ground undulated in a series of ridges beneath her fleeing feet, threatening to twist an ankle.

Then her lungs and legs gave way to exhaustion. Her body went horizontal as it declared its hundred-meter dash complete.

The brown grass twisted thick, tall, and coarse around her body. She gasped for air as the world grew dark around her.

Don't let the maggots get me.

RYAN PUT a round in each of the knees of the two men who had held Jenna. Maxine shot the one with the laptop in the shoulder. Barry came in behind them and helped Maxine secure the weapons from the Cuban mafia.

Ryan looked around the barn one last time, ensuring the scene was safe for his team. All the assailants rolled on the ground, clutching injuries as they screamed and swore.

"Go, man," Reece said. "We got this."

Ryan sprinted in the direction Jenna had escaped. She had fled like a bunny from foxes. With bullets flying, he felt relieved she'd run and avoided catching a stray.

He exited the broken back door. His eyes roamed the tall grass, but he couldn't see her. He slowed to a jog. "Jenna!"

Silence.

Flat, unkempt land spread before him. Cool, dry air brushed against his cheeks and forehead.

Deep in the brittle brown reeds, he caught a glimpse of something white. As he approached, he saw her white sleeveless T-shirt and spandex exercise shorts as she lay crumpled in the grass.

"God, Jenna," he gasped.

She didn't move even as he knelt near her. Her knees were scrapped, and her bruised arms looked like someone clobbered them with a baseball bat.

Cursing, he holstered his weapon.

When he leaned over her, he could see that she was still breathing. The cool, clammy extremities lax around her had him worried about shock. He lifted her gingerly into his arms.

She mumbled something indiscernible, but her body remained limp and her eyes closed.

Did she just call me a maggot?

Hopefully, that meant she still had some fight left in her. In his field experience, people in shock didn't hurl insults.

He walked back through the field toward the farmhouse.

. . .

By the time Ryan got Jenna back to the barn, Maxine had pulled the SUV up the driveway.

With Reece's help, they loaded Jenna in the back seat and wrapped a thermal blanket from the medical kit around her. They left Maxine and Barry behind who were calling the police for cleanup detail. Reece drove as Ryan sat with Jenna in the back of the vehicle.

He watched her rest in his arms.

Thirty minutes into their planned route to the nearest urgent care facility or hospital, Jenna stirred awake.

Large green eyes slowly focused on him.

"Ryan."

His heart instantly swelled at hearing her say his name with such relief and pleasure.

She sat up and buried herself in his arms. It was the closest he had ever been to her, and the embrace stole his breath. He hated the circumstances, but was grateful she was alive and the role he'd played in ensuring her safety.

"You're safe, Jenna." Ryan stroked her disheveled copper hair. "We're taking you to a medical facility to get checked out."

She sat up slowly, blinking away tears. "I'm okay. A few scrapes is all."

"Jenna—"

"Ryan, I promise I'm okay. I need my own bed and nourishment. That's all."

He looked at her for a long moment, trying to decide if he would have any success disagreeing with her.

Nope.

With pursed lips, Ryan nodded. "Reece."

"I'm on it."

Ryan handed Jenna a bottle of water.

She gave him a grateful look as she snatched it and downed it.

"I'm sorry for calling you. And I'm grateful you brought the cavalry."

"Well, Wyatt brought the cavalry. I turned green and angry."

Jenna chuckled. The sound warmed Ryan to his core.

"Thank you, Reece." Her eyes glanced upward at the rearview mirror briefly.

"Anything for Ryan's ... uh ... friend."

Jenna finished the last drop of water and looked at Ryan, blushing. He preferred those rosy cheeks to the ashen color they'd been in the field.

She looked down at his chest as though wanting to find her way back into him but unsure how.

"Come here," he said, pulling her toward him.

She curled up in his arms.

"Just rest. We'll get you home."

He resisted the urge to probe her with questions. How much of what happened did she understand? She didn't have the benefit of a computer whiz gathering information for her. Had Jenna learned anything from her captors? Did she comprehend that her rescue was only the beginning of the battle to come?

CHAPTER 15

*J*enna woke to the smooth softness of her own sheets against her skin. Her limbs felt battered and looked like one of her ICU patients after multiple failed intravenous line attempts. Her mouth felt like someone had stuffed it with gauze.

She remembered resting in Ryan's arms in the car. Then, he'd carried her, laid her in bed, and dabbed something wet on her cuts. She slipped into an afternoon post-abduction nap.

Sitting up slowly and blinking, she looked around her bedroom. She was alone. She slapped away the creeping tendrils of disappointment. Of course, Ryan wouldn't be here. Certainly a man like him had more important activities than watching a semi-comatose person sleep and—she looked down at her pillow—yep, drool.

Shower. Need a shower.

She flung off the covers and looked dismally down at her dirt-smeared, tattered exercise clothes.

The sound clanging of dishes caught her attention as her nostrils filled with the smell of coffee and bacon.

You are my hero.

She opened the door to see Ryan in her kitchen cooking. He appeared to have changed out of his camouflage and into slacks and a blue collared shirt.

Crap.

She froze. She knew she looked hideous.

He looked up at her and smiled. "I thought you could use some food."

She smiled back and nodded sheepishly. "I'll run through the shower."

She walked in the opposite direction down the hall to the bathroom and started the shower. After stripping and climbing in, the warm water on her aching muscles felt heavenly. She had to take her fingernail brush to scrub the dirt off her hands, knees, and elbows.

She assessed and palpated her injuries. The red spot on her jaw would turn purple in a few days, but at least nothing was broken. A tender lump throbbed on the back of her head. She suspected that was acquired from when they threw her in the van. The pain had set every nerve ending on fire up until the pain, fear, and hyperventilation culminated in unconsciousness.

She knew she had been hypocritical in not getting examined. If a friend of hers had been accosted like she had, she would have forced a CT head on her at the very least. Yet Jenna knew if her injury had been life-threatening, she would have died in the barn instead of waking on the floor.

She shuddered. She almost had died in that barn were it not for Ryan Walsh—tall, dark, and luscious.

In ten minutes, she was clean and dry and ... and without clothing. She didn't bring her clothes with her into her small bathroom because there had never been a gorgeous man in her miniature kitchen cooking her a dinner of breakfast food. She wrapped the towel around her torso and tried to tiptoe back to her room.

Right, because the former Ranger, private security investigator isn't going to notice a half-naked woman creeping down the hall.

She didn't make eye contact because it would adversely affect her ability to deny to herself that he had seen her.

Once dressed, she emerged. Her hair hung damp, but no way was she missing a hot meal to take time to dry it.

Her stomach did flips seeing the plates of food—omelets, bacon, coffee, and she sat down across from him at her small round table and ate greedily.

"Thank you," she said between bites.

"Unconventional meal since it's not breakfast."

"I meant for the rescue."

"I'm glad you're okay. I'm glad you called me."

She absorbed his rich, soothing voice.

"Me too. I had no idea that you were capable of doing what you did. You're a better tracker than a bloodhound."

He smiled, revealing his deep dimples. She could lose herself in that smile.

Who am I kidding? I'm already lost. I was lost to him in Antigua.

"We retrieved your purse and your cell phone. It's cracked, but it worked. I took the liberty of putting it on your charger."

"Thank you."

She finished a piece of bacon and half of the omelet.

Grabbing the cup of coffee with both hands, she said, "I would like to do dinner again. I feel like I said 'no' when I meant 'slow.'"

The corners of his mouth turned up a little, but his eyes looked sad. Not a good sign.

"I like you, Jenna. I do want to see where this may go. But you've been through a lot. I don't want you to make any decisions under that kind of stress."

Jenna was a little taken aback. Was this the same man who'd courted her in Antigua? Kissed her silly outside her room?

Then it clicked. "You think I'm acting out of gratitude. Like I want to pay you back for saving me. Like some type of hero worship."

He started to protest, but she stood and walked over to a kitchen drawer. She opened the drawer filled with pens, stamps, scissors, and other miscellaneous items. She withdrew his business card, closed the drawer, and laid the card on the table in front of Ryan.

She sat back down and watched him inspect it. The worn edges were frayed, and the embossed writing was faded.

"I have looked at the card every single day since I let you walk away in Antigua. I've held it in my hands every day. When I finally did summon the courage to call you, I only let it ring twice before idiotically hanging up. I am interested in spending time with you, Ryan, and that predated this kidnapping mess."

He looked up at her with a wolfish grin. "I believe you turned me down because I was the troublemaker who might bring danger to your doorstep."

"Yeah, apparently, I had it backward." She reached out to take the card back, but he took her hand in his. His large hand felt warm and calloused. Her heart raced at his touch.

She bit her lip as she stood and tugged lightly at his grip. He followed her to her small couch in a room that was some compressed version of a living room, office, and lounge, though half the size of what might be considered normal for anyone of those.

They sat together. Then she curled up in his embrace.

"I think this is the right spot."

He leaned back and accepted her into his arms. She heard him take a large, satisfied sigh.

She ran her fingers over his calloused hands, feeling the rough contours as she listened to his beating heart. "You seem to be exceptional at your job."

"I've acquired the right skill set for it. Maxine, my boss, does a pretty good job of screening the cases. She makes sure we're on the moral high road. None of us want to be taken advantage of." His voice turned a little frosty at his last sentence. "It feels good to help people."

Jenna thought of his previous job and surmised he must have felt they had taken advantage of him.

"I can relate to that." Her medical training enabled her to help people. The emotional reward of helping patients displaced the negativity from the many lives she couldn't save.

She threaded her fingers between his as she enjoyed the rise and fall of his chest, reminding her of the waves on the shores of Antigua. Thinking of Antigua made her recall his succulent kiss. She needed that kiss again.

Stretching her body toward him, she arched to touch and taste him again. He interpreted her intentions flawlessly and moved to accept her lips.

Just as delicious as last time.

The excitement of the kiss built until she found herself straddling Ryan, tongues hungrily exploring each other's mouths. He ran a warm hand up her leg and grasped a buttock. She let out a groan. As he swelled beneath her, she instantly decided too many clothes separated them.

"Jenna," he began breathlessly, "I don't have any protection."

"Good. I'd be a little worried if you carried those around on all of your rescue missions."

He gave a throaty laugh as he caressed her neck with his lips.

She moaned.

"I.U.D.," she managed to get out between breaths.

His hands slid up her back.

She shifted her weight on top of him in anticipation of their interaction continuing to escalate. She'd delayed three months calling him. Now that he was here, she wouldn't delay a second longer.

Ryan relished the feel of Jenna's soft skin.

He wanted her more than he wanted his next breath. He also didn't want to take advantage of a woman who had been victimized in the last twenty-four hours. He didn't want to be a fleeting escape from her fear and stress. The lovemaking needed to be real. She needed to choose him—all of him—not the man who rescued her. He wanted to be her lover, not just her savior.

His body steam-rolled his brain's attempts to slow down the building sexual fervor. She had, after all, obsessed over calling him so often that she had nearly disintegrated his business card in her hands over three months—which was an excellent reason to date her, but didn't necessarily justify sleeping with her under these conditions.

She shifted her weight on top of him and took in a sharp breath. She must have moved something that had been injured during her kidnapping. Considering her multiple bruises, the source could be any number of locations. As she was still kissing and caressing him, she seemed intent on ignoring her pain.

He swung his legs down onto the floor and hoisted her into his arms. As he carried her into the bedroom, her large green eyes stared at him with raw desire.

But Ryan's desire had been squelched the instant he was reminded of her injuries. He refused to have the much-craved moments of passion between them be punctuated by her pain. When they made love for the first time, she was going to enjoy every moment of it.

He set her down carefully on the bed and took a step back from her.

The most adorable whimper of protest escaped her lips.

"We're not doing this with your injuries."

"But—"

"Jenna, roll over."

She shot him a puzzled look.

"Roll over." He motioned with one hand.

She complied hesitatingly and turned her head to eye him suspiciously.

He sat on the side of the bed and settled his hands over the muscles of her back. He firmly massaged the tightened lumps along her neck, shoulders and spine.

"Relax, Jenna."

The stiff tension along her spine eased beneath his fingertips. He worked his way down her tan, muscular legs, careful to avoid the places he most wanted to explore. At first she let out a few groans and then she quieted. Lastly, her breathing slowed and slipped into the rhythmic tide of sleep.

RYAN LEFT Jenna sleeping and stepped into the kitchenette to phone Reece.

Her incredibly tiny apartment left him no room to distance himself. There was no place he could walk where he couldn't be heard from her bedroom.

"What's the status?" Ryan kept his voice a low whisper.

"Maxine's wrapped up at the farmhouse. All the perps are in custody. Paperwork's done. How's sleeping beauty?"

Ryan felt grateful to have competent friends who were willing to keep working when he was otherwise indisposed ... nearly sleeping with the woman he was protecting. "Battered but better."

Ryan rubbed his neck. "So how do we neutralize the threat?"

Reece made a tsk noise over the phone. "Not sure if our little display of force will scare them off. They're not a large gang, but they might be willing to try harder depending on the sum. Claire is still working on uncovering the sum. Did Jenna say how much they're after?"

"I haven't debriefed Jenna yet, but we know it's enough to send a team up to Chicago to try to collect it. Can we get something on the leader—this Ernesto Busta?"

"You mean to land him in jail? I don't know if that'd be enough. He might still be able to reach her from behind bars."

Reece was right on all counts. Ernesto may be sufficiently motivated to come after her even from prison if the price was right. Rider SI was not an organization that performed targeted assassinations, even of criminals like Ernesto.

Ryan had finished leaving dead bodies in his wake long ago—they all had. Reece, Mason, Barry, Maxine, and Billy. Even though no one knew the mysteries of Dorian's past, he had been an agent, which meant he'd done someone else's dirty work, which meant he'd killed. Claire was the exception. She was the only innocent among them. Clean hands. Clear conscience. Well, except for that dot-com thing, but nobody died.

So they needed to eliminate a deadly threat without deadly force.

"Witness protection?" Reece asked.

Ryan sighed. "She doesn't have anything to exchange. Brad might, but neither she nor I would let her and Cal go into witness protection with him."

"We'll figure it out," Reece assured him.

"Thanks."

As he disconnected the call, he looked around at the small apartment, which had grown dark as evening settled.

He could work out a solution tomorrow. Tonight, he needed rest. His eyes fell on her credit card-sized couch—barely more than a love seat. He frowned. Wearily, he made his way to the bedroom and lay down quietly on an unoccupied sliver of Jenna's queen-sized bed.

After setting his gun on the nightstand beside him, he closed his eyes.

⁂

RYAN BLINKED at the setting sun outside Jenna's window. He'd slept maybe an hour. Something had woken him. He listened. Footsteps.

A knock came at the door.

Slipping silently out of bed, he left Jenna sleeping. As he eased his gun out of his holster, he approached the door and looked through the peep-hole. A sloppy thirty-something with a round, bearded face was sniffing his own armpits and checking his breath.

Ryan eased the door open, keeping his gun out of view. "Can I help you?"

"Oh." The man's eyes widened. He had clearly been expecting Jenna to open the door.

He wore flip-flops and no coat. Neighbor then. The type of neighbor who felt at ease dropping in unannounced.

"You must be the guy," Jenna's neighbor said, awe filling his voice.

"I'm the guy." Was he? Sure, why not?

"Jenna said your name was Ryan, right?"

I am the guy.

Ryan was curious to know the context in which Jenna had given his name to her intrusive neighbor. He also wanted the man to leave before he woke Jenna.

"I'm Brandon, her neighbor. I was checking on her because she didn't come home the other night. Usually if she goes out of town, she asks me to feed her fish."

Ryan could tell his body language intimidated poor, harmless Brandon, who was obviously an infatuated neighbor who didn't know he smelled like cat litter.

Ryan leaned against the door to appear more casual, careful to keep his gun concealed. "Yeah. That's my fault." Ryan gave a guilty quirk of his lips.

It was his fault because it took him so long to get to her at the abandoned barn. Ryan knew Brandon would leap to a different conclusion, probably that Jenna had stayed at his place.

He kept an easy smile as he watched Brandon's reaction. The man nodded and scratched his beard. Acceptance settled into his brown eyes.

Ryan was now certain of the context Jenna must have dropped his name. She likely insinuated a relationship. Was it because she wanted a relationship or because she needed to deter busy-body, beer-belly Brandon?

"She said you're a consultant. What type of consulting?"

Seriously? The guy wanted to small talk as he stood in her hallway?

Ryan lowered his voice. "Hey, Brandon. Jenna's sleeping. Thanks for checking up on her. Maybe we can chat another time."

"Oh, yeah. Sure. Nice meeting you."

"You too. It's good she's got a neighbor looking out for her."

Brandon smiled briefly at Ryan's words before he turned and slunk away from Jenna's door. Ryan shook his head. Jenna was sweet enough to be a nice neighbor to Brandon, who repaid the kindness by taking care of her fish.

For the sake of those around her, including harmless neighbors, Jenna might need to relocate until this danger with the Cuban mafia was resolved.

CHAPTER 16

As Ryan walked to the kitchenette, fresh steps approached Jenna's apartment from the end of the hall. Apparently her apartment was not only the size of a silver dollar, but the walls were thin as paper. The click of heels grew louder—a woman's quick, short stride.

Ryan walked back to the door with his gun in his hand. He sighed at Jenna's apartment door with its woefully inadequate single deadbolt. Well, whoever clicked her way down the hallway was hardly a stealthy assassin.

Ryan opened the door, again keeping his weapon concealed behind his back.

The tiniest Asian woman, the size of Mini-Mouse and as adorable, startled back from him as she withdrew the hand with which she had been about to knock on the door.

"Who the hell are you?" she snapped at him, all four-feet nothing of defiance. Even with her heels, she didn't reach five feet.

He arched an eyebrow. "Jenna's guest." He kept his voice calm. Bellied-Brandon was likely with his ear to his door, eaves-dropping.

The small woman attempted to peer around him into Jenna's apartment. "Where is she? She's not answering her phone."

"She's had a rough few days and lost her phone. She's currently sleeping. And you are?"

"I'm her damn best friend." Large, hoop earrings jangled about her head.

Ryan suppressed a grin. The feisty little woman was already riled and would likely be insulted if he laughed at her.

"I'm Ryan Walsh." He produced a business card with his free hand and gave it to Jenna's friend.

She snatched it with a scowl. "I'm Jessica Ong."

"Dr. Ong?"

As Jessica read his card, her mouth fell open. "You're him."

"Beg pardon?"

No longer a ball of fury, she placidly handed his card back to him. "You're Antigua. I mean, the man she regretted letting leave. Did she finally call you?" Jessica looked him up and down appraisingly. "I told her she should have slept with you."

Ryan chuckled. "Thanks. I think." He opened the door wider to let Jessica inside the apartment.

She walked in and made herself comfortable on Jenna's loveseat. She froze, watching intently as Ryan holstered his gun. "You always answer the door before people knock with a gun in your hand?"

Ryan put a finger to his lips as he closed the door. Softly he said, "Jenna is sleeping. She was kidnapped."

"Kidnapped?"

"Shh. Yes. Apparently, Brad is in debt to the Cuban mafia, and he suggested they reclaim the money through Jenna." Ryan sat down in Jenna's desk chair in her living room-office-dining room combo.

"Cocksucker," Jessica swore.

Ryan shook his head. The small Asian fireball reminded him of Maxine. "I wouldn't know about that, but Jenna's safe for now."

Jessica's eyes widened. "What about Cal?"

"Cal is safe and knows nothing about this."

She relaxed slightly. "So Brad gambled his way into trouble, and Jenna's supposed to bail him out? She divorced his sorry sack of saggy balls so she wouldn't have to bail him out anymore."

Well, that's a mental image of Brad I didn't need.

"We'll have to get creative to make sure this is the last time."

"We?"

"Rider Security and Investigation."

Jessica nodded with a grunt. "Jenna's a good person. Good doctor. Good mom. She doesn't deserve this crap." She flipped long strings of straight black hair off her shoulder. "Fucking Brad."

"Agreed."

She narrowed her eyes and scrutinized Ryan again. "You like her?"

"I do."

"You want to sleep with her?"

Did he ever.

"In addition to having a meaningful relationship."

Jessica snorted. "She needs both."

"Agreed."

"You don't gamble, drink excessively, or break the law?"

"No. No. And I'm not at liberty to say."

She huffed out a breath as she stood. "Fine. Tell her to call me when she wakes." She walked over to the door and opened it. "And treat her good." She pointed a short, purple polished nail at him. "Or else."

"Yes, ma'am."

She narrowed her eyes at him.

"Yes, Dr. Ong," he corrected himself, containing his amusement.

Jessica strode down the hallway, the sound of her heels reverberating off the walls.

Ryan closed the door, chuckling to himself. He liked Jenna's friend. He'd also been in enough relationships to know you don't piss off the best friend—least of all when they wore six-inch heels and swore like a Marine in a room full of subordinate men.

<hr>

Jenna woke pleasantly in Ryan's arms.

They both still wore clothing, reminding her of what she had wanted and been denied last night. If her aching muscles were any indication, Ryan had made the appropriate decision.

He pulled her close to him and kissed her forehead.

"I hope it's okay that I had Barry check on Cal. He's okay."

"You did?"

She wanted to kiss this man. Again. But not with morning breath.

Suddenly self-conscious, she excused herself to freshen up.

When she emerged, Ryan had made them bagels with cream cheese, orange juice, and coffee.

She dove into the meal.

"I need to ask you some questions about the kidnapping."

She looked at him as she chewed. He seemed hesitant. Surely he didn't think she would fall to pieces reliving it. The terrible event had ended. She was okay. All was well.

Was it over?

Crap.

It wasn't over. The Cubans didn't have their money. Ernesto didn't have his money.

Swallowing the bite of food, which had suddenly taken on the consistency and flavor of a rice patty, she nodded. "Ernesto Busta wanted me to pay Brad's debt—three hundred thousand dollars. We didn't get as far as me explaining how I don't have that kind of money before you and the A-Team arrived."

He arched an eyebrow, and she recalled how he didn't like mixing analogies.

"You and the Avengers," she corrected herself.

Ryan shook his head, releasing a quirk on one side of his mouth. "That's as far as the conversation got?"

She nodded, sipping her coffee.

"And three hundred thousand dollars was the amount he said?"

"Yes."

Ryan pursed his lips. "Jenna, this is bigger than a few grand."

She cleared her throat. "Three hundred is a few?"

"Apparently, Brad got in debt to Ernesto and promised to pay him back with some accounting work. He botched that, and twelve million dollars went missing."

Jenna choked on her coffee. "Twelve million?"

He turned the face of his phone to her and showed her a text message on his phone from someone named Claire, *12 mill.*

As she unceremoniously cleaned her coffee dribbles off the table, he continued. "Claire is our information technologist. She's the one who helped track you. She also uncovered the exact amount. I think they were going to make an example of you, Jenna. I think after you gave them whatever funds you had, they were going to execute you."

"Jeez, Ryan. Why are you telling me this? I'm a dead woman?"

He took hold of her hand, but in the face of twelve million and a shallow grave, the gesture hardly felt comforting.

"I am going to talk to Ernesto, see if I can broker some kind of deal," he said.

She slid her hand away from him. "Ryan, I already owe you for the rescue mission. I can't afford to pay you to broker a deal with a drug lord on my behalf."

His jaw tensed as his voice hardened. "And I'm not doing it for the money, Jenna."

She blinked at him, surprised by his tone and a little aroused by his intensity. "I'll talk to him with you."

"Out of the question."

"If he signed my death warrant, the least he can do is talk to me first. Judging by the doom and gloom reality talk you're giving me, I'm dead if this doesn't work anyway, right?"

"No. We'd go somewhere. Keep you safe."

"From a man who lost twelve million? Not likely."

"You're not going, Jenna."

She ignored him. "Don't they have some type of parlay or something until we meet?"

"Those are pirates," he said wryly.

"There must be something like that."

"I'm not putting you in harm's way, Jenna." He sounded as though his patience was cracking.

She looked him in the eyes, not caring if he turned big, green, and ugly. If she didn't face this—get out in front of this—the Cubans could go after Cal.

To hell with that.

"This situation outcome leaves me fifty shades of dead, so I'm going to be part of the solution."

He worked to restrain a grin. "I'm pretty sure death is a black and white thing."

"Hmm. Maybe in your world, Ranger. Come to my ICU, and I'll show you the gray shades of death."

"Touché," he said quietly. He leaned back and bit his bottom lip.

She had the sudden, inexplicable sensation of wanting to be the one biting those lips. She crossed her arms, more to restrain her strange impulse to want to resume yesterday's couch activities than to convey impatience.

Watching him silently, she waited for him to acquiesce.

Her mind continued to wander to the kisses they'd shared. She wanted to feel his warmth and strength. She wanted to smell his cedar scent and feel the way his fingers curved into her flesh with desire.

Ugh! What's wrong with me?

She was ogling him like a diabetic in a doughnut shop who hadn't savored an apple fritter in half a dozen years.

She had shifted from rejecting him to calling him for help in a life- threatening situation to trying to jump his bones. He must think she was bizarre, which would be true.

He looked at her curiously, making her wonder if the man was reading her mind or if she was exceedingly transparent.

"Okay," he said at last. "I'll talk to Max. We'll set up a meeting."

ERNESTO SAT AT HIS DESK, staring at Juan as he explained what had happened in Chicago. He'd been introduced to Dr. Masters when their meeting was abruptly interrupted. Hours had eked by before they acquired information about what events had transpired.

Dr. Masters had hired protective services. Surprise. Surprise. She was smarter than her ex-husband had insinuated.

Ernesto felt his eye twitch in irritation. No one on his team knew she'd hired a security team. Nor had they taken any precautions to ensure they hadn't been followed. Because they all now had bullet wounds, perhaps they would remember to be less careless next time.

He picked up the fingernail file on his desk and began smoothing the edges of his nails. "Who is protecting her?"

"A company called Rider Security and Investigation. Small group based out of Atlanta."

Ernesto's eyes flickered irritably to Juan and then back to his fingers. "And they want a meeting?" Someone from the company had called requesting to speak directly to him, but he declined, letting Juan take the call.

"*Sí.*"

Ernesto ran his tongue along his teeth as he turned his gaze to look out his office window. "Bayfront Park, as they requested. Set it up. Ground team. Sniper team."

He needed to squeeze funds out of Dr. Masters before he killed her. If she had money to pay a security team, she had money to pay him. Killing her at this meeting would be counterproductive, but he would be prepared for defensive measures if needed.

A small security team wouldn't have the resources or audacity to affront the Cuban mafia. They obviously wanted a negotiation, and Ernesto was willing to help Dr. Masters workout a payment plan. Abducting her had perhaps been a hasty maneuver. Because she had savvy and resources, he could be magnanimous enough to find a mutually beneficial agreement—one where he drained her funds and she lived a bit longer.

⸺ ⁂ ⸺

JESS RUSH into Jenna's room and threw her arms around her in more emotion than Jenna had ever seen the small woman express. She'd found coverage and left work to come see Jenna.

"I'm so sorry, Jenna. Ryan told me about Brad's colossal screw-up. Jackass."

"Thanks."

Ryan sat back down on the couch to work on his laptop.

Jenna released the hug and walked with Jess into her bedroom. "I'm going to meet with the Cuban mafia, see what options I have."

"You're going to go confront this guy?" Jess's voice dripped with incredulity and concern.

"I don't have a choice. I can't pay him. I have to see if I can reason with him." Even as Jenna said the words, she realized the improbability of success.

She remembered Ernesto's cold, dark eyes. Her life was unimportant to him. Inconsequential. How do you reason with a cold-blooded killer?

Jenna packed her suitcase as Jess stood staring at her.

"I was an indentured servant to Brad for years. Maybe Ernesto will accept monthly payments."

"For something that isn't even your fault?"

"I'm short on options, Jess. I can only hope."

Jess's face transformed from devastation to pity. Jenna knew that look. She'd shared it with families who clung to hope of their loved one's survival in the face of certain death.

When her eyes moistened, she looked away. She wrapped her phone charging cord into a small, coiled ball. "If anything happens to me—"

"Don't."

"Jess—"

"Don't say it."

"I need you to look after Cal." The lump in Jenna's throat threatened to choke her.

"Shut up." Jess said harshly. She crushed Jenna to her in a hug. "Of course I will."

Burning tears ran down Jenna's cheeks. "My life insurance policy should—"

"I got it. But you're going to be fine."

"I love you, Jess."

Jess sniffed. "Yeah, well. I'm unique." She wiped drops from around her eyes and straightened her scrub top.

Jenna had never known the woman to shed a tear.

"I have to go to my shift. I want text updates every few hours. Keep me posted—when you land, when you go to bed, when you faceoff with asshole-Ernesto. All of it. Don't leave me hanging."

"Yes, ma'am."

Jess gave her a wry smile. "And try to enjoy that hunk of yumminess in the next room, will you?"

"Get out," Jenna said playfully. She ushered her friend out of the bedroom, down the hall and to the door.

Before leaving, Jess gave her one last look. They didn't exchange further words or hugs. Thank god. Jenna thought she'd crumble if they went another round of sharing emotions.

She closed the door as Jess left. As she pulled out her phone, Jenna took a deep breath to compose herself. She had another call to make because she wanted to keep her job if she survived this ordeal.

"Hi, Jenna."

"Brody, I'm heading out of town on urgent family issues," she told her boss.

Twelve million urgent issues.

"My next shift is covered, but I wanted to let you know in case I can't resolve things quickly."

In which case, I won't be around for any shifts … ever.

"Everything okay with Cal?"

"Yes, Cal is good."

"Jenna, I heard you were maybe looking for another job. I know you want to be near Cal."

"Brody—"

"But you're one of the best physicians I have. Do you know, as a supervisor, how much I value you? You're always on time, always thorough, and you have a good bedside manner. And you don't complain. You make my job easier."

"Brody—"

"Don't leave. Don't leave, Jenna, and I promise I will get you a year-end bonus."

She pinched the bridge of her nose. "I'm not leaving."

"You're not?"

"I'm not working elsewhere. I'm going to Miami."

She could hear him rubbing his bald head.

"Oh. That type of family issue."

Brody knew she'd left her ex-husband back in Miami. She had made it clear that no information about her was to be given out to anyone. Not wanting him to think she was a fragile abuse victim, she had told her boss the details.

"I'm going to hold you to that bonus, though."

"You got it."

Unless I get killed by the Cubans.

CHAPTER 17

An odd sense of nostalgia and dread filled Jenna as they neared the Miami airport. She stared out the plane window with Ryan silently seated beside her.

She'd left Miami after she and Cal had made plans for Cal's boarding school. After closing the doors on the mistakes of her past, she didn't need to live in a city that would remind her of them.

Yet Miami was also where so many memories of Cal lingered. The best memories of their time as he grew up took place in Antigua, but Miami held its share. Aside from the many beaches and parks, she had taken him to a puppet show at the Adrienne Arsht Center for the Performing Arts. They had climbed the white lighthouse at Bill Baggs Cape Florida State Park. They saw animals at Jungle Island. In the heat of the summer, she would take him indoors to the Miami Children's Museum.

She moved to Chicago, not only because the hospital offered a great job, but because she wanted a new city without constant reminders of how much she missed her son.

I can't keep him forever.

With her current situation, she felt grateful he wasn't caught in the middle. Perhaps she could resolve the problem with Ernesto without Cal ever having to know the danger in which his mother had been involved.

Jenna walked through the doors of a hotel in downtown Miami.

The last forty-eight hours blurred in her mind through the haste of packing and rearranging her work schedule.

A stocky woman with untamed brown hair filled with coarse, unruly gray sparklers greeted them at the door. She shook hands roughly with Ryan before turning a set of tired yet friendly blue eyes on Jenna. The woman appeared to be in her mid-fifties with stern lines around her eyes and lips.

She extended a hand. "Dr. Masters, I'm Maxine Rider." Her mouth sagged in what appeared to be a perpetual frown, but her voice remained relaxed.

Ryan had told Jenna that Maxine was a former Marine. Jenna wondered if a hard military life was where her many facial lines had originated.

Jenna shook her hand. "I'm grateful to your team, Mrs. Rider."

"Call me Max. Ryan is the least pain in my ass of my employees, and he doesn't cry wolf. He needed help. We helped." Maxine appeared to be appraising her and Ryan, gauging their stance and the closeness of their bodies.

"Thank you, Max."

Maxine scratched her chin and seemed uncomfortable yet appreciative of the gratitude Jenna expressed.

"I would have introduced myself sooner, but I used your recovery time to try to get a pulse on the severity of the situation."

No pulse. Just flat-line. The kind of flat-line an entire syringe of adrenaline wasn't going to revive.

Jenna's mouth grew dry. "Thanks."

"You realize when you go meet Ernesto and all hell could break loose? Have you thought about what your absence would do to Cal? All he'd be left with is a sorry excuse for a father." The Marine was gruff, but Jenna appreciated the woman being thoughtful enough to consider her son.

"I understand." Jenna had thought about Cal in the event of her 'absence,' which was one of the reasons she needed this debt issue settled. She didn't want to spend one second turning Cal's life upside down with the havoc his father had created. She needed to end this chaos ... somehow.

"Barry is in Boston. He's going to provide surveillance for Cal until this thing blows over. Barry is good. Cal won't know he's watching his back."

Jenna embraced Maxine. She swallowed the lump in her throat and blinked away moist eyes. "Thank you, Max."

She felt the way the other woman stiffened in her arms before patting her back awkwardly. Maxine's emotional barriers made it easier for Jenna to pull herself together, though her gratitude overflowed.

Maxine turned and walked beside Jenna toward the check-in counter.

Ryan followed, carrying his overnight bag.

Fifteen minutes later, Jenna rolled her suitcase into her quiet hotel room.

Ryan gave her a nod. "I'll be back at six, and we'll go to dinner." He left to join Reece in a room.

As the door clicked shut, Jenna turned to look out the window. The swaying palm trees and billboards glinting in the sun towered in bright contrast to her somber mood.

Tomorrow she would meet with Ernesto Busta and try to have a rational conversation with a gun-wielding crime lord who probably thought she was nothing more than gum on his shoe, a diverticula in his colon, a mole on his back, a sliver in his finger, a—

Ugh.

She flopped down on the bed.

After this, maybe she could go back to her normal life where she dealt with blood and death daily—just not her own. If she got lucky, she could also engineer a way to punch Brad in the nose for his part in this nightmare. She felt a surge of burning fury toward him. Her divorce was supposed to be the hallmark conclusion of their involvement together. How dare he be so careless when he had a son to consider. She felt impotent as she pondered a way out of this disaster and how to prevent ones in the future.

Curled into a ball, she rubbed her right hand, remembering how Ryan had held it. He'd held it after she video-conferenced with Cal, pretending that all was well and needing to hear him talk about his mundane school day. Ryan had also held her hand on the plane as she stared out the window, flying toward some incomprehensible fate.

She pushed herself up, walked to the mini-fridge, and opened it. What she wouldn't give for a drink. But she wasn't about to pay ten bucks for a single shot of liquor. She closed the fridge and pulled the water thermos out of her carry-on bag and took a long gulp.

Ryan had promised to take her to dinner at six. Perhaps she could have a glass of wine then. Wine at one's last supper seemed appropriate.

⁂

RYAN STRAIGHTENED his tie again before he knocked on Jenna's door. He felt a little foolish with butterflies annoying his abdomen.

Former Rangers don't get butterflies.

Besides, he certainly shouldn't be feeling like this was a date. This was a planning dinner in preparation for their conference with the Cuban mafia tomorrow. They needed to discuss strategy.

Had he missed his opportunity to be with her the other night in her apartment? She had undeniably wanted him, and instead of taking what she'd offered, he'd tucked her into bed. He couldn't tell if she felt rejected as a result. She hadn't made any further moves since, but then she'd been a little preoccupied worrying about shades of death.

Jenna opened the door looking as radiant as she had the first time he had seen her in Antigua. Her caramel skin glowed as her copper hair spilled over her shoulders. She wore a blue cotton dress that dipped low into her cleavage, a spot his lips had a sudden raging desire to explore.

"You look beautiful," he said, his voice sounding foreign and hoarse in his ears.

She must have caught his eyes roaming her body because the corners of her mouth turned up slightly.

"I like this polished look," she said. "Little different from khaki shorts and palm tree shirts."

Stepping aside, she let him into her room.

"When on a tropical island undercover, one wears unsightly Hawaiian shirts."

She turned around and slipped on her earrings from off the counter. By the time she turned back around, Ryan had moved in close. At first he wanted to smell her floral, coconut scent. Now that he stood mere inches away from her radiant eyes and succulent lips, he knew he needed a taste. Just one, if she was willing.

He ran his hands lightly down her bare arms. Her breath caught as her nipples visibly tightened beneath her dress.

She was willing.

He moved in for a kiss, and she met him halfway. Her sensual lips felt soft and smooth. The kiss began gentle and probing before escalating to raw desire that had them both gasping for air. His arms wrapped around her perfect curves as he drew her body closer.

She released a sensual noise, a mix between a moan and a purr.

God, she mesmerized him. They were never going to make that second date at this rate.

He slid down the fabric over her shoulder as they kissed.

Her delicate hands undid the buttons of his shirt.

For an instant, he abandoned all rational thought, picked up Jenna and laid her on the bed. He pulled his shirt off and lay beside her. The sight of her made him catch his breath. Her eyes filled with sheer desire, staring at his naked chest. Ready and undaunted, her hungry gaze roamed his body.

He trailed his hand from her cheek to her shoulder and down to the curve of her breast. She was so close but still too far away from him.

He stilled and swallowed. "Are you sure, Jenna?" He wanted to devour her, and once he did, there was no going back.

Beneath him, she wriggled out of her dress over her head, offering every inch of her flesh to him. She lay unabashedly exposed. "Oh, yes."

He kissed her again, hard and hungry as his hands moved over her like he'd been waiting years for the chance—up her warm ribs, over the soft curve of her breast, feeling her arch into his touch as if she'd been starving for it. He'd been starving too. Ever since that first kiss—he'd wanted this. Wanted *her*.

When he bent to taste the delicate line of her collarbone, the small of her back, he memorized the way she shivered for him.

When he kissed her mouth again, she was hot, hungry, and demanding.

Every press of her body against his made his urges harder to control. She melted under his hands, into his chest, into him, like she trusted him with every need she'd kept tucked away.

He slid lower, kissing down her stomach, savoring the way her breath hitched. Her fingers slipped into his hair, tightening just a little—God, that did things to him.

"I want you inside me," she breathed.

Ryan paused. That voice—low, rough, needy—shot straight through him.

He lifted his head, grinning. "We'll get to that."

He kept moving lower, slow on purpose, wanting to feel every moment of her unraveling. But then he felt a tension ripple through her—a subtle, startled stiffness.

"Whoa. I've never ... no one's ever ... " Her throat bobbed in a swallow.

He looked up at her, heart catching. "That's a damn shame," he said softly. "I promise you'll like it."

"What do I do?" she whispered.

"Enjoy it."

And when he touched her—really touched her—she came apart in a way that stunned him. Watching her lose herself under his mouth, hearing the sounds she made, feeling her fingers twist in his hair... it wrecked him in the best way.

When he crawled back up over her, she blinked up at him, dazed and beautiful after her climax.

"Was it supposed to be that fast and furious?"

He laughed, brushing his thumb over her cheek. "When it's the right two people? Yeah. My ego's thrilled, too."

Her smile—soft, open, wanting—hit him hard.

"Keep going?" he asked.

"Yes," she breathed aloud. "Oh my goodness, yes."

When he slid up and into her, heat surged through him so fast he had to grit his teeth. She wrapped her legs around him, meeting his rhythm, her hips rising to match every stroke. Hearing her whisper his name—"Ryan"—in that voice made something inside him snap.

Soon they were both slick with sweat, bodies sliding together. Her nails traced along his back, leaving fire in their wake.

Then he angled his hips just right—felt her gasp, felt her tighten—and the way she clung to him pulled him straight into the edge. She convulsed around him, pleasure rippling through her in waves so strong he felt them all.

The world blew apart.

He whispered her name, over and over, moving in slow, drawn-out strokes, unwilling to leave her body too soon. He buried his face in her hair, breathing her in, holding her close until the after-shocks faded and they stilled—still joined, still breathing hard—her chest rising against his, the air warm between them.

SATIATED IN A WAY she never new possible, Jenna took pleasure in exploring Ryan's body. She'd considered his appearance rugged at first glance, now she knew why. His face had multiple small scars—one at his bottom lip extending down to his chin, another over his left eye, and a last jagged one by his right ear. They had been well tended, only visible under scrutiny. She adored the way his smile illuminated dimples that softened the appearance of his face. On his chest staggered a linear, jagged scar.

His rich sable eyes watched her watching him.

She touched the scar near his lip. Every mark he bore repre-sented a story from his past, a past about which she knew very little.

Regardless of the details of his past, events had led him to Rider SI, which put him in her path in Antigua. Because of his past, she was alive. Without hesitation, he'd come to her aid. Without hesitation, he stayed with her now.

"You're deep in thought."

Her eyes wandered back to his. "I'm savoring this moment."

Sadness tugged at the corners of his mouth.

She worried he thought she meant she savored it because she was worried it was her last. Lying with him after making love, she'd momentarily forgotten an uncertain future awaited her.

She leaned forward and kissed him, wiping the concern from his expression.

"I'm afraid I made us miss dinner," he said.

She shook her head. "Food has been less than appetizing under the circumstances."

He drew a finger along her clavicle, delighting her senses.

"I can't believe I passed this up in Antigua," she admitted.

"You weren't ready to let a stranger in. Considering what you've been through, I don't blame you."

She had no idea it could be so—

"Amazing."

He smiled. He kissed her bare shoulder before easing her body on top of his. "You say that like it's over."

***

RYAN SAT at the square breakfast table in the hotel lobby. Jenna sat in the chair to his right, Reece to his left, and Maxine across from him. Ryan watched Jenna nervously arrange her scrambled eggs on her plate in an anatomically accurate form of two bean-shaped kidneys. Given the stressful circumstance of her situation, she was holding up remarkably well.

Maxine had already finished her omelet. Ryan sipped his coffee between bites of his yogurt parfait. Reece drank orange juice and ate a side of bacon.

Maxine wiped her mouth with a napkin as she spoke to Jenna. "Claire investigated further into the details of Brad's screw-up. The small clerical error Brad made put Ernesto Busta in debt to Russian mobster Vladimir Pronin."

Jenna's already drawn face paled further. Ryan wished he could kiss away her worries, but nothing in life was so simple.

"That sounds worse than the Cuban mafia." Jenna put her fork down on the plate.

"It is," Reece confirmed.

Ryan scowled briefly at his partner. Scaring Jenna more than she already was could be counterproductive.

"Don't you have a connection?" Ryan asked Maxine.

Maxine pursed her lips. "Vladimir and I have an understanding. Not the type that affords me the ability to wipe away seven hundred fifty million rubles."

"What understanding?" Jenna asked.

"As long as his interests and the interests of my clients do not run counter to each other, I won't take the risk of damaging his organization, despite the fact that he's a criminal."

Ryan added, "She doesn't want to start a war."

"With the Russian mafia? Who would?" Jenna leaned back and sucked in a deep breath as though she thought it might be her last.

"What's wrong?" Ryan asked.

Other than the obvious that you're wearing a bull's-eye on your back.

Jenna looked hard at Maxine as she laid her hands on either side of her plate. "Would a man like Vladimir be willing to forgive that sum of money to repay a debt?"

Ryan frowned. Debts and favors with the Russian mafia were

not good practice. Furthermore, one would not likely find a debt worth twelve million dollars.

"I saved his nephew's life."

Reece's eyebrows shot to his hairline.

Except for that debt.

Jenna looked back and forth at Maxine and Ryan. "In February, Mikhail was in my ICU with the wrong diagnosis. I found the problem and fixed it. I don't consider the patients and families I treat as owing me a debt, but Vladimir thanked me and told me to call if I needed a favor."

Maxine's jaw appeared to come unhinged. Not an expression Ryan had ever seen the woman wear.

Ryan cleared his throat. "That could work, Max. At least let's offer a proposal that he forgive the debt. Let him negotiate it down if he's not willing to settle for the full twelve million."

Maxine nodded slowly as she looked at Jenna. "He's a man of honor. He'll remember his debt to you, but something of this magnitude will need to be discussed in person."

"What do I do about Ernesto in the meantime?" Jenna asked.

"*We* still have to meet with him," Reece said.

Ryan glanced at his watch—forty minutes until their meeting.

Maxine opened her phone and began texting while speaking. "*We* will need to buy time to meet with Vladimir."

Ryan appreciated the way Jenna's eyes warmed to everyone, expressing that they made her feel like part of the team.

"How do we do that?" she asked.

"Done," Maxine replied.

Jenna startled at her word. "You are on texting terms with the Russian crime lord?"

"Not exactly. Well. Yes, close enough. Like I said, we have an understanding."

Jenna shot Ryan an incredulous look.

He smiled at her and winked. He knew Maxine and Vladimir had a run-in during Mason and Billy's tennis player protection duty. Maxine had met with the mobster and former FSB Russian Intelligence. Not only had she left unharmed and unthreatened, she'd secured the safety of the tennis player from anyone under Vladimir's influence. Because Maxine never boasted or discussed personal meetings, no one knew all of the details.

Maxine stood. "First stop, Bayfront Park. Next stop, Moscow."

CHAPTER 18

Forty minutes later, Jenna stood rigid with Maxine on one side of her and Ryan on the other as Ernesto greeted them with a feral smile. His eyes were narrow and spaced far apart giving them a catlike appearance.

Jenna recognized Ernesto's disconcerting smile from their video chat. At the time, she thought his face may be the last face she would ever see before she died.

Too early to say it won't be.

She smelled the familiar salty air at Bayfront Park. The humid air was vastly different from the ever-blowing dry breeze of Chicago. She recalled the times she had taken Cal for walks along the waterfront and through this very park.

Cal.

Her gut clenched.

Maxine had ensured a public meeting place. Nearby people played in the park and strolled down by the water. At the amphitheater, a crew was setting up for an outdoor concert later that day.

She tried to draw on the strength and solidarity of the two

armed negotiators on either side of her. They somehow appeared simultaneously at ease and battle-ready. Ryan had made assurances that nothing would happen to her.

Sweet, but how much resided in his control?

They stood outnumbered two to one, and those were the gunmen she could see. Did they have snipers just as Maxine had Reece on a rooftop somewhere?

Rolling her shoulders, Jenna felt the weight of her Kevlar. Because she knew a shot to the head, brachial artery, or femoral artery could be as fatal as a shot to the chest, the vest brought limited comfort.

"*Señor* Masters led me to believe you were with limited funds, Dr. Masters, however, I see you hired a security team," Ernesto said.

Not any team. The Rider SI team.

Having been instructed to let Maxine handle the communication, Jenna kept silent.

"We do pro bono," Maxine said casually. "It's good business."

Ernesto looked down his long, tan nose at Maxine. It seemed his thin stature and shimmering purple suit disapproved of her short, round body and cargo pants.

Jenna sensed he immediately underestimated Maxine.

Jenna liked Maxine immensely. Ryan had explained Maxine's heroism in the Marines. She was tough as steel and fierce as a wildcat. Jenna wondered if Ernesto had spent even a fraction of the time investigating her organization as she had his.

Ernesto was well funded and ruled with an iron fist, but his tactics suffered flaws, Maxine had explained. He had loyalty problems in his organization because he often shot first and asked questions later. If Brad had misplaced a smaller sum of money, he likely would have been dead already. As things were, Ernesto needed to first sort a way out of his problem with the Russians before he could shoot anyone over the missing money.

But bullets flying are a matter of time.

Ernesto looked slowly at the three of them. "None of you appears to be carrying my money." His voice sounded cold despite the Spanish accent.

"We are working on a solution," Maxine replied. "We will need a few more days."

Jenna's gaze flickered to Maxine and then quickly back to the Cubans. Maxine didn't mention Vladimir. Surely, explaining they planned to discuss the funds with Vladimir was a pertinent addition to the conversation.

Jenna continued to keep silent. The intensity of the tension in their circle made her feel like she stood in an autoclave. She began to sweat, recalling the time in residency when the air conditioning broke during her ER rotation. Fully draped in a sterile gown, hat, and gloves, she bent over a patient as she started a central line. The sweltering room, smell of blood and body odor mixed with a long, exhausting shift culminated in overwhelming nausea.

At Bayfront Park, she swayed slightly like the palm trees around her.

Ryan eased his body close, touching her arm with his torso. The proximity of his strength helped her find hers.

"I cannot guarantee your safety if you take longer to bring me my money," Ernesto said, breaking the silence.

Jenna suppressed an incredulous look. The man who threatened her safety was surely the one who could guarantee it.

Salsa music burst forth from Ernesto's suit pocket. Jenna startled slightly, but no one else moved.

"You should answer that," Maxine encouraged him.

The Cuban narrowed his eyes at her.

"Slowly," she added.

Ernesto opened his blazer cautiously and withdrew his phone. *"Hola."* As he listened, his face paled. His Adam's apple bobbed nervously.

Vladimir Pronin, Jenna surmised. Maxine is a remarkable woman.

"Yes, *señor.*" He snapped the phone shut. After a brief swallow, he straightened. "It appears you are granted an eight-day extension. We will meet again when you return to Miami."

He refastened the buttons on his suit, turned on his heels, and walked down the sidewalk. His assistants followed like puppets.

Jenna felt like the weight of a hospital bed eased off of her. She knew this was an irrational sense of relief because meeting with the Russian mafia was next on her to-do list.

Next stop, Moscow.

She turned to Ryan, who wrapped a reassuring arm around her. His face betrayed a pride that made her girlishly giddy.

All I did was stand here.

"I need to talk to Cal before I go."

He nodded, eyes filling with concern. The man who only moments ago had appeared stoic facing armed gangsters suddenly brimmed with compassion for her. Her heart swelled before she remembered more pressing issues.

What the hell am I going to tell Cal?

***

MAXINE CLOSED her hotel room door and unloaded the weapons she had carried to the park—Sig Sauer P226 and 938 as well as her seven inch Marine Corp American Legend KA-BAR. The knife had seen more bloodshed than some biker bars.

She retrieved her phone from one of her cargo pants' pockets.

She unlocked it, grabbed a beer from the mini-fridge, and plopped down on the small chaise lounge. After taking a long swig, she looked at the ongoing chess game on her phone.

After taking Vladimir Pronin's rook with her bishop, she continued to stare at the board. She'd won the last game, but she wouldn't underestimate this formidable adversary. They'd been playing chess for almost a year since he'd invited her after their first and only face-to-face meeting in the Atlanta airport.

She never should have accepted his invitation to play, but something intriguing smoldered in his eyes as they vacillated from deadly to playful. He was not a charismatic man the way actors and politicians were. His appeal emanated from having seen and lived through violence, terror, and loss; yet he was still capable of finding both humor and serenity in the world.

Be that as it may, she had no business allowing herself to be pulled into his magnetic personality. The FM-92 Stinger surface-to-air infrared missile may be an awe-inspiring piece of equipment, but one did not want to be on the receiving end. Becoming familiar with someone likely to detonate and take those around him with him was a dangerous undertaking.

Where do you want to meet? She sent the message through the chess game they played.

Kafe Pushkin, he replied.

My client is unlikely to cordially eat under the circumstances, she texted.

Dr. Masters was not accustomed to high-stakes negotiation as Maxine and Vladimir were. Suturing knife wounds was not the same level of stress as the threat of receiving one. The physician would likely be unable to conduct herself in a manner befitting Russian culture if she was forced to endure an entire meal with a Russian warlord.

He replied, *Very well. My office off Varvaka.*

He took her bishop with his queen.

Her team and the physician would be vulnerable within his fortress. They were no less vulnerable anywhere in Moscow. Unlike Ernesto, however, Maxine had an element of trust with Vladimir. Perhaps trust seemed too strong a word. Mutual understanding and respect were more accurate. Should anything happen to any of Maxine's team or clients, she would unleash the full force of Rider SI. Her team may not be able to destroy his massive organization, but they could cripple it sufficiently, enabling other predators to seize the weakened creature and finish the kill.

Another text came from him: *Afterward, you and I will go to Kafe Pushkin.*

Maxine stared at the screen and mumbled a stream of expletives. What was his endgame? Chess was one thing, but meeting in person was an entirely different level of interaction.

Vladimir had agreed to meet with her and her client. He'd agreed to extend Dr. Masters' immunity within his organization and Ernesto's. Maxine felt obligated to agree to dinner. It may not only facilitate Dr. Masters' debt forgiveness, but future negotiations.

Shitballs, Maxine thought. *Are there going to be future negotiations?*

She started her company to help people who needed difficult-to-find skill-sets. She did not start her company to Hopak with the Russian mob.

I don't dance. She mentally sighed.

Finally, she replied to Vladimir, *I accept.*

She took his queen.

Jenna stood in the hotel room as Ryan inspected it. When he gave the all clear, she shrugged out of her Kevlar and dumped it in the chair.

Ryan pulled her into his arms. "You did well, Jenna. We'll get through this."

We.

'We' sounded wonderful. She closed her eyes for a moment, reveling in the feel of him.

"Will you stay while I talk to Cal?"

"Sure." His eyes lit with delight at her request.

He sat down on the small sofa beside her. She opened her laptop, connected to the hotel wireless Internet, and waited for Cal to answer the call. Ryan took her hand and squeezed gently.

Please answer. Please answer.

If Cal didn't answer now, she didn't know when she would have the opportunity to call him again.

At last the screen flickered and Cal's face appeared.

"Hi, Mom." He spoke the familiar words, but faltered at the end as he noticed Ryan.

Jenna fought to contain her relief at seeing him. To Cal, they had spoken a few days ago. To Jenna, she was seeing her son after seventy-two hours of agonizingly feeling like the clock tick on borrowed time in this world.

"Hi, Cal. This is my friend, Ryan Walsh."

"Friend?"

"Yes."

"Hello, Cal. I've heard a lot of great things about you."

Cal continued to look at his mom. "Your friend that you sit close to on a couch that isn't yours?"

Damn, he noticed that.

"Yes. He is that type of friend."

Silence stretched for a long moment, but Jenna could see Ryan grinning beside her.

Cal looked toward Ryan. "That's cool, man. Mom needs that type of friend. What do you do?"

Cal had asked the question casually, but Jenna knew the answer was important to him. He'd seen his father mooch off of her for years. He wouldn't want to see that happen to her again.

"I work in private security and investigation, which is often some combination of exposing criminals and protecting people."

Her son seemed to mull over that description.

She hadn't thought to discuss with Ryan how he might be introduced, but she liked that he gave candid answers to her son. She strived to be truthful with Cal when he asked questions, though she often didn't volunteer information. She didn't inundate Cal with how dismal marriage to Brad had been. She didn't discuss much of what she saw and treated in the hospital intensive care unit. She certainly wouldn't divulge the tangled web of organized crime his father had spun around her.

"Are you packing?" Cal asked Ryan.

"Cal," she reprimanded in surprise.

"When I need to," Ryan answered.

Cal narrowed his eyes at the former Ranger. "You'll protect my mom?"

"With my life."

Cal gave an approving nod.

Jenna wanted to accuse them of being overprotective, but that wasn't true given her current situation.

Cal leaned back, picked up a half-eaten apple and took a bite. The crunch transmitted crisply through the speaker on the laptop.

"How'd you meet?" Cal asked, still chewing a mouthful of Fiji Red.

"I watched her save a man's life in your grandparents' bar in Antigua. After that, I knew she was the woman of my dreams."

Cal chuckled in approval.

Ryan shot Jenna a wry smile.

She leaned toward the screen. "I'm calling to see how class is going."

"Fine, Mom. You should get an email copy of my report card next week." He took another bite of apple.

"And skiing?"

"Cross training now with all the snow melted."

Cal nodded toward Ryan. "You got a car?"

"Cal," Jenna cautioned. She turned to look at Ryan. "He's on me about driving lessons. The excuse of me not having a car—I can walk or take the L wherever I need to go in Chicago—is wearing thin since some of his classmates now have learning permits."

Ryan chuckled. "Yes, I own a car."

The sound of tinny drums interrupted their conversation. Cal picked up his cell phone and looked at the screen.

"Gotta go, Mom." He started to stand. "Cool first-time boyfriend."

"I love you." She called quickly.

"Love you, too."

The screen went blank, but she continued to stare at it. She wanted to say more, but suddenly the conversation had ended. "Maybe it's better this way. I wanted to throw out a lot of reassurances, but that would have alarmed him." She felt her bottom lip tremble.

Ryan put an arm around her and pulled her to him. She enjoyed his warmth and swallowed to keep the tears at bay.

"He likes you," she said.

"I like him."

"I liked how honest you were with him. You treated him like an adult."

"I suppose, not having children, I only know one way to treat them."

Her hands fiddled with the collar of his shirt. She was amazed that, with the world spinning out of control around her, life felt calm and perfect in his arms.

"So pack for Russia?"

"Pack for Russia," Ryan confirmed.

"Good thing I already have a passport."

"You're going to be okay, Jenna."

The way Ryan said the words made them feel like truth.

Impossible.

Logic dictated her life was insignificant to the criminal underworld, but she shouldn't be snuffed out over someone else's twelve-million-dollar mistake. Yet the situation appeared bleak.

"Jenna." Ryan's warm hands cupped her face.

She looked into his deep brown eyes. The worry they transmitted radiated intensity.

"I'm sorry." She knew she should be stronger, rather than making mental funeral arrangements.

Carnations or roses? Classical music or classic rock? How about Queen's 'Who Wants To Live Forever'?

Ryan's thumb stroked a cheek. "You have nothing to apologize for. You're an amazing woman doing a remarkable job of keeping yourself together under stressful circumstances."

She covered his hands in hers.

How was Ryan able to simultaneously ease her worries and spark her passion?

She leaned closer to him. His hands slipped around her waist as her tongue slipped between his lips. In his arms, the world beyond them vanished. She felt transformed from a working mother, ex-wife with a bounty on her head to a hungry, insatiable seductress. She would analyze that transformation some other time.

She gasped as Ryan claimed her mouth the way he was about to claim her body.

CHAPTER 19

*S*leeping Jenna. Her beauty took his breath away. Ryan would have to wake her soon, though. Moscow beckoned.

Quietly, he exited the room and called his brother.

"Ryan, what's up?"

"Sonny, I need to know what time frame you could liquidate everything if needed."

A long pause hung on the other end of the line. "What's going on?"

"How long?"

"Three days, man. What's this about?"

"I'm on my way to Moscow for a job, and things might get dicey."

"Dicey?"

"Dicey. I might need to vanish fast."

If his brother could move his assets to cash, Claire could move them to safety. She could work on new identities for him and Jenna. And Cal. Ryan grit his teeth and hoped to hell it didn't come to his last resort plan.

"Vanishing sounds ominous."

Ryan remained silent. He certainly didn't have enough funds to help pay off Jenna's debt, but he had enough to go into hiding.

"And permanent," his brother added when Ryan didn't reply.

"This is a last resort, but someone's in trouble."

"A client?"

Ryan walked through the hotel lobby to the continental breakfast area.

When Ryan didn't answer, Sonny added, "You said you were on a job."

"She's more than a client. She's the woman I met in Antigua."

"And you might have to disappear with her?"

"As a last resort," Ryan emphasized again. He positioned the phone between his ear and his shoulder while he fixed two coffees.

"Do I get to meet the woman who's sweeping my brother's life savings out from under him?" Sonny's tone stung with bitterness.

"It's not like that. She doesn't know anything about my funds."

She hardly knows anything about me.

Doesn't change the fact that I love her.

"You love her?"

Damn, had he said that aloud?

Ryan added a splash of cream to the drinks. "Yeah. I do."

"That's new."

"Yeah."

"I mean. You've never said that to me about a woman."

"I know." Ryan paced the hallway.

"Ever."

"Yeah."

"You said she's a physician?"

"She works in an ICU in Chicago."

"How's a doctor get so deep in trouble that you're going to

Russia and you've got DEFCON one on speed-dial if things go to shit?"

"Ex-husband," Ryan said.

Sonny huffed out a breath, but he didn't pry any further. "Well, if you don't go to ground. I want to meet her."

"Yeah, of course."

"I mean before it gets more serious."

"Yes, Sonny."

"I'm not joking. You're already in love with her. I don't want you showing up on my doorstep married. I get to meet her before this relationship goes any further."

"I said I loved her. I didn't say the feeling was mutual. She's dealing with a lot, and marriage is definitely not a leap either of us would entertain right now."

"Uh-huh. Well, if you love her, then you're pulling all your psychoanalytical punches, which means you're telling her exactly what she wants and needs to hear. That means she'll fall in love with you in no time."

Sonny could jokingly claim Ryan had such abilities, but they both knew that wasn't true. Still, Sonny had never brought his dates to meet Ryan for fear that his intuitive skills would elucidate from the woman's body language that she wasn't interested in Sonny or have her flocking to Ryan's arm with a few witty and insightful words.

Sonny sighed. "I'll have some emergency funds ready for you from the Red Funds. I'll keep my phone close by. Let me know when everything blows over so I can stop worrying."

"Thanks, Sonny."

Sixteen hours later, Jenna sat beside Ryan on the plane as he squeezed her hand.

He'd tried to be supportive, teaching her bits of Russian and distracting her from the dread tugging at her insides. She adored him for his efforts.

As the plane circled Moscow, he pointed out landmarks. The sun glistened off the golden dome of the Cathedral of Christ the Savior. The Red Square burst with color, including the domes of St. Basil's Cathedral. She saw the Moskva River, which Ryan explained stretched over three hundred miles long.

They landed, quit the plane, and made their way through customs. Jenna watched with a mixture of fascination and dread as her passport was stamped with her visit to Russia. She'd never been anywhere outside the States except Antigua. Once her parents sunk their savings into the tropical island resort, why would they want to go anywhere else? After marrying a man with a gambling problem, trips remained limited to those taken by car. Others would be either too expensive or raise awareness that she was moonlighting and saving money on the side.

Jenna, Maxine, Reece, and Ryan took a rental car from Domodedovo Moscow Airport to the Hotel Mercure up the A-105. Reece drove, and Maxine sat beside him. Jenna and Ryan sat in the back. During the hour drive, the landscape changed from woods and pasture to commercial buildings.

Ryan extended an arm and rubbed along her shoulders. "If we have time before we leave, we can tour the Kadashi Church. It's elegant in its baroque style."

Maxine added, "It was a KGB archive until they finally gave it back to the Russian Orthodox Church in 2006."

Jenna swallowed, struck with the sudden lurching reminder that she knew very little of the man to whom she entrusted both her life and her heart.

"You should take her to the Red Square," Maxine said.

Jenna turned to Ryan. "How many times have you been to Russia?"

"Tri, solnirshko moyo."

She blinked at him.

"Three, my sunshine," he translated.

He seemed to sense her unease as he added. "They were all business related, but I always imagined how I might come back with someone special."

How little she knew about this man. She couldn't imagine the sudden chaotic portion of her life without him. Self-sufficient Jenna Masters found herself in a world she didn't understand, reliant upon those that did. Not unlike patients who found themselves in her ICU.

She didn't know Ryan well—his past, his present, his future plans. She'd leaped into a relationship—an intimate relationship—with a man she hardly knew. Had she learned nothing from her past mistakes?

Glimpses of her moronic nineteen-year-old self making hasty relationship errors made her feel claustrophobic. She cracked her passenger window open.

Sleep with the handsome, mysterious man with a dark past. What could possibly go wrong?

What would Cal think of his mother rushing headlong into the unknown?

Her world seemed to be imploding in on her. She was being sucked into an impossible situation with no hope of escape.

RYAN KNOCKED on Reece's hotel door. He scowled at Reece's surprised expression. Ryan pushed past his friend and tossed his luggage bag onto the small ottoman. He sat down on the lounge chair.

"Something vexes you?" Reece asked.

"Jenna needed some space."

"Oh. I thought you two—"

"We are."

"Did she say why?"

"Didn't have to."

Reece flopped on the bed, his large bare feet and gangly toes pointed toward the muted television.

"She's overwhelmed," Ryan said. "She spent fifteen years learning how to rely on no one but herself. Now, her life is in danger. Suddenly, she has to rely on Rider SI. And me."

Reece stretched his arms behind his head with two pillows behind his arms. "Her instinct on being overwhelmed is to kick you out?"

"Her instinct is to assert her independence."

"Sucks it's at your expense."

"Yeah, sucks."

"You try to talk to her?"

Ryan stood, grabbed a soda out of the mini-fridge, popped the top and took a swig. He sat back down. He kicked off his shoes and closed his eyes as the beverage bubbled its way down his throat. "No. I will. But not the night before she has to meet the Russian mafia. Right now, she needs to know I respect her enough to back off when she says she needs space."

"You know, there are less complicated women out there." Reece frowned. "Nope. Forget I said that. They're all complicated. I just try to keep uninvolved in the complications."

"I don't mind complicated as long as I know the end result."

"She'll come around, Walsh. Give her time."

Ryan was quiet a moment before saying, "I appreciate you coming to Russia."

Reece shrugged. "Doesn't need to be said, man."

"It does."

"Okay. Guess that means I'm ahead."

Ryan took another sip of his soda. "By my count, we're even."

"Nope." He flipped through channels on the muted television.

Ryan scowled. "How so?"

"Tokzar."

"No. I evened Tokzar when I snuck you across the Russian border to that *pivnaya* where you hooked up with the pub owner's daughter."

Reece set down the remote and grinned at Reece. "That was a nice night. But I was already up."

They bantered for a few minutes about the score in their friendship. Despite his efforts, Ryan couldn't get the count even.

Ryan huffed out a breath. "Okay. Allison Merriweather."

"Oh, Ali," Reece said wistfully.

"I covered for you when you snuck out of your house to make out with her."

Reece chortled. "We're going all the way back to high school now?"

"Seems we are."

"Your Old Man."

Ryan went silent. Reece had him there. In fact, there was no equivalent reciprocation for a friend who consistently got Ryan out of his broken home and away from his father. After high school, they'd joined the military together through basic and advanced training, airborne, and into the Rangers.

"Sorry. I didn't mean to drudge up bad memories."

Ryan chugged the rest of his drink. "You didn't. But you made your point. I'll always be indebted to you."

"You know it's not about that, right?"

"Yeah, I do."

Reece began flipping through the channels again. "But if you feel obligated to try to even the score, you can find me a smokin' hot physician to date."

⁂

JENNA TOSSED and turned alone in bed. With jet lag and stress, her body vacillated between wanting to curl up in the fetal position or do a hundred-meter dash.

Run. She needed to run.

After throwing off the covers, she dressed in shorts, a T-shirt, and running shoes. She pulled her hair back in a ponytail and grabbed her key card.

As she exited the hotel room, she careened with a tall figure, solid as an ox. She started to scream when thick, familiar hands embraced her shoulders.

She clutched her chest. "You scared me."

"I'm sorry." Ryan released her and leaned against the wall. "Going somewhere?"

"How did you know?"

He blinked. "The 'S' of Rider SI is *security.*"

She crossed her arms. She hadn't made much noise getting ready. Not enough to be heard across the hallway.

"Audio bug is in your hotel room. Camera above your door."

Jenna looked up at the small round device, no bigger than the tip of a toothbrush.

He added, "I placed them for your protection, not to spy on you."

She noted the flash of concern in his voice. She may be worried about the many changing aspects of her life, but she would never suspect Ryan of ulterior motives. "I believe you. I'm surprised I didn't even notice you planting the devices."

"I'm not an amateur. But I wasn't consciously trying to deceive you. I guess I've placed them secretively so many times, it's the only way I know how. In retrospect, I should have told you about them and then perhaps you would've felt more at ease."

Jenna pressed her lips together. She suspected the only way she would feel at ease was in his arms, but since she didn't want to appear indecisive and flighty, she opted for silence.

She flipped her key cover over in her hands. "I'm going to the gym for a run."

Ryan gestured to his own exercise clothes and running shoes. "So I suspected."

She gave him a weak grin. "You knew that based on the sound of me dressing?"

His expression sobered. "It's late, you're emotionally exhausted, and you like to run. Stands to reason you would feel like running if you were having trouble sleeping."

She noted that he hadn't assumed she was getting out of bed to come find him, to come retract her request for solitude. Part of her wanted to be back in his embrace—where she had slept soundly —and part of her needed distance to get her head reattached correctly.

In the span of a few days, she had gone from a highly independent professional to completely reliant on the Rider SI team and at the mercy of a future beyond her control.

"Okay, Banner. Let's run."

CHAPTER 20

Ryan woke early the next morning and joined Maxine for coffee. They both poured their beverages black and then sat in the hotel lounge.

"How's Jenna holding up?" Maxine asked. She wrapped her hands around her cup.

"Better than expected." Ryan leaned back, inspecting the bags under Maxine's eyes. In the span of a few days, she'd flown from Atlanta to Chicago to Miami to Moscow. The ordeal would take its toll on her.

"Thanks for doing this, Max."

She shrugged. "What's the point of having our unique skills if we don't use them to rescue good people? Despite the hell Jenna is going through and worry about Cal, she asked me conversationally about Rider SI and my hobbies. I bet she does that with her patients. All those years knowing her rotten sack of shit husband gambled her hard-earned money and cheated on her, and she's solely focused on maximally caring for her patients."

"I imagine it would be devastating to know you worked hard to provide for your family while your spouse sabotaged you."

Maxine's jaw twitched briefly in annoyance. She had apparently caught the parallel he referenced between Jenna's past and her own.

She looked back down at her coffee. "At least her son likes her."

Ryan decided not to push. Instead, he changed the subject. "I need you to know about my plan B."

Maxine arched an eyebrow.

"If negotiations don't go well, I'm disappearing with Jenna and Cal."

Maxine scrutinized Ryan's face. "Does Jenna know about this?"

"No. And I'm hoping it doesn't come to that, but if we can't get the target off her back, then I need to get her out of range."

"You might consult the woman whose life you're considering uprooting before you do so."

"Her life is already uprooted. I may have to replant it somewhere she isn't expecting. But if I start talking about altering identities and hiding, she's going to be more spooked than she already is."

Maxine still appeared skeptical of his plan. "You have everything you need to pull it off?"

Ryan nodded. "Funds and IDs. It would be helpful if you let Barry know you're backing me. That way he can extricate Cal without hesitation if need arises."

She pursed her lips. "Will do." She took a long, slow sip of her coffee. "You would disappear with a woman you hardly know?"

Ryan gave her a wistful smile. "I know Jenna. She's an amazing mother. Dedicated physician. It would crush her to have to give up medicine. She would hate the loss of autonomy in a life of hiding. I don't want it to come to that. I want her to keep her steady ICU job, see Cal every month, and continue to savor long escapes to the Caribbean. But our job is to be prepared for the worst. If it comes to it, I will disappear with Jenna and Cal."

Maxine's piercing blue eyes bore into him. "It's also our job to make sure it doesn't come to that."

He raised his cup of coffee. "Here, here," he agreed.

⁂

JENNA TRIED NOT to gape at the opulence of Vladimir Pronin's office building. It appeared more like a small castle—a miniature Versailles. The windows were decorated in tapestries, real fabric, not vinyl blinds like modern offices. Oil paintings framed in eloquent gold hung in the hallways—portraits of Catherine the Great, Peter the Great, Boris Godunov, and others.

Jenna wriggled her shoulders under the weight of the Kevlar vest. Ryan had insisted she wear it, and she didn't take much convincing.

She looked to Ryan, whose large physique bore his vest like a second skin under his buttoned shirt. His dark eyes were narrow and his jaw was set. Ranger mode. Pre-Hulk mode. Damn if he still didn't look good enough to eat.

He glanced sidelong at her, and she flushed as if he might have read her thoughts. The brief quirk on his lips had her suspecting he had read her mind.

The only person missing was Reece, who was keeping an idling car on standby in case they had to flee their meeting with the mob. Ryan had put a small plastic device in his ear and explained during the car ride to Vladimir's office that he would use it to communicate with Reece remotely. Maxine had one as well.

Jenna stared at the high ceilings, arched like a church. In fact, all the interior opulence felt a bit like being in an Orthodox church. She felt small and insignificant compared to the grandeur surrounding her. She'd spent immense time and effort becoming a physician so she wouldn't feel small and insignificant. What she'd spent years building crumbled in mere days at the hands of a few crime lords.

They entered a large office with a stout mahogany desk in front of a wall of books. Tolstoy, Pushkin, Lermontov—all Russian classics.

Vladimir Pronin walked from behind his desk. He smiled warmly as though this were a family reunion. His gray suit shimmered as he moved.

"Maxine, *dobro pozhalovat'*." He gave a bow as he grasped her hand in his.

Maxine gave a strained smile. "*Spasibo*."

Jenna thought she detected a hint of a blush on Maxine's face.

Vladimir's smile deepened before he turned to Jenna, blue eyes sparkling. His full head of gray and white hair lay in immaculate waves. "Dr. Masters, it is such an honor to have you in my hometown." His voice held surprising sincerity.

Here comes the kiss.

Vladimir moved in and kissed one cheek at a time.

Next, he extended a hand to Ryan. "Mr. Walsh, I presume. Recipient of the distinguished Service Cross for heroic actions in Afghanistan. I'm told this is the US Army's second highest honor."

"I served my country. Now, I serve others in need of help." His tone was relaxed and modest. "I believe you, too, once served your country."

Vladimir nodded as they shook hands.

Jenna glanced up at Ryan, the guilt of her selfishness coursing through her. She hadn't asked Ryan about his past except for the one night at dinner. He'd been reluctant but willing to talk about his past. She knew about the Rangers but not that he had remarkable achievements. He was humble, though. He wouldn't have told her about his accolades.

She made a mental note to peruse his online profile later. As a man in investigative work, he had probably already checked her background. He didn't need to investigate her. He already knew the best parts—Cal, Antigua, and her work as a physician—and the worst parts—Brad and ... Brad.

"Please, come. Sit." Vladimir motioned to a sitting area in one corner of his office with a couch and two chairs.

Jenna followed Ryan to the couch and sat with him. Maxine and Vladimir each took a chair.

Vladimir introduced his assistant, Boris, who remained standing. He wore a black suit like Ryan's.

"It is a pleasure to have you all here, though I understand the circumstances are less than ideal. Maxine gave me the details. I believe Dr. Masters' only crime here is an unfortunate relationship. We are all in agreement that she should not be punished for someone else's mistake."

Slowly, Jenna allowed herself to exhale.

Ryan slid his hand into hers, which had a soothing effect.

"That being said," Vladimir continued, "twelve million dollars are missing. Someone must be held accountable."

ONE HOUR LATER, the discussions to formulate a resolution were complete. Ryan sensed Jenna's mixture of relief at the arrangement between her and Vladimir and dread about the terms of the agreement.

Ryan glanced at the uneaten cherry *pirozhki* lying on a platter on the small table between them. The food and tea had been a polite gesture, but no one wanted to eat pastries under the circumstances.

A knock at Vladimir's door sounded before it opened.

Vladimir stood as he smiled and opened his arms. "*Otlichno, Mikhail. Dobro pozhalovat.*"

Ryan, Jenna, and Maxine stood.

Vladimir greeted his nephew and his nephew's tall girlfriend. The Russian supermodel wore a short skirt and a glittering silver top. Her thick lips accentuated her razor-sharp cheekbones.

Rider SI had prior dealings with Natasha Bodrov when she'd been sending hate mail to one of their clients. Ryan's understanding was now that Natasha was under *dyadya* Pronin's watchful eye, she kept her sociopathic tendencies under control.

Vladimir turned to Jenna. "Dr. Masters, my nephew Mikhail, wishes to see you again. He is still grateful to the physician who saved his life."

Mikhail, in contrast to Natasha, stood shorter with tightly buzzed hair and an abundance of tattoos visibly emerging from his short-sleeve shirt.

Ryan wondered at Vladimir calling Mikhail "nephew." He wasn't a blood relative, so he had either endeared himself to Vladimir through service to his organization or he and Natasha—Vladimir's niece by blood—were close to tying the proverbial knot.

Alternatively, perhaps Vladimir had only claimed to be Mikhail's uncle when Jenna treated Mikhail so that he would be allowed to speak with the treating physician. In that case, he would have to be very detail-oriented to think to call him nephew again now to keep up pretenses.

The mystery of Mikhail and Natasha relationship as relatives of Vladimir—blood or otherwise—could be pondered another day.

After Vladimir and Mikhail embraced briefly, Mikhail turned and embraced Jenna. The young *myfia's* motions were relaxed and friendly. He didn't seem bothered that Jenna reciprocated with surprised stiffening before she awkwardly accepted the greeting.

"Thank you, Dr. Masters, for all you did for me during my stay in the hospital."

She tucked a loose strand of hair behind her ear. "It's my job and my pleasure. *Pozhaluysta.*"

Mikhail beamed.

Ryan suppressed a prideful grin as Jenna perfectly pronounced 'you're welcome.' He hadn't had a lot of time to give her a crash course in Russian, but 'thank you' and 'you're welcome' were key phrases he'd taught her on the plane ride.

Natasha bent low to hug Jenna and give her a personal greeting.

Mikhail said, "I'm told you looked beyond stereotypical diagnoses for a young man in my line of work. For that, I am grateful."

Ryan watched Jenna swallow and wondered at the story behind Mikhail's words. Jenna had said Mikhail had "the wrong diagnosis" and she fixed it. Ryan speculated that a man of Mikhail's appearance might by stereotyped as a drug user—if one took note of his expensive yet casual clothes and sharp, attentive eyes, junkie would be taken off the differential diagnosis. Ryan liked that Jenna had that level of attentiveness.

Mikhail spoke warmly to Jenna. "Perhaps sometime under less stressful circumstances for you, you can return to Russia and we will give you the full tour of Moscow."

"That's very generous of you. Ryan has already mentioned coming for a leisurely visit."

Mikhail's pale green eyes found Ryan as Jenna stepped back to Ryan's side. The young Russian's brief appraising look was nonconfrontational, but his eyes flickered between Jenna and Ryan as he seemed to sense the presence of a relationship.

He extended a hand to Ryan.

Ryan accepted the firm handshake. As he met Mikhail's eyes, they connected. Soldier to soldier.

"*Kak pazhivayesh*?" Ryan asked how he was.

"*Neeploha*." Not so bad, was the leisurely reply.

After their introduction to Ryan, Mikhail and Natasha met Maxine.

Mikhail exchanged words in Russian with his uncle about taking Natasha shopping. He helped himself to a cherry pastry before wishing everyone well and disappearing out the door with Natasha.

<hr>

RYAN KEPT his body close to Jenna as they exited Vladimir Pronin's office building. The meeting had gone well, and a plan had been formulated. The plan would keep Jenna safe. How safe she would feel after face-to-face encounters with both the Cuban mafia and the Russian mafia would be determined in time.

Today, she had done remarkably well under pressure—not an easy feat with one's life on the line.

As they walked down the steps to the sidewalk, Ryan allowed a moment of relief that one segment of Jenna's journey concluded without incident. She and the Rider SI team would go back to the hotel. Hopefully, she wouldn't distance herself from him again. If she did, he would continue to employ patience.

Vladimir and Boris exited the building beside them, having explained they had other, unrelated business to attend.

"Reece, we're exiting," Ryan said into his earpiece.

"Copy."

Vladimir's departing words echoed through Ryan's mind. "Per our agreement, Maxine, I will see you this evening."

Maxine hadn't mentioned a separate, private meeting. When

Ryan had shot her a questioning look, she dismissed his inquiry with a scowl. He would have to wait for an explanation. What had Maxine agreed to on behalf of Jenna—on behalf of him?

He felt a guilty, acidic lump in his throat. He wouldn't want Maxine to agree to anything illegal or immoral on his behalf. Yet she'd consented to something with Vladimir, and she hadn't told the team about it.

A large, silver SUV awaited Vladimir and Boris. The afternoon sun glinted off the polished chrome.

Reece, who'd been circling the block, would be coming soon. They wouldn't leave their getaway car idling in front of the Russian mafia's building like a target.

Jenna stood beside him on the curb, her expression a mixture of relief and anticipation.

Boris held the door open for his boss as Vladimir bid Maxine farewell before their clandestine meeting tonight.

A whistle cut through the sound of car engines and distant jack hammering.

"Bogie!" Ryan yelled. He curled his body around Jenna.

Boris must have heard it as well because the large Russian was already taking Vladimir down to the ground.

Vladimir's car burst into flames.

Ryan's body engulfed in hot air as it lifted him off his feet. He kept his body protectively around Jenna as the explosion hurled him against the concrete steps of the building. Pain seared through his back.

Everything went black.

CHAPTER 21

Maxine's ears rang as she fought disorientation. She coughed to catch her breath, her lungs feeling as though they had been singed on the inside.

She let out a string of curse words even as her eyes scanned the perimeter for threats while she gripped her Sig in her hand. Blood running down from her forehead impaired her eyesight, but she could still see out of her right eye. No visible assailants. She couldn't see if a second grenade launcher was at the ready.

She surveyed her team's injuries. Ryan lay twenty feet away and out cold. At least she thought he was unconscious. Jenna inspected him for injuries without the panicked expression of someone looking at a corpse.

Vladimir was using his coat to put out the flames on Boris' body.

Pedestrians evacuated the area, screaming as they fled.

"Reece, extraction one block north."

"Copy." His voice sounded strained, but she knew his training would make him reserve questions for later.

Questions like: what just happened and who was the intended target? Vladimir or Maxine? Vladimir's car was the one torched.

"Vladimir, I have a car coming. One block north. Can you manage?"

"*Da.*" He nodded as he helped Boris to his feet.

He stumbled under the weight of the large man. He caught himself, but a bullet whizzed between him and Maxine.

"Shit! Sniper!"

They crouched behind the burning SUV, waves of heat threatening to catch her hair on fire.

Glancing at Jenna and Ryan, she feared they were open targets. Jenna was struggling to drag Ryan behind a large van parked on the side of the road. Unfortunately, that positioned them further away from Max and Vladimir. At least her cover wasn't on fire. The side of the van read KOVER. Maxine guessed it was a carpet cleaning crew.

Jenna started tugging Ryan's gun out of its holster.

Does she know how to use that thing?

Boris spoke through gritted teeth of pain. "Sonya, sniper." He was talking through an unseen communication device to someone on his own team.

They were pinned down with no way to make it to Reece's car.

Craning her neck to look around the SUV, Maxine spotted two armed men advancing on them. They wore jeans, black thick-soled boots, and gray cotton shirts. Maxine's Sig against two automatic weapons didn't bode well for her. She fired two shots that hit a brick wall behind one of the men.

One man opened fire as Maxine ducked back out of view. Bullets sprayed the flaming car and concrete around them. All he had to do was keep them pinned while his associate crept around for a clean shot.

Three shots sounded. Maxine looked to see Jenna firing from under the van at one attacker.

Jenna, we're going to have a talk about not hiding beneath a tank of gas during a gunfight.

The man wasn't hit, but rolled in surprise, which gave Maxine time to flatten herself against the concrete walkway and fire at the assailant. Her bullet didn't miss this time. The man hit the pavement in a heap of bleeding flesh.

The other gunman rounded the van and poised to shoot.

Jenna screamed, trying to scramble out from under the vehicle.

Maxine knew she wouldn't be able to turn and fire in time.

Another shot sounded—sniper rifle again—but the bullet struck the assailant. He crumpled to the ground.

Maxine rolled back behind the SUV.

"Sonya took out the sniper," Boris said weakly.

And had the knowledge to turn the gun to their advantage.

Maxine raised her eyebrows in unconcealed admiration.

"She will cover us," Vladimir said.

Maxine holstered her weapon.

"You got him?" She asked Vladimir of Boris.

"*Da.*"

She hoisted herself to her feet and scurried to Ryan, ignoring the splinters of painful protest in her arthritic knee.

"How bad is he?"

"Concussion at best. Internal hemorrhage at worst," Jenna replied, her eyes wide as she seemed to fight for control of herself over her fear.

"We need to move. One block north of here. The sniper threat is gone. The new sniper will watch our backs." Maxine hoped that was true. Sonya worked for Vladimir, so she was technically only obligated to watch her boss' back.

Jenna nodded.

Maxine moved around behind Ryan and squatted. She wrapped her arms around his torso. "You get the legs."

Jenna complied. Kneeling and facing away from Ryan, she cradled one leg in each arm.

"Stand in three ... two ... one."

They stood together, grunting under the weight.

"Move. Steady pace. Don't run."

Neither woman was tall, so their brisk paces matched nicely. They fell in behind Vladimir who helped Boris limp through each step.

In the distance, at the next intersection, she could see Reece's car.

Jenna reached the SUV panting. She helped hoist Ryan into the rear where she quickly joined him. She pulled the Rider SI first-aid bag toward her.

They needed a bigger vehicle. Reece sat in the driver'd seat, and Maxine crawled in next to him. Boris and Vladimir crammed in the back seat.

They drove away from the scene of the crime.

"Safe house," Maxine told Reece.

Boris protested, "No. We have a *ubezhishche*."

"Like hell I'm going to your safe house. That attack was on Vladimir's life."

"He stays under my protection."

Jenna didn't think Boris looked capable of protecting anyone in his condition.

"Any place you own must be treated as compromised. *Skompro-metirovan*."

"Bred sivoy kobyly."

From his tone, Jenna guessed Boris had begun swearing.

Great. Swearing and bickering. Very productive.

She pursed her mouth shut and catalogued everyone's injuries. Maxine's scalp bled, leaving a trail down one side of her face. Judging by the blood, the gash would need stitching. Ryan needed close observation. The physician in her wanted to get him to a hospital, but she didn't know if such a thing would be safe considering their current predicament. Vladimir had some scrapes, nothing detrimental. Boris had second-degree burns and possible torn ligaments in his ankle.

Jenna looked at her body, for the first time assessing her own injuries. She had fresh scrapes and contusions to add to the healing ones from the kidnapping, but nothing more serious. Ryan had cradled her and protected her head and body. The vest had helped, too.

Vladimir finally put an end to the disagreement. "Boris, it's okay. We go to Maxine's *ubezhishche*."

"Yes, sir."

Jenna checked Ryan's pupils. She may not have access to a CT scanner, but she could perform frequent neurological checks to ensure he had no catastrophic intracranial bleeding.

JENNA PACED the floor in the room adjacent to where Ryan slept. She'd made him comfortable and bandaged his lacerations. He had a nasty scalp cut that took her forty minutes to suture, working gingerly. Maxine's cut took half as long. As she sewed, Marine Max verbally grilled Vladimir on the speculated identity of assailants.

Vladimir had narrowed his list down to three enemies.

Guess I'm lucky to have only the two mafias after me.

Jenna didn't have to wade through a list of possible threats to find who was holding the smoking gun—smoking grenade launcher.

When Jenna finished patching up Maxine, the bickering couple moved their discussion to a different room. Bickering couple? Yes, that was how they sounded.

She wondered how deep the relationship between Maxine and Vladimir ran. He seemed enamored and intrigued by her in his office. Then, he looked worriedly at her injuries as they rode in the car. Did she care about him as much as he seemed to care about her?

Jenna rubbed her temples, her ears still ringing with sounds of the exploding bomb.

"He's okay?" Reece asked.

She looked at Ryan's partner, the only one unscathed from this event.

His mouth twitched, causing his mustache to wiggle.

"Concussion and some scrapes."She sat in a nearby chair, feeling defeated. "I'm sorry. My mess has put everyone's life in danger."

Reece scowled. "The attack had nothing to do with you. Vladimir has to get his house in order."

Jenna shook her head. "We wouldn't be in Moscow if it weren't for my debt."

His scowl deepened in an expression that made her feel like she'd insulted his mother. "Stop talking like you own this debt. This is your jackass ex-husband's mess, and all of us would like to beat him to a pulp right now. Nobody blames you."

His voice still sounded harsh when he added, "But you obviously care about Walsh, so why are you pushing him away?"

Jenna startled at the hostility in his voice. It reminded her of Jess. Jess would give Ryan the same grilling if he'd distanced himself from her.

She pinched the bridge of her nose. "I'm not great at relationships."

"Who the hell is?" Reece blew out a breath in a huff and sat down in a chair across from her.

She glanced up at Reece. "I do like him."

"Well, Walsh'd tell you it's none of my business, but if it was my business, I might be inclined to let you know a few facts about him. Since he was a teenager, he avoided relationships, fearing he would be a womanizer like his father. As a Ranger, he worried he'd leave some woman a widow during one of his missions. Then he thought his combat past would be a deterrent. He's finally figured out he'd make a good man—someone worth worrying about. I don't want the first real relationship he is fighting for to bite him in the ass."

"I feel the same way about my first real relationship."

Reece looked at her carefully. In a gentler tone he said, "Walsh would cut off his hand before he did or said anything to hurt you."

Jenna swallowed. She locked eyes with Reece. "I won't hurt him. I may take longer to get where he is, but I won't hurt him."

Reece nodded as if those were the words he needed to hear. After pushing himself out of his chair, he sauntered into another room.

Jenna texted Jess, *Meeting with RM (Russian Mafia) over. Went well.*

The meeting had gone well; the concussive blast immediately after had not. Jess didn't need the extra worry of that part of the trip.

Jess, *K. Come home safe.*

Jenna, *Will do.*

It occurred to Jenna that she should be in a ball, crying about nearly being incinerated. Instead, she thought about Ryan. She thought about how she'd forced distance between them, even if only for a day. She thought about Reece's words.

She called Antigua—international charges be damned.

"Mom, can I talk to you about relationships?" Jenna looked at the slumbering giant on the bed who hadn't stirred. She kept her voice low.

"Of course."

"You remember you said I have been self-sufficient and alone for so long?"

"Yes."

"I don't know any other way, Mom. I met someone. Someone I want to lose my independence to. How do you and Dad do it?"

Jenna knew her parents were inseparable but highly functional. They shared a mutual respect where each one was their own person but synergistically stronger with the other. Their relationship was both fulfilling and required a daunting level of trust.

"We trust each other wholly. What we relinquish in independence we gain by sharing a love together. It takes a leap of faith."

Jenna fumbled with the zipper on the first-aid bag.

Her mother continued, "Think of the patients who put their lives in your hands. That leap of faith requires them to lose some of their independence and rely on someone to help them. If you have feelings for this man, let him help you, heal you."

"You always said happiness can't come from another person. It comes from within."

"Which is true. But people thrive on relationships to help further their inner happiness."

"Okay."

"You're ready, Jenna. Take that leap of faith."

Jenna chuckled. "Mom, you haven't even met him."

"Since you are having this conversation with me, I have no doubts that you have chosen someone worthy. You're a mature adult with impeccable rationality."

Jenna recalled a conversation she'd had with her mom about Cal's boarding school. She struggled to let him go, but she couldn't let her own selfishness stifle his dreams. Her mom had accused her lightly of 'impeccable rationality.' Of course, in the many times her parents had urged her to leave Brad and she had stayed out of some delusional desire to avoid a broken home, her parents had also accused her of impeccable rationality.

"Okay."

"Leap, Jenna."

"Okay."

Easy as a champagne tap lumbar puncture.

JENNA USED the cold faucet water of the warehouse to clean. She scrubbed dirt and blood off herself and off her clothes, but still had to put the filthy clothes back on. Clothing drenched in sweat and smeared with blood and dirt seemed to be her trend lately.

She crept into bed beside Ryan who occupied most of the thin mattress and rested her head on his bare chest. His chest rose against her cheek in a deep breath as he rolled to embrace her.

"Jenna." His voice was barely a whisper.

She took a measure of awe and relief to know that if he felt a woman beside him as he slept, he would immediately assume it was her without opening his eyes.

"Jenna!" His eyes flew open as he grasped her.

"Easy there, Banner. You're okay."

His gaze and hands roamed over her.

"I'm okay," she assured him.

He reached for the bandage on his head, but she gently brought his hand back down to his side.

"You have a nasty cut, but it's stitched."

"I slept through stitches?"

"You have a concussion. I'm benching you for a week."

"Max?"

"Maxine is okay. Reece and Vladimir are fine. Boris has some burns and a sprained ankle. Their driver died. They killed three of the attackers—I think. They believe the attack was orchestrated by someone after Vladimir. We're at our safe house." She tried to ramble off as many facts as he might find relevant.

He looked at her again and stroked a hand along the side of her head. "You're okay?"

"Thanks to your cocoon of muscle, yes. You took all the force."

He pulled her to him and enveloped her in his arms. Home.

This is what home feels like.

He looked down into her eyes, then down at her lips. She realized he was trying to restrain himself because, per their last conversation, she'd asked for space.

She moved toward him for a kiss, and he needed no further encouragement. He claimed her lips tentatively at first, growing bolder. They pulled away after the fervor left them both breathless.

She smiled. "Lot's more of that, but when you're healed."

"I'm a picture of health."

"Um. I had to restrain every iota of physician training to not take you to a hospital during the hours of your unconsciousness."

He wriggled his body against hers. She bit back a groan.

"We didn't take you from the barn to the hospital."

She narrowed her eyes at him. "By that time I was awake, so I knew I was okay. I've been doing pupil checks and reflexes on you every thirty minutes to make sure you don't have a head bleed."

He nibbled on her ear, sending warmth coursing through her body. "Thank you, Doctor."

"You'll be fine as long as you take it easy."

He kissed her neck. "And your prescription?"

"Lime. Coconut. Call me in the morning."

The deep rumbling of his chuckle where his torso pressed against her delighted her.

She sucked in a ragged breath as his lips reached her collarbone.

Putting her hand on his chin, she lifted his eyes to her. Her voice sobered. "Me, Ryan. My prescription is me and you, together, like this."

"In a warehouse, on a dilapidated twin bed, after a harrowing explosion?" He gave her a wry smile.

She gave him a playful scowl. "You and me in a relationship," she explained, though she suspected he knew what she meant but wanted to draw it out of her.

"Intimate and dating?"

"Yes."

"For how long?"

As long as I'm alive.

His brow furrowed, and she suspected he interpreted her doleful expression as reluctance when it was more a fear of an unknown future.

"As long as possible," she replied, kissing him softly and briefly on the lips.

Leap taken.

She stared into his rich brown eyes.

Yep, I'm a goner.

"I plan to be fairly proactive in this relationship. 'As long as possible' could be a long time."

"I'm counting on it."

The look he gave her of pure affection and desire had her heart melting.

He pulled her to him again, savagely kissing her until all sense of time and space vanished. Fear of the past and future dissolved. She simply existed in this moment, in this amazing man's arms.

CHAPTER 22

*J*enna's gaze roamed the warehouse.

They gathered in a large, mostly empty room, leaning against walls or sitting on crates and looking like a ragged group with torn clothing, dried blood, and various bandages.

Aside from a few bruises elsewhere on his body, Ryan's head had taken the brunt of the damage. Jenna felt relieved to see him upright. He, too, observed the group.

Reece sat leisurely on a crate, stroking his mustache like a gunslinger, cool under pressure. Although both men radiated serenity, she was certain tumultuous thoughts churned under the surface.

Boris was in the most obvious pain. The first-aid kit Maxine's team had put together was complete with a suture kit, silver sulfadiazine cream, and painkillers. Boris had declined the morphine in favor of ibuprofen and acetaminophen, explaining that he wanted to stay alert during the threat. She gave him maximal doses of both before cleaning his burns—which involved picking out pieces of scorched clothing from flesh—and applying cream and bandages.

Vladimir stood with arms crossed, looking like a statue of ice and fury born from the cold Ural Mountains. He was ready to strike back at his attackers with calculated and deadly force. Jenna hoped always to remain in favor with the frightening man.

Lastly, Maxine sat in the only chair in the room, a worn-out blue lounge chair. She stared at one wall of the warehouse with a contemplative gaze as though the Mona Lisa perched on the spot rather than chipped plaster.

Maxine turned to look at Vladimir. "What are we up against?"

"I have many enemies. But the most recently upset with me are the Argentinians."

Reece's lips twitched. "That leaves two possibilities—human trafficking or drugs."

Boris crossed his bulky arms. "Mr. Pronin does not deal in human trafficking."

Jenna watched the group silently. Reece and Ryan shot disbelieving looks at Maxine. She seemed to simultaneously confirm Boris' claim and silence her workers with a single solemn nod.

"White charcoal," Vladimir said.

Jenna frowned.

"Cocaine," Ryan explained.

"In Argentina? I thought cocaine was a Colombian thing?" she asked.

"Sure. In the 1970s." Reece snickered.

"In the last forty years, the drug trade has spread throughout South America," Ryan said with calm patience. "In the last twenty years, Argentina has been trafficking drugs from Bolivia and expanding local growth and markets. They've been escalating from micro-trafficking to international trade. Business is good. Demand is high."

"Nothing like a homegrown product," Reece added.

"Presumably, Mr. Pronin wants to expand his business there."

"*Da*. They have great market potential, but no experience. Is like Wild West there. Chaos is bad for business."

"Who'd you piss off?" Maxine asked as amicably as though she had asked if he preferred white or red wine.

"Lautaro Fernandez."

"Super." Reece threw up his hands in exasperation.

Jenna looked back and forth from Maxine, whose right hand looked like it wanted to wrap around a bottle of whiskey—or maybe a gun—and Ryan, whose only indication of alarm was standing a little straighter.

Tension blanketed the room. It reminded Jenna of the seconds in between CPR when the team stops all activity to check for a pulse. Nope. Still flat-line. Resume CPR.

Jenna was about to ask her question when Ryan spoke. "Lautaro Fernandez is the third most powerful drug lord in South America."

Not the first. That seemed like a plus. Fernandez was apparently still powerful enough to take a swat at Vladimir on his own turf. Powerful enough or stupid enough? Perhaps both.

So the Cubans were after her, and the Argentinians were after Vladimir. She sat down on a nearby crate, feeling the exhaustion of the last several days—kidnapping, plane flights, explosions. When could she get back to chest tubes, septic shock, intubations, family meetings, and lumbar punctures?

She scrubbed her hands along her face. "Can we pit the Cubans against the Argentinians and call it a day?"

Everyone turned to stare at her.

Damn. I said that aloud.

Reece's lips twitched in amusement.

After an uncomfortable silence, Vladimir said, "Perhaps."

She blinked at him. She swiveled her body to look at Ryan who gave her an appreciative grin.

"For now," Vladimir continued, "I strike back at Fernandez. I will get you safely back to Miami so you can deliver my message to Ernesto per our agreement."

Jenna gave Vladimir a grateful bow of her head. Whatever war the Russian mafia planned to wage wasn't going to include her.

———— ⚜ ————

RYAN TUCKED JENNA INTO BED. Well, an uncomfortable wire box spring they were using as a bed.

"We'll leave at daylight." He kissed her lips briefly.

She closed her eyes and pulled herself into a tight ball.

She would be sleepy, he thought. After suffering repeated surges of adrenaline, she'd had to patch up everyone at the warehouse except Reece.

Yet, she'd tackled all the hurdles with fortitude, never recoiling with debilitating fear. She was the Jenna who intervened after a bar fight to save a man's life, the Jenna who escaped the barn skirmish with bullets flying around her, and the Jenna who stared down her Cuban executioners.

His Jenna.

He needed to feed her something more than granola bars and water, but that was all anyone had. Tomorrow, when they returned to the hotel, he would buy her a wholesome breakfast.

When he walked back into the makeshift conference room, he rejoined the conversation.

"They have a plant outside Aldao," Boris explained. His voice was deep, and his English thick with his Russian accent. "They package the drug then send it down river to Rosaria. From there it is transported to the airport, batched with deliveries from Bolivia and Mexico, and prepared for international travel."

"We can eliminate that production facility," Vladimir said to Boris.

"It will take many men and some planning, but it is feasible."

"No," Maxine interrupted. "It will take one man."

"Max—" Ryan began, but she held up a hand to silence him.

Was she truly planning to help Vladimir? To get in bed with the Russian mafia? Ryan had enough dark and shady deals in his prior employment that he had no interest in helping the mafia.

"No casualties," Maxine said. "If you honestly know the location of their drug manufacturing plant, we send in one man to mark it. He doesn't have to be close."

Ryan felt his throat constrict. She was talking about engineering a precision missile strike. One man to paint the target with a laser, then boom.

Vladimir gave her a speculative look.

"I have a friend in Buenos Aires," Maxine explained. "For the right price, he could destroy the manufacturing plant with a Hellfire."

Ryan caught Reece's wide-eyed stare. Maxine referred to an AGM 114 Hellfire. She was going to launch one—probably from a small boat off the coast of Argentina to make it least traceable—into a cocaine facility owned by Lautaro Fernandez.

"I like your friends," Vladimir said.

"You make sure all the credit goes to you. I don't want my help in cleaning up your shit to come back and bite me in the ass."

"No ass biting," he assured her with a grin.

"A heat signature drone goes up one hour before the launch. If the place isn't cold, my man doesn't press the 'go' button. I don't care how you do it, but you get that place evacuated first."

Vladimir nodded.

Maxine blew out a breath. "They use child labor in those drug shops, and I'm not killing a bunch of kids."

"No casualties, Max," Vladimir said softly.

Ryan relaxed slightly. Max was agreeing to help, but she wasn't letting herself be manipulated. She seemed to want the opportunity to take a bite out of crime. Wasn't that why she started Rider SI? Perhaps this was different from a paying client, but it was still a win for the good guys.

Clever Max.

She had Vladimir eating out of the palm of her hand, and he seemed to genuinely enjoy doing it. Something more hovered between them than a strained business relationship. Fate kept throwing them in each other's path, but neither of them seemed to resist their merging.

Curious.

Ryan looked over to his partner, wondering if Reece held any suspicion of the two leader's relationship. Reece was cleaning dirt from his fingernails with the tip of his pocketknife.

Oblivious.

Ryan looked back at Maxine. He had faith in her in all levels of business management and operation execution, but something in her dealings with Vladimir felt disconcerting. Her interaction with the Russian felt as much personal as business. Business dealings with the Russian mob invited risk. Personal dealings with them were downright deadly. He would have to talk to Maxine alone about the situation.

And how the hell did she know a civilian with a Hellfire missile?

JENNA REVELED in the feel of the hot shower now that they were back at the hotel. She scrubbed until her skin gleamed. She felt lucky to have suffered little more than a few scrapes and bruises.

Tomorrow she would leave Moscow and go back to Miami. The switch was like exchanging typhoid for cholera, one unstable situation for another. She hoped the plan with Ernesto would work.

When she got out of the shower, she dried off and walked from the hotel bathroom to the bedroom. All was quiet. Her laptop sat open on a little desk across from the bed. A note rested on the keyboard.

I'm picking up lunch. Reece is outside your door. Internet is
connected if you want to call Cal.
—Banner

She dressed quickly and was still drying her hair when she called Cal for a video chat. What time was it on the East Coast? After 5 a.m.?

"Mom?"

"Hey, Cal." She choked back the longing to hug him.

He scrubbed his hands across his face. "Where are you?" He inspected the backdrop of a hotel room bed behind her.

"Hotel room. Sight-seeing. Sorry to call so early."

And meeting the Russian mob. And dodging bazookas. Had it been a bazooka?

"Oh. Are you with Walsh?"

"Yes." She felt her face flush. Ridiculous. Women in their late thirties didn't blush.

Cal's face beamed. "That's great. He seems cool. Are you going to bring him next time we visit?"

"Sure. Yes. Are you okay with that?"

"Mom." He used his teenager scolding tone. "You're all glowy at the mention of his name. You haven't been this excited since you got that ICU job in Chicago."

"Oh."

"So yeah. I wanna meet him."

"Okay."

"When are you back to work?"

"Two weeks."

Hopefully back to the ICU with deadly adventures behind me.

"How's school?"

"Good."

"What did you end up getting the girl you like?"

"Scarf, and we spent an afternoon at the campus game room."

"Oh, what games?"

"Ping pong, pool, foosball. She won most of them."

"I like this girl so far."

The hotel door clicked, and Ryan entered the room. After setting down a bag of Chinese takeout on the desk, he gave Jenna a kiss on the cheek. He'd showered and applied a fresh bandage to his head, though Cal wouldn't be able to see it from his angle.

"Hi, Cal."

"Hi, Mr. Walsh."

"Ryan is fine."

"Cool. Ryan. Okay, Mom, gotta get my last hour of sleep."

"Okay. Love you."

"Loves. Bye."

Jenna stared at the blank screen.

Ryan came and squeezed her shoulder.

"It's a good school. Very rigorous. The kids are up at six thirty in the morning to start the day with cardio followed by skiing, when there's snow. Five hours later, they're in the classroom. Then they stay up studying or waxing their skis." She looked up at Ryan through glistening tears. "Ninety percent of them go to college."

He pulled her up into his embrace. "You are an amazing mother. You're doing a great job with Cal. Look at how happy he is. You've given him this remarkable opportunity."

Jenna squeezed her body into Ryan's.

He continued, "In a few days, these crazy events will be contained, and you'll be making plans to take Cal to Antigua."

She pulled away and looked up at him. "How about the three of us?"

Ryan's face lit up with a smile. "Yeah, the three of us."

CHAPTER 23

The next morning, Jenna woke to an empty room. She'd grown accustomed to silence when Cal had left for boarding school. In her peaceful apartment, she was free to follow her own schedule. The eighty-hour workweek for weeks on end of residency became a thing of the past.

She missed Cal, and suddenly she also missed Ryan.

A knock came at her door.

She pulled on the closest shirt—one of Ryan's—and walked to the peephole.

"Jenna, it's Ryan."

Swinging the door open, she let him into the hotel room. She looked down at the paper cups in his hands and said, "Coffee. My hero." She took the one he handed to her.

"Raf-coffee."

She gave him a quizzical look.

"It's a Russian favorite. Espresso, cream, sugar."

"Sounds perfect." She took a sip. "Tastes perfect."

She took another sip and savored the warmth as it slipped

down her throat. Setting the cup down, she ran her hands along her arms. "Can we lie together? Can you hold me for a while?"

He set his coffee down and pulled her onto the bed with him. "I can do that."

She curled against him and laid her head on his chest. "I never considered myself a snuggler, but there's something magical about this spot. Like I could rest here in any room in any country and it would feel like home."

He squeezed her shoulder.

"It seems crazy that I could feel that way even with the fabric of my own reality unraveling around me."

"It'll get better. But I don't mind accepting the compliment."

She fidgeted with a button on his shirt.

He spoke in a soothing, confident voice. "In a few days and lots of jet lag later, Ernesto will have what he wants. You'll be able to walk away. Life will resume some semblance of normality."

"I was shaken up after that explosion."

"As expected."

"You weren't scared."

"I was unconscious."

She flicked a finger at his chest. "You know what I mean."

He chuckled. "I'm trained to react differently. But I've been afraid for you. Afraid of what all of this would do to you. You're holding up well." He ran his hand along her arm and down to her hand where he linked fingers with hers.

"Thanks to you."

"I don't mind accepting the compliment," he repeated.

She stayed in his arms, marveling at the comfort they offered. His presence blanketed her fear like a snug sleeping bag, keeping it contained until the warmth let it dissolve.

AFTER LUNCH, Jenna insisted they leave the hotel room and do some type of walking tour. She couldn't be stuffed inside a hotel room one minute longer, and their flight back to Miami wasn't until tomorrow.

Ryan considered the request carefully. He seemed to finally convince himself that since both Rider SI and Pronin's team concluded Vladimir was yesterday's target, little risk existed in being tourists for half a day.

Nevertheless, he took a dizzying route in the vehicle downtown. Jenna was certain they crossed the Moskva River three times before finally parking near the Red Square.

She closed her passenger car door. "That seemed thorough."

"Making sure we didn't have a tail."

She nodded. "What do you suppose Max and Reece are up to?"

"They're looking into the attack on Pronin with Claire's help. She might be able to confirm that the Argentinians are culpable."

"You don't shield me from details. I appreciate that." She leaned against him. "I don't want kid gloves."

He put an arm around her, leading her down Ilyinka. "You've repeatedly proven how tough you are—the bar, the Cubans, the Russians. I won't insult you with secrets and half-truths. If Rider SI continues down this path of entanglement with the Russian mafia, it might get more dangerous. I don't know."

"I feel safe with you."

"I'll keep you safe. Seems like that goes both ways. Max told me you pulled my gun and fired a few rounds at our attackers."

Jenna cleared her throat. "In their general direction. I don't think I was any real threat."

"It gave Max time to get in position and take advantage of the distraction. Are you holding up okay?"

Jenna swallowed. "Surprisingly, yes. Though I'll feel better when everything is behind me."

Ryan kissed her forehead. "Soon, Jenna."

She cherished the few hours with Ryan close to her in the Red Square, so named, he explained, because *krasnaya* meant both 'red' and 'beautiful' in Russian. They meandered together simply as tourists enjoying the historic landmark.

She relaxed into the role, encouraging him to talk about what Russian history he knew. The Red Square transformed from a marketplace to ceremonial grounds over the decades. Numerous fires and demolitions over hundreds of years had resulted in many of the original buildings being replaced.

The breathtaking St. Basil's Cathedral had been built under Ivan IV. Its vibrant colors stood in stark contrast to the pale blue sky beyond it. They walked hand-in-hand from the cathedral to the Kremlin to the state historical museum.

"Previous work brought you to Russia?" Jenna asked.

Ryan nodded. "Protection detail for an American business-man's daughter. She was eight, and he hired Maxine's team for three months—the duration of his stay overseas. I took an online course in the month before the trip to learn about the culture and a little of the language. Dorian has the best Russian."

"Dorian. I haven't met him yet."

"He's on another assignment, but you will. He has a daughter starting college soon. You'll meet everyone on the team eventually."

She squeezed his hand. Because the Rider team was like family to him, the plan to meet all the team felt moving and inti-mate. "I'm looking forward to it. I'll have to ask Dorian for some advice since Cal is only a few years from college."

"And who else on the Jenna Masters' team should I meet?"

"Well, you met Jess. She's the main event. We've been inseparable since residency. Carmen is another critical care doctor and a friend. Kat, one of the nurses I work with, is also a good friend. She and I have done occasional trips to the museums in Chicago and Navy Pier."

Jenna took a shaky breath and, stopping, turned to Ryan. His expression, with his rich brown eyes and curve of his lips, warmed her to the core. "Thank you for everything. Thank you for your persistence in Antigua, your card, your rescue, your affection."

He cupped her chin in his hand—warm, rough with callouses but still gentle. "You're welcome, *solnirshko moyo*."

———

THE TRIP back to Miami was uneventful. In yet another hotel room, Jenna paced the carpeted floor as the phone range. A awkward sensation crept along her spine as the the phone rang on speaker and Ryan and Reece listened and recorded. She hadn't spoken with Brad in a year, but she was too emotionally exhausted from all of the travel and meetings to give him the tongue-lashing he deserved.

"Hello?"

"Brad."

"Jenna! You're okay. Thank god. Things got out of hand, and the Cubans got carried away. I'm okay. I've been recuperating."

"It must have been so hard for you." Her voice was devoid of sympathy.

"Yeah. I thought they were going to kill me. I'm lucky to be alive."

Jenna kept her voice flat. "I could have used a heads up." She was done wasting energy being upset with Brad or expecting anything but failure from him.

He is who he is.

Nothing she could say or ever had said would change him. He would always be a troll. Now, the cards were dealt, and Brad's fate was sealed.

"God. I know, babe. I wanted to warn you, but I was beaten to a pulp."

Not that he asked, but, "Cal is okay."

"Right, Cal. Good. He's safe?"

"I've worked out a plan. We're meeting with Ernesto tonight." She gave him the address and time. "Bring your passport."

"Jeez, Jenna. Where are we going?"

"Twelve million is a lot of money, Brad."

"I'm sure we can work something out. You make a physician's salary."

There he was, muddling through and still expecting her to pay for his mistakes. He didn't consider what portion of her hard-earned money went to Cal's boarding school—to which Brad contributed nothing. What remained would not cover his debt. Not in this lifetime.

"I did work something out. I'll see you there." She turned off the phone.

Ryan took off the headphones and gave her a solemn nod.

"Think he'll come?"

"He'll come," Ryan replied.

"He didn't even ask if his son was okay. Ernesto could have kidnapped Cal to begin with instead of me. Brad didn't even consider that."

"I hate that he still has the power to upset you, but I can't say I'm surprised at his behavior. He's a certifiable asshole."

"Am I going to extremes?"

"No." Ryan walked up to her, placing his hands on her shoulders. "If you ask me, he deserves worse than what you've arranged."

She looked at his strong features, feeling the power radiating from his aura.

"One day, I'll have to tell Cal what I've done."

"What you were cornered into doing," he corrected her. "I'll be there to help you."

She leaned into him.

BRAD PHONED Ernesto repeatedly and left several messages. Finally, on the fourth dial, he answered.

"Brad, I'm trying to enjoy a poolside afternoon. What is so *urgente*?"

"Jenna called me about the meet."

"*Si*, we are meeting. Everything is arranged."

"I want to be straight with you, Ernesto. I know I messed up before, but I'm being upfront now. I think my ex-wife is planning something. She told me to come and bring my passport." He wiped a sweaty palm on his jeans as he paced his apartment living room.

"You think she is planning to flee the county?" Ernesto's tone sharpened.

"I don't know what she's planning, but I want you to know that I'm not part of any double-cross."

What was the crazy bitch thinking? Bring a passport? He wasn't going to run away with her. Maybe he should be touched by the gesture, but the idea of living in another country terrified him. He knew enough Spanish to live in Mexico, but one did not hide out from the Cuban mafia in Mexico. Where could they hide?

What country had modern amenities and didn't despise Americans? Australia?

Besides, he wasn't going to be tied down to her and on a stipend like she had done before, treating him like a damn teenager with an allowance.

"You think she has no intention of repaying me?" Ernesto asked.

"It didn't sound like it." He knew he was throwing her to the *chupacabras*, but not only was fleeing ridiculous, the ability to conjure such a scheme meant she had a sizable stash of money. He knew she'd been playing him. Holding out on him. Stingy bitch. Instead of paying Ernesto a token of good faith, she was going to get them both killed by trying to run.

Jenna didn't usually think outside the box like this. She must have hired help. Brad remembered the phone call he had received after Jenna's kidnapping—some guy looking for Jenna. His voice was demanding and authoritative. Brad had holed up in his apartment for the next few days, wondering if police would come for him. No one came. Had she hired protection? How would she have done that so soon?

"*Brad, gracias para tu honestidad.*"

"I don't want to screw things up again."

"Smart thinking."

"What do you want me to do, Ernesto?"

"Play along tomorrow night. Join us, bring your passport or not. I will make sure she's cornered like a mouse. She won't escape."

***

JENNA ROLLED her neck and shoulders under the weight of the Kevlar vest as she listened to the pouring rain striking the SUV.

She hadn't had any caffeine, but she felt wired despite it being nearly midnight.

Ryan gave her a squeeze on her thigh.

Show time.

Jenna, Ryan, Reece, and Maxine exited the vehicle. They walked through the pouring rain into the warehouse. Jenna felt her now damp navy yoga pants cling to her skin. Ryan had advised her to wear clothing she could be mobile in so cotton pants and a loose shirt were an easy choice. Her sneakers felt slightly slick on the smooth surface of the warehouse. Another empty warehouse.

Doesn't anyone use storage space these days?

In the middle of the vast empty building stood Ernesto Busta and five of his goons. No, four. One man stood to Ernesto's right looking smug—Brad.

The creator of this entire debacle stood casually as though he were Ernesto's right-hand man. As though tonight's meeting was about relieving his obligation. As though he thought he should be redeemed. As though he hadn't nearly made their son motherless.

"Maxine Rider," Ernesto greeted her with a wolfish smile. "You must pardon my behavior the last time we met. It seems I underestimated your resources and skills."

"Apology accepted."

Jenna glanced at Maxine with her cargo pants and gun on her hip.

Ernesto seemed to realize she was a contender given her meeting with Vladimir. Did he understand she towered above him on the badass food chain? Perhaps. She had the clout to go above Ernesto, straight to the Russian mafia. Jenna's role in saving Vladimir's nephew eased negotiations, but only Maxine's reputation and relationship with Vladimir made the meeting possible.

Ernesto turned his winning smile toward Jenna. "Dr. Masters, you have had an eventful few weeks."

You have no idea, Busta.

Since he didn't know about the Argentina hit, he didn't know the half of it.

He continued, "It delights me to know my unpleasant role in your life has concluded."

"*Gracias*," she said.

Brad's brow wrinkled in the first sign of confusion. He was obviously realizing he'd missed a few events that transpired. Since no one told him about the Russian mafia, he would be confused.

"*Bueno.* Let us conclude our *negocio, sí*?"

Jenna nodded grimly.

On cue, Vladimir's team materialized—Mikhail, Sonya, and Ruslan. Raindrops on their black suits glistened under the fluorescent lights of the warehouse. Tattoos snaked up their necks—black ink on pale skin. They looked like a hit squad. Merciless.

Ernesto and his men took several relaxed steps back, leaving Brad exposed.

His eyes grew wide. "Jenna, what the hell is going on?" Brad's voice cracked.

She felt a pang of sorrow for Brad, but the deal had been sealed. Twelve million wiped off the record in exchange for the debt on Mikhail's life fulfilled and Brad Masters' involuntary servitude to the Russian mafia.

Jenna steeled her resolve. This was the only solution, the only way to keep Cal safe from his father's idiocy. "You're accounting error cost Ernesto twelve million dollars of debt to the Russian mafia. The Russians are forgiving Ernesto in exchange for you."

"Jenna, no. Don't do this." His face blanched. "Think about Cal."

"I am thinking about Cal. You are a danger to him. You have to be kept on a leash."

Privyaz', Vladimir had told her the word for leash in Russian.

The Russians stood on either side to escort Brad.

"Mr. Masters, come with us, *pozhaluysta*."

Brad shook and appeared as though he might vomit. The two men supported his arms as he walked away with them.

How long would Brad survive? Vladimir had made it clear to Jenna that if she chose to forfeit his life to the Russians, they would end Brad if he was ineffective or dangerous. She would have to tell her son that his father was never coming back to visit. She needed to accept that one day his life insurance check would arrive unannounced because he'd screwed up something with the Russian mafia.

"*Mucho gusto*, Maxine Rider." Ernesto gave them a polite tip of his head as he slipped out of the warehouse with his men.

Jenna released a shaky breath into the empty space before them.

Reece stroked his mustache. "So many assholes in one room, and I didn't get to shoot anybody."

Maxine turned to walk out of the warehouse. "It's called conflict resolution."

Everyone followed her.

"Yeah, so is my Beretta." Reece looped his thumbs in his pants pockets.

"Nonviolent conflict resolution," she amended. "That is the purpose of Rider SI."

Reece snorted. "So says the woman who can launch a Hellfire with a phone call."

Maxine pursed her lips.

As they climbed into the car, Jenna asked, "What's a Hellfire?"

"I'll fill you in," Ryan said, kissing her lightly on the cheek.

CHAPTER 24

Ryan held Jenna close as she lay sleeping. Her silky hair fanned around her. Her smooth, bare skin pressed against him. A hint of coconut swirled around her. He could imagine every morning like this. Could Jenna?

Lovemaking last night had been exquisite, both a deepening of their intimacy and a release of tension. He could spend a lifetime exploring her body.

Thankfully, everything tumultuous in Jenna's life was settling. She'd been through a tornado in the last few days and the wreckage would need to be mended, but she had survived and Cal was safe.

Maxine and Reece were headed back to Atlanta today. Maxine had missed her mysterious dinner date with Vladimir. Ryan still needed to confront his boss about that detail. Perhaps he'd loop Dorian in to get his take on the situation.

Barry was leaving Boston, Cal never knowing he had secret protection.

Ryan had texted Sonny last night to let him know everything

had stabilized and he could put the funds back into investments. Sonny reminded him he wanted to meet Jenna.

Ryan anticipated planning the next few months with Jenna—working around their schedules to see each other. They would sort out when he could meet Cal and she could meet Sonny. Maxine would have another job lined up in no time, but maybe he could eke out a week to spend with Jenna.

Direct flights between Chicago and Atlanta were easily accessible. He could see more of her if she lived in Atlanta because it was the company's home base. And Atlanta was a shorter flight distance to Antigua. Both O'Hare and Hartsfield International had direct flights to Boston to see Cal.

Slow down, Walsh.

Time. He needed to give her time. She needed to recuperate before he started spewing long-term plans and talk of relocation. He wouldn't pressure her to move. He knew where he stood in the relationship and knew he loved her, but she needed it to progress at her pace.

⁂

"You look happy," Ryan commented over his newspaper. They sat in the Miami hotel dining room over breakfast.

Jenna smiled, the joy within her reaching her eyes. "I'm amazed at how this simple domestic moment feels reassuring and comfortable."

He lowered his paper and sipped his coffee. "Good. Because I'm not sure I can maintain the level of adventure you've had over the last week."

"Good. I don't want that level of adventure." She sipped her orange juice and glanced at the cut on his head. Most of it was concealed by hair, but probably reminded of the danger they'd encountered.

"What level of adventure do you want?"

Her eyes sparkled at him. "Like last night will do."

Last night had been phenomenal but also limited by jet lag. "I believe I can top that."

"Oh?"

"But first, I need to come clean about some plans I made."

Her smile faded.

He continued, "My line of work requires contingency plans. Situations can become beyond one's control."

Such as when ex-husbands lose an insurmountable amount of money.

Ryan imagined Jenna's ex would have a lifetime of servitude to the Russians, however long that would turn out to be. Ryan wondered if Ernesto would ever find the clerical error or if Brad had even made an error at all. Perhaps the money was hidden somewhere, though Brad didn't strike Ryan as having the *cojones* to pull off a theft like that.

"And?" she asked.

"I had an escape plan if our meeting with Vladimir and or Ernesto hadn't worked out. A plan that involved you, me, and Cal running and hiding. Out of reach of the Cubans. Out of reach of the Russians."

"Oh."

"I didn't share the back-up plan with you because I didn't want to cause you more worry than what you already faced, but I'm telling you now because you need to know I will always have a back-up plan."

"Sounds reasonable," she said cautiously.

He hesitated for a moment before deciding to elaborate further. Keeping his voice low, he said, "The company I worked at for two years had many shady deals. One of which was sex trafficking—protection for the transport of high-end prostitutes. Most of the girls weren't voluntarily in the business."

He hated to confess his cowardice in not stopping Titan Enterprises. He had been caught between his training to be loyal, his morals, and the immense danger of what he had gotten mixed up in.

"By the time I put all the pieces together, the most I succeeded in doing was covertly getting a few girls their freedom. If I'd had resources or ingenuity, perhaps I could have blown the lid off their illegal activities. I left after that, left all of those victims, past and future, to a terrible fate."

Silence settled between them. Chatter from other tables and the clinking of dishes hung in the surrounding air. He didn't look at Jenna's face for fear of the judgment he might find.

A small, warm hand gripped his. He stared at Jenna's hand.

He took a breath. "I never spent a dime of the money I made at that company. I gave it all to my brother, Sonny, who invested it for me. It's not a lot, but it's enough to pay for new identities and disappear. If I never need to do that, then perhaps it will find its way to a charity someday."

Soft lips touched the back of his hand. He looked up into Jenna's compassionate expression.

"I appreciate you having a backup plan, Ryan. I'm thankful it didn't come to that, but I'm glad you told me—now rather than earlier. Because, yes, it might have tipped me over the edge. I'm sorry that your last employer was a monster, but I think your days before and after that time reveal your true character. You've helped people. You'll continue to help people.

"Sometimes in medicine I wonder if I had done certain things differently, would the outcome have been better for the patient. I can't change the decisions I made, but I can learn from them and make different ones in the future. Better choices. You've done that. Those events, terrible as they were, have motivated you to help people."

"Thank you."

She straightened in her chair. "You would have left your family and Reece to go into hiding with me?"

"They would have understood."

"But they're family."

"You wouldn't survive in hiding without me or someone like me. Reece and I have been friends since high school. Maybe our idea of an ideal relationship isn't the same, but he would have understood."

"I would never want to be responsible for separating you from Sonny or Reece like that." Her eyes dropped to the rest of her uneaten eggs and bacon.

He leaned forward, still gripping her hand. "And you wouldn't be responsible. The jerks who put your life in danger would be."

She seemed to struggle with her thoughts for a moment.

Looking up into his eyes, she cracked a mischievous smile. "Okay. Now, what's this you mentioned about topping last night?"

He grinned. "Oh, I have ideas."

⁂

MAXINE POURED herself a glass of whiskey. When she raised the bottle in offer, Dorian politely declined with a wave of his hand.

She sank into her chair opposite her couch where the slender British man lounged. She felt bone deep tired from so much travel. She wasn't a spring chicken anymore, but she needed to personally handle negotiations with Ernesto and Vladimir. At least that ordeal was behind her.

"How are Kate and Dia?"

Dorian smiled. "Splendid. Kate's on her third novel. Dia is starting college in the fall. Enter a whole new list of fatherly worries."

Maxine took a sip and let the amber liquor pleasantly singe its way down her throat. She knew those worries. Her son, David, fortunately seemed a ball of ambition. He'd been pre-med from the beginning and never lost focus.

Maxine had never met any girlfriends, but suspected, with his level of determination, anyone he perceived as a distraction would be swept aside. He didn't seem to form lasting relationships, and she wondered if she were to blame somehow. The lack of a relationship made for a remarkable career. And a remarkably lonely life.

"Thank you for going to Buenos Aires."

Dorian nodded.

"So the spook doesn't want to sign on?"

Dorian pursed his lips. "He finds the idea of the occasional odd job acceptable, but he doesn't want anything permanent."

Odd jobs she could provide. Someone with Mort Hutchinson's talents would be helpful on an as-needed basis.

Dorian crossed his legs and leaned back on her worn suede couch. "I think you won him over when he got to launch a Hellfire into the heart of a drug manufacturing plant."

Maxine smiled. "Firepower is one way to win a man to my side."

"You seem to have won over Vladimir Pronin."

She sucked in a deep breath and scratched her chin. "I'm still not sure what's brewing between us. I once thought it was mutual respect." She ran a finger around the rim of her crystal glass. "Now, it feels more like we slipped into bed together."

"Do you want to be in bed with him?"

Her eyes shot up to his. "I was speaking metaphorically."

"I know. I was not."

She narrowed her eyes at him.

"Max, have you considered the simple possibility that he is a man seeing you as a woman? Not a game. Not a conquest. Just a woman he fancies?"

She shook her head slowly as she took another sip of whiskey. "No. There's a play he's making. I don't know what it is yet."

A long silence settled between them.

"Well," Dorian spoke at last. "You're not in bed with the Russian mafia. You teamed up to kick a beehive in Argentina. You haven't any other business together."

She felt reassurance at his words, except—"Beehive, huh?"

"For every action there is an equal and opposite reaction except in the underworld where the reaction is usually worse than the action. They tried a hit on Vladimir, and you blew up their compound. As an example."

She set her now empty glass down on the coffee table, leaned back, and crossed her arms.

"Mort mentioned a new player in town in Argentina's white chalk market. Someone wanting to optimize the trafficking."

"Oh?" Maxine knew those had been Vladimir's plans before the violent message '*leave to Argentina alone*' was conveyed.

"A faceless man or group called The Phoenix."

"Oh, shit." Maxine scrubbed her hands over her face.

Dorian arched an eyebrow at her response. "Someone you know?"

"Maybe. Probably." Crap. She needed Claire to dig for confirmation, but Lucius Titan, mastermind of the security company Titan Enterprises had once executed a military operation entitled the Phoenix. The massacre gave him the reputation of someone who cleans up others' messes without pesky moral impediments.

Few people knew of the covert mission. Fewer still knew its code name.

"Is that going to be a problem for us?" Dorian asked.

"Maybe. Probably." She needed another drink.

JENNA ADJUSTED the strap of her red dress. She looked around the club as she clutched her glass of water. "What are we doing here, Ryan?" She had to raise her voice over the music playing.

"It's Miami. No one leaves Miami without first going to a nightclub." He winked at her.

"I lived in Miami. I've been to nightclubs."

Two shot glasses arrived filled to the brim with golden liquid.

Ryan leaned over and slid one hand along her thigh. "Not with me you haven't."

She sucked in a ragged breath at the instant heat she felt from his touch. They'd spent a glorious day together, beginning with conversation over a breakfast of eggs and coffee. The conversation was delightfully normal; they discussed work and travel and Cal. They planned when next to visit Antigua, and Ryan talked about his next job with Rider SI. She explained how rotations worked in the ICU. They planned to go together to pick up Cal when school was out for the summer. Later they walked in a park, sipping lemonade and holding hands. When they came to a women's clothing store, he mysteriously had her buy a dress.

Ryan slid one of the shot glasses over to her. "Drink."

She tipped her head back and downed the shot. The liquid burned down her throat before landing in her stomach with a thud. "Whew. I don't remember the last time I had a shot of tequila." She took the lemon he handed her. After sucking on it, she dropped it into the empty shot glass.

"You'll remember this time." He stood off his barstool and pulled her up with him.

"Banner?" She narrowed her eyes at him.

With a smile and those sexy dimples, he led her to the dance floor. Holding her close, he started to sway.

"What are we doing?" She moved with him.

The surrounding crowd danced to the rhythm of the band playing.

"We're dancing. No more running. No more fear. No more threats. You and me and the music."

He spun her and then brought his arms down around her, his fingertips caressing her skin.

"Oh my god, you know how to salsa." She felt the rhythm with him and moved to the beat. The hem of her dress swirled slightly with the swish of her hips.

"You sound impressed." He smiled at her.

"I just fell in love with you."

He laughed. "You mean all of this effort I've put forth over the last week, and all I needed to do was salsa with you?"

"Definitely. If we had done this the first night, I would have asked you to marry me."

"I didn't know you liked salsa back then."

"I love dancing, but particularly salsa."

Their bodies moved in synchrony. He took her into a cross-body lead.

"So you want to marry me? First a vacation invitation and now a proposal? I admire your ambition, but it's all a bit fast-paced for me."

Her cheeks warmed. After the thing they'd done with each other—to each other—in the bedroom, she hadn't suspected he could still make her blush. He was twisting her words again, and she suppressed a smile that might encourage him.

"I want to get to know you better first." She didn't want to be that nineteen-year-old girl again, rushing into a relationship.

Then again, she had waited a long time for the right man—Ryan Walsh—to come into her life. Why wait longer?

"I like the sound of you getting to know me better." His voice was a seductive purr.

"I meant your personality, your history, your likes, and dislikes."

He pulled her into him and moved his waist against her. Her heart raced like a thoroughbred and hummed with excitement. He was driving her hormones insane, and by his expression, he knew exactly what he was achieving.

He gave her a boyish grin. "I was talking about the same thing. What's on your mind, Doctor?"

She pursed her lips to avoid giving him the satisfaction of an incredulous open-mouth gape.

He sidestepped into the next move, leading her left and then right.

"Call me your sunshine again."

He leaned toward her ear. "*Solnirshko moyo.*"

"I am in love with you." She watched the words she spoke float into the air, into the troposphere. Unleashed, for better or for worse.

Ryan gave her a wry grin as he leaned close to her ear. "You're only saying that because you want to sleep with me."

She laughed as he pushed her away and spun her.

Their bodies came back together flawlessly, drawn like magnets.

"I do want to sleep with you. But I am also in love with you."

CHAPTER 25

EIGHT MONTHS LATER

Giddy anticipation delighted Claire as she rode in the cab to Hartsfield International Airport.

Maxine sat next to her with her usual brooding scowl. The woman barely displayed an emotional range, but Claire knew that provided Maxine with a barrier to the world. Deep inside, she cared, maybe even more than most. Maxine had erected walls to a lifetime of hardship—the poverty of her youth growing up a coal miner's daughter, the brutality of war as a Marine, and the rejection of her husband and son.

Maxine had built a new family through her company. Though she wouldn't admit it, she liked seeing her recruits happy. Claire knew Ryan Walsh was one of Maxine's favorites. Claire silently bet she would see at least one tear fall from those steely Marine eyes at the wedding, despite the way Maxine would grumble about having to wear a dress.

Maxine crossed her arms as she stared out the window. "He could have gotten married in Atlanta."

Claire scoffed. "I know, right? It's so inconsiderate of him to drag us to a tropical paradise."

Maxine snorted.

Mason Stone and former Rider SI client, Aurora Meridian, had gotten married on Aurora's parents' vineyard in California. The wedding dazzled, and the reception had been positively magical. They had strung LED lights throughout the backyard. Between the lights and the lush greenery, Claire felt like she was in Tolken's Rivendell. As beautiful as that location had been, Claire was certain she would like Antigua more, having never been to the Caribbean.

Ryan and Jenna's wedding would also mark Claire's first role as a bridesmaid. When Claire finally met the physician in person, Jenna had wrapped her arms around her in a fierce hug and thanked her. After a brief conversation, Claire knew the beautiful, intelligent, and practical woman was perfect for Ryan—the older brother Claire had never had. When Jenna asked her to be her bridesmaid, Claire had leaped with joy. Ryan laughed heartily at her reaction before giving her a hug and tussling her hair.

"I guess Billy is next?" Claire wondered aloud.

Billy, the only other woman on the Rider SI team who was currently working overseas, remained exceptionally private about her personal life. Claire knew from her background check that the woman had never been married. She knew from Maxine that Billy's intimate life consisted mostly of a few one-night stands. Billy didn't care much for commitment.

Maxine grunted. "From now on, you screen the applicants to make sure they are married. No more drama. No more weddings."

Claire shot her a quick look of dismay as the cab pulled to the curb. "I screen for quality ex-military, Max. I do not discriminate based on age, gender, race, sexual orientation, or marital status." She wanted to add that Maxine of all people should know that marital status did nothing to convey personal stability or lack of drama, but that would hijack their playful discussion into a darker realm.

Maxine unleashed a few choice curse words at Claire's insubordination as she climbed out of the cab. Claire paid the driver and got out as well.

"This isn't the military, Max. You don't get to discriminate, and I don't have to blindly follow orders."

Maxine's mouth quirked in a mixture of annoyance and amusement.

Claire grinned. She picked up her luggage from the curb where the driver had set it.

Antigua, here we come.

JENNA SAT stiff as a hospital bed mattress as Nora, part-beautician, part-sadist, applied make-up.

Jess stared out the bungalow window wearing a pink, flowing, and strapless dress. Her jet-black hair shimmered in the streaming sunlight. "The beach is all set up. It's going to be a beautiful wedding. Oh! Cal is so cute in his tux. And he's talking with Ryan. They look like buddies."

Jenna smiled, wishing she could be the one watching them. She knew if she moved, Nora would glare menacingly at her and probably poke or pull something to induce pain.

"Ryan has been phenomenal with Cal—hiking, fishing, kayaking. He even gave him driving lessons. He's made male bonding look effortless."

Jess turned back to look at her with a soft expression. "You've got a keeper." She turned back to the window. "Bitch." Her voice was a playful grumble.

Jenna laughed but was forced to stifle it when Nora halted her blush application to shoot Jenna a warning look.

Jenna had spent several hours each day for the last two days with the beauty specialist. Three days of plucking, cleansing, and coloring. The woman seemed to enjoy inflicting discomfort, as though the suffering was directly proportional to how beautiful she would look walking down the aisle. Jenna hoped the torment would pay off, but mostly she wanted to see Ryan again. They'd decided to get separate rooms in Antigua ... that absurdity ended tonight.

"You don't have to sleep separately for appearances, Mom," Cal had said during a walk on the beach.

"Shush. We're not having a conversation about my intimate life."

Cal rolled his eyes. "You're always asking me about mine."

"Yes. I'm the mom."

Jess shifted in her dress. "Wow. Natasha looks gorgeous. How could she not look gorgeous with that bone structure? She could wear a burlap sack and heads would turn. Her man's a looker, too. Bet he had to tell her not to wear heels, or she'd be a foot taller than him. What'd you say his name was?"

"Mikhail."

Jess turned to Jenna. "I can't believe you invited the nephew of a—"

Jenna gave her a silencing, wide-eyed stare. Nora didn't need to know details about Jenna's bizarre guest list—ex-military, Russian mafia, Russian supermodel.

Besides, she had invited Mikhail and Natasha to be polite. Who knew they would actually come to Antigua?

"Wait. If Mikhail is his nephew and Natasha is his niece, isn't that incestual?" She crinkled her nose.

"I don't think that's a word, but, yes, it would be except that Mikhail was adopted so no blood ties."

"Oh. Who's the old guy?" Jess had turned her attention back out the window as Nora worked on Jenna's eyelids. "He kissed your friend Maxine on the cheeks."

Cheeks. Pleural. Jenna's stomach hit the floor. Her mouth went dry. "Salt and pepper hair?"

"Yeah."

"Central bulk but not too overweight?"

"Yeah."

"I'm gonna be sick." She would have closed her eyes in mortification if they weren't already closed for Nora.

"Is that him? Him, him?" Jess asked, her voice rising in excitement in contrast to the foreboding Jenna felt.

"Yes. And I didn't invite him."

"This is the coolest wedding ever."

VLADIMIR STEPPED BACK from Maxine after kissing her cheeks. The new flush in them gave him warm satisfaction.

"It's good to see you," he said with a smile

"Jenna didn't mention you on the guest list." She smiled in return.

He detected a hint of strain in her voice.

"*Da.* I am not on the guest list. However, when I discovered you would be here but with no plus one, I considered that my invitation."

She examined his face, no doubt trying to calculate how he might have gained access to Dr. Masters' guest list. As she had her computer savvy Claire, so he too had resources.

"Do you think Dr. Masters will be offended?"

"Offended? No. Terrified? Possibly. But she'll be pleased to know you think the event worthy of attending."

"Wonderful. Then we should not spoil her pleasure by revealing that I primarily came to see you."

The color rose back into her cheeks. She looked lovely in her mint green dress and pearls. His Catherine the Great. Maxine the Great.

She stared hard at him. "Do I need to be concerned about that?"

"I am no threat to you, Max. I stand before you unarmed, hoping only that you will agree to dance with me after the ceremony. We never did get that dinner date after all. You, on the other hand, have me surrounded by your top soldiers."

Her eyes flickered around the two of them. As he had approached the wedding grounds, the groom—Ryan—, groomsman—Reece—, and loyal guard—Barry—had quietly positioned themselves in an offensive circle.

After letting out a deep breath, and she visibly relaxed. She gave a subtle hand gesture, which he assumed was the signal for her men to stand down.

"One dance," she said.

"Wonderful. And to keep appearances that I am here for the bride and groom, I will dance with Dr. Masters as well."

"Anyone with whom you desire."

He smiled again. She truly was magnificent. She had tight control of the fear she felt in his presence. No, not fear. Concern.

Does she fear anyone?

She controlled her emotions well. And she had not an ounce of jealousy or fanfare. He had waited these last twenty lonely years for a self-assured woman of Maxine's maturity. Here they stood, so close, but on opposite sides of the chessboard, and he didn't know how to bridge such a gap. She saw only the criminal side of him, only what she wanted to see. Black and white, like chess pieces.

She knew nothing of his charity foundations and nothing of the chaos he brought under control in the Russian underworld. Sure, he moved guns and drugs. They were lucrative. He didn't force anyone to buy them. What they did with the weapons and drugs scorched their souls, not his.

Tough little *liska*.

How to lure the sly fox into his arms?

BUTTERFLIES DANCED in Jenna's stomach as she stared at the guests. The rows brimmed with family, friends and ... and other people too dangerous to call friends whom she could only hope to never call enemies.

Vladimir had found a spot near Maxine, the woman who had made this day possible. Boris stood on the other side of Vladimir. Natasha and Mikhail stood one row ahead of them along with Barry. On the other side of the aisle stood her mother, hands clasped and smiling as she intermittently dabbed at tears. Friends of theirs encircled them.

Jenna swallowed and began walking down the aisle to the music. Her father, looking dashing in his tuxedo with his gray hair smoothed, walked beside her.

In the background, waves lapped against the shore. At the erected altar stood her friends—Jess and Carmen and Claire. Cute Claire with her blue hair, who had saved Jenna's life as much as the rest of the Rider team by tracking her phone.

On the groom's side stood Cal, Reece, and Sonny—Ryan's brother whom she had the pleasure of meeting three times before the wedding. Cal looked mature and handsome in his tux.

Jenna blinked back tears. Heaven help her. She couldn't start bawling before she ever made it to Ryan. Her father patted her arm.

Her eyes fell on Ryan, and her heart skipped a beat. He looked ravishing in his tuxedo. She could imagine nothing lovelier than the man she loved in a tuxedo on a gorgeous beach. Except perhaps without the tuxedo. She grinned at the image.

Ryan gave her a wry smile as he narrowed his eyes at her.

She felt her cheeks blush. How did he always know what she was thinking?

As her eyes remained fixed on Ryan, the rest of the world faded into light. At this sublime moment, she had not a single worry. She felt no reservation, no hesitation. The event had been eight months in the planning and had superseded her expectations.

Ryan superseded her expectations.

She basked in the moment—this gift—of blissful happiness.

***

ON THE DANCE FLOOR, Ryan looked down at his amazing bride. She radiated beauty and love. Love for him. Never had he imagined he could feel this happy. Never had he thought he deserved to feel such wholeness. Jenna thought otherwise. When she looked at him with emerald green eyes filled with adoration, he felt worthy of happiness. His Jenna. His sunshine.

She even had a great son. After spending time with Cal, he liked the skinny spitfire. Cal was witty and smart. Most important was the love and respect he had for his mom.

The wedding party was a little unconventional, but then so was the way they had met and met again. His eyes casually roamed the dance floor. Mikhail and Natasha danced together.

Claire had sweetly asked Cal to dance. Reece and Jess were dancing and laughing. His partner looked quite enamored by the small Asian woman. She was a feisty hellion, but maybe Reece needed that—someone to unravel his notion that a lifetime of one-night stands were sufficient nourishment for the soul.

Ryan's gaze fell on Vladimir, the unexpected guest. Yet, for a twelve-million-dollar forgiveness, the man could come to the birth of Ryan and Jenna's child if he wanted. Vladimir stood staring in the distance, his face heavy with concern. Ryan followed Vladimir's gaze to Maxine. Her face looked pale and stern as she spoke on her phone. Trouble brewed.

Ryan made eye contact with Claire who gave him a puzzled look. He nodded in Maxine's direction, silently urging her to check on the woman. Claire looked at Maxine, realization dawning on her face. She whispered to Cal and excused herself from the dance floor. Cal's grandmother stepped in to take her place.

Ryan's eyes came back to Jenna, and she smiled at him, setting his world alight. Whatever next turmoil awaited Rider SI, he had this moment with this woman and many more pleasurable ones to anticipate. The rest of the world could wait.

MAXINE HAD LEFT THE DANCING, drinking crowd to answer her phone. She felt a measure of relief in excusing herself. She had enjoyed the ceremony and nearly cried, which she attributed to some mixture of sand blowing into her eyes and menopause. Vladimir offered her a handkerchief but withdrew it in a chuckle when she glared at him.

As she walked in search of a quieter spot, she glanced back at Vladimir with whom she'd first danced. She felt oddly comfortable and aroused in his embrace. What was he playing at coming all the way to Antigua?

She raised the phone to her ear. "Hello?"

"Maxine Rider," a male voice purred.

Despite the chill that ran down her spine, she forced casual cheer into her voice. "Lucy, what can I do for you?"

"I've been keeping tabs on you, Maxine." His voice dropped an octave. "It's how I know you're throwing Hellfires around South America where you have no business meddling."

Her blood ran cold as icicles formed along her spine. "Is that so?"

"Yes. First you interfered with my confiscation of Sharp's prototype then you launch missiles into territories under my purview. I haven't unearthed your contacts yet to know how you pulled it off, but I will. You need to rethink your strategy, Maxine. Taking on a titan such as me has consequences."

"Apparently it does, because you're interrupting my relaxation." She fought to keep her voice even despite her racing mind.

How did he discover she had ordered the strike eight months ago in Argentina? She paced the beach. Her heart kicked into a fast race. Consequences brought to bear by Titan Enterprises had an ominous ring.

He continued, "When people come after my organization, I take it personally. Do you want to make this personal, Max? You have a family, don't you? A son? Tragedies happen to emergency room physicians all of the time."

A roar like a jet plane sounded in Maxine's ears, devouring the sound of music, ocean waves, and wedding guest chatter. Her vision blurred, and an aching pain thudded with every heartbeat.

"Taking out a drug manufacturing facility isn't personal. But if you do anything to my son, I will cut off your—"

The phone disconnected.

Maxine swore before channeling her fury into her legs to will herself to stay standing. She clenched her phone in her hand. The ache in her chest magnified. Was she having a heart attack?

"Max?"

Maxine's eyes focused on the color blue. Blue hair. Blue Claire. Her vision cleared. Her gaze flickered toward the festivities to ensure her state of panic wasn't noticed by anyone else. Only Vladimir stared in their direction.

"I need to make a quiet exit," she told Claire. "Tell everyone my conversational abilities have reached their limit."

Claire shrugged. "They won't have a problem believing that."

"I need you on the flight back with me."

"You're scaring me, Max. What's this about?"

"We need to get back to the office, and we need to start tracking David."

"David?"

"Yes, my son, David."

Claire's eyes went wide.

"I want location updates scheduled to my phone every thirty minutes. I want a tracker on his car and security cameras in his apartment."

"Okay. Yes, absolutely. Why?" Claire's face grew paler and worried.

"Lucius Wallenius Titan declared war on me."

****QUICK NOTE FROM THE AUTHOR****

ARE you ready for more clash between Lucius and Maxine? Want to know what happens to David Rider, Maxine's son? Find out in *McMillan File, The Rider Files Book 3.*

She's investigating a murder. He's trying not to become the next victim.

Mica McMillan, savvy PI and scrappy street fighter, is trying to track down a murderer and doesn't have time for delays or relationships. As she tries to unravel the mystery of who murdered her last bounty, she finds herself in the deadly web of crooked private security contractor— Lucius Titan.

Dr. David Rider snaps out of his dreary ER work when confronted with Mica's fascinating life and magnetism to danger. But when a drug dealer working for Lucius puts a hit out on David, the mismatched couple find themselves on dangerous ground. Mica will have to rely on help from The Rider SI team, and David reunites with the owner—his mother.

Can Mica and Rider SI bring the criminals to justice or will she and David become Lucius Titan's next victims?

DEAR READER

Want to keep in touch?

If you enjoyed this book and want to know about future releases by CB Samet you visit www.cbsamet.com to sign up for my mailing list! I promise I won't spam you. I only send an email when I have a new book released, giveaways, or special discounts. You can also unsubscribe at any time.

If you loved this book, kindly let others know by posing a brief comment on social media or leave a review where you purchased it so readers can find their next favorite romantic suspense series.

Even more ways to follow me below!

Thank you for reading,
CB Samet

THE RIDER FILES SERIES

Meridian File / Masters File / Box Set 1

McMillan File / Maltisse File / Box Set 2

Storm File / Sullivan File / Box Set 3

Sharp File / Sizani File / Box Set 4

Rivera File / Rucker File / Box Set 5

Richmond File / Redwood File / Box Set 6

Atlas File / Angel File / Box Set 7

Buy 4book box sets direct from author and save 10%

Payhip. Use code E152MoGZG4

OTHER BOOKS BY CB SAMET

Looking for more romantic suspense? How about with an urban fantasy twist? Check out my supernatural adventures...

The Shadow Guardians Trilogy

Urban fantasy Norse Mythology Adventure

Get *Raven's Flight, a prequel novella* for FREE. In my newsletter, you'll learn about me, special discounts, and new releases.

Raven's Flight, prequel novella

Raine Down, Book 1

Rosalyn's Run, novella

Storm Surge, Book 2

Anka's Orb, novella

Sky Fall, Book 3

Olympian Awakenings Trilogy

Urban fantasy Greek Mythology Adventure

Grab the prequel exclusively HERE.

Stone Hearts

Winds of Destiny

Flame and Shadow

The Dr. Whyte Adventure Novels

Thriller Series

Black Gold

Whyte Knight

Gray Horizon

Sweet Romantic Suspense

"Well-written... tales of love and ghosts."

— KIRKUS REVIEW

IN BOXED SETS

Romancing the Spirit Series #1

Sadie's Spirit / Willow's Windfall

Cassie's Chase / Phoebe's Pharaoh

Vanessa's Valentine / Autumn's Angel

Romancing the Spirit Series #2

Carol's Christmas / Allison's Alibi

Gracelynn's Genie / Michelle's Miracle

Heather's Hero / Chloe's Cupid

Romancing the Spirit Series #3

Sabrina's Storm / Jenny's Justice

Stella's Star / Gigi's Gift

Phoenix's Phantom / Fiona's Freedom

**Love action/adventure and strong female leads in a fantasy world?
Check out my other genre:**

The Avant Champion Fantasy Series

The Avant Champion: Rising

Malakai: Origin of Malos Story (prequel)

The Avant Champion: Honor

The Avant Champion: Ashes

Brothers' Bond: An Avant Champion Malakai Story

The Avant Champion: Conquest

Isabel: An Avant Champion novelette

The Avant Champion: Redeem

FREE EBOOK WITH NEWSLETTER SIGNUP

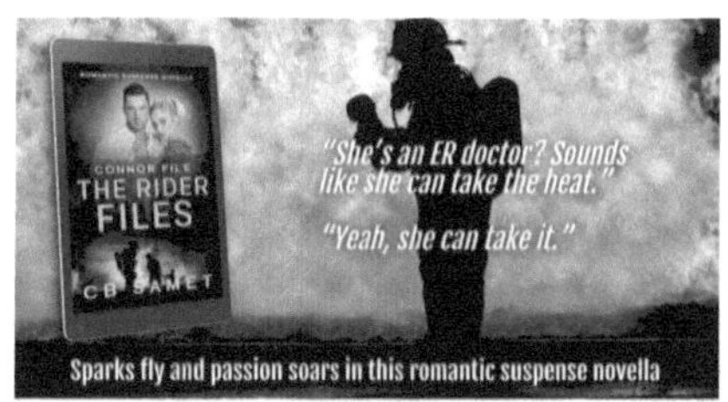

Rick Swanson loves his job as a firefighter, but his world is sent on a tailspin when an arsonist has an agenda of revenge. He needs to deal with this threat if he's going to get his life back on track.

Mackenzie Rivera is falling fast for fireman Rick, until he inexplicably distances himself. When she learns he's trying to protect her from a crazed arsonist, she won't be idle. And she won't back down from danger. But will her determination and his strength be enough to save them both from the fire?

*~~~***<<<SIGN UP HERE>>>***~~~*